Blade of the Phoenix

RIVIAND LOST
BOOK 1

KRISTY DIXON

The Blade of the Phoenix (Riviand Lost- Book 1)

Book Cover by Miblart

Edited by Lawrence Editing

1st edition 2025

ISBN 978-1-960841-30-8 Paperback

ISBN 978-1-960841-32-2 Hardback

ISBN 978-1-960841-33-9 ebook

To Ellena Kathryn

Colter's Lake
Troll City
Troll's Retreat
Kinton
Serpent's Hill
Dragon's Cove
Desert
Tyran
Rivland
Pyramid
Goblin Mountain

1

CHAPTER 1

Queen Claret sat on her stiff, uncomfortable throne and tried to look confident as she listened to Odious, the spokesman of the goblins, speak. She hated dealing with Odious. He could maintain eye contact to a degree that made her uncomfortable. She would prefer talking to an actual goblin, but they always sent him since he was the only human who lived with the goblins. Her advisor stood quietly by her side, observing.

Odious consistently wore a cape crafted from black feathers and dark attire. His brown hair was slicked back and stiff, and the comb marks were noticeable on the top. He had a black ring on his pinky that he would occasionally twist while he was talking. She guessed he was around her age, probably sixteen or seventeen. His pet puffin was never far, and at this moment was perched precariously on his shoulder. Claret worried it would fall. Puffin's webbed feet were not meant to perch, and Odious's puffin was obviously overfed.

"I thought the gold I gave you last month was sufficient," Claret said.

Odious's mouth turned down, and he sighed. "We believed it was too, but unfortunately, the ingredients the goblins need to perform the spell are quite pricey and scarce."

"I thought that once they performed the spell, Riviand was safe?"

"We must cast the spell every time the continent begins to rise. I'm afraid it is the only solution, unless the Blade of the Phoenix is found."

Claret resisted the urge to rub her temples. The sword needed to be found. If she had to keep paying the goblins for their help, the treasury would go completely broke and she would have to raise taxes. If they didn't keep the continent down, Riviand would break through the sky, and the ocean would flood in and kill them all.

"We are searching for the sword, but we have no leads, and we've had no luck," Claret admitted. The continent of Riviand had been taken under the ocean thousands of years ago, and the Blade of the Phoenix was the key that kept them safe. It was carefully guarded and should have been safe, but someone had stolen it, putting everyone in danger.

"That is unfortunate," Odious said. "We take no pleasure in asking for more money, but the goblins have little, and the ingredients are out of our reach if we cannot secure the funds."

Once this was all resolved, she hoped Odious stayed out of Tyran. She would be happy to never deal with him or the goblins again.

Claret stood and walked toward Odious. He scared her a little, but that was something she wanted to keep to herself. "How many times will we have to pay?" she asked, handing him a bag of gold.

He placed the bag somewhere inside his cape and shrugged. "With any luck, this will be the last time. We hope that the more times the spell is done, the more secure Riviand will be."

The puffin grunted, and Claret turned her attention to him. He was easier to digest than his master. "Hello," she said, rubbing a finger over his head.

"Careful," Odious said, taking a step back. "Gregor is dangerous."

Claret raised her brow. The bird appeared harmless. "Gregor?"

"Gregor, the Destroyer. I'm the only one who controls him, and I cannot even foresee his unpredictable nature."

"I see," she said, returning to her throne. "I do not wish to keep you."

Odious bowed and plucked Gregor from his shoulder. He threw something against the castle floor. The sound of breaking glass met her ears, followed by a large plume of blue smoke that partially obscured Odious's retreat. He ran from the castle; the puffin tucked tightly under his arm.

"Does he really think we believe he can disappear?" Claret asked her advisor, who was also her aunt.

"I am certain he does," Durdessa said, pushing a long blond strand of hair over her shoulder. "I cannot imagine he would keep doing it if he knew how ridiculous he looks."

"I wish he wouldn't break the glass on the floor. It just makes more work for the maids."

"Well, with luck, we won't be seeing him again. We should ban him from Tyran. He may appear to be helping us, but I'm sure there is something else under the surface."

Claret let out a shaky breath. "How did I do, Auntie? I feel like an impostor every time I meet with anyone. I wish Father were still alive."

Durdessa gave her a squeeze. "You did fine, love. Don't worry, it will get easier."

"I hope so. I hope there is time for it to get easier. If Riviand can't be kept down—"

Durdessa shook her head. "No, don't say it. Riviand has survived worse things, and it will survive this."

Claret was glad to have Durdessa. She didn't know her aunt's age, but she was at least as old as her father had been, which made her at least forty. That meant she had more experience than Claret, and she needed someone like that in her life. People in Riviand always took notice of Durdessa. She was beautiful and had a commanding presence.

"What if we run out of gold before everything is secure?"

"I do not trust the goblins," Durdessa said. "It wouldn't shock me if they were the ones behind all this. Goblins are greedy and unethical. They may have caused this problem to grow their gold supply."

"But if it goes wrong, they would suffer as much as we would. And why would they do it now?"

"You're young and inexperienced. It is possible they see you as an easy mark."

"If the goblins are behind it, I'll make them sorry… But if they are, what can we do? Without the Blade of the Phoenix, we're helpless. Only the goblins have strong enough power to keep us from drowning."

"We will just have to do the best we can."

"I hope it is enough."

Odious ran down the drawbridge with the speed of a dragon. He didn't stop to check if the guards were paying attention to him. He liked to think he was fast enough to go unseen. Gregor squawked under his arm, and Odie darted into the dense trees surrounding the castle. Once he was sure no one could see him, he slowed to a walk.

Odie couldn't believe the goblins trusted him with something so important. Goblins were suspicious creatures, and it had taken some of them years to respect him. Well, respect probably wasn't the right word, but at least they trusted him.

He ignored the guilt that tried to bubble up inside of him when he thought of the look on Queen Claret's face when he told her they needed more money. He shouldn't feel guilty. Her father and grandfather had pushed the goblins farther and farther away from the good parts of Riviand. The kingdom owed the goblins, and he was only helping them get what was rightfully theirs.

He was only feeling guilt because the queen was pretty. Her long golden hair flowed down to her waist and her green eyes sparkled like emeralds. He didn't enjoy seeing the worry in them. No sense dwelling on it. She was the enemy.

"Did you get it?"

Odie spun around to see a gray goblin in a green tunic and black pants.

"Of course I did," he said, holding up the bag of gold.

The goblin stomped his feet, and a portal ripped open in front of them. Odie was always impressed when a portal opened. It looked like a tear in the air before them. Odie jumped through, followed by the goblin, and ended up in his father's throne room.

"Odie!" Ummi, the king of the goblins, exclaimed. "Did you get the gold?"

"Right here," he said, throwing it to the king.

King Ummi caught it as he sat on his black throne. He opened the bag and smiled. "Good job, Odie. You too, Greg."

"His name is Gregor the Destroyer."

"Did the queen give you any trouble?" he asked, ignoring the correction.

"None."

"We are lucky to have such a gullible child on the throne."

Odie crossed his arms. "She's no child." If they thought of her as a child, then they must think the same about him.

"Don't get defensive, Son."

The king's black obsidian throne sat at the top of five black steps. Almost everything in the castle was made of the shiny black stone. Odie went to the steps and sat on the second one to the top.

"I don't think we should take any more from them. If we get carried away, they might get suspicious."

"Don't let the queen get in your head. There's a lot of gold in Riviand and a lot of it belongs to the royal family. We haven't asked for enough to even dent their supply."

He wouldn't argue with the king. King Ummi had taken him in and raised him as his own. Now he had a chance to repay him.

"If the royal family limited our land, shouldn't we ask for the land back?"

Ummi narrowed his eyes and twisted one of his golden rings around his finger. He loved his rings. He piled them on so high, Odie sometimes wondered how he used his hands at all. "We don't need more land, but we can always use more gold."

Odie studied the king. His tall golden crown caused him to appear taller than most of the goblins. Ummi liked to wear more than just rings and was adorned with as much jewelry as he could comfortably allow. Even with all the jewels, he still appeared frightening with his pointed teeth and grayish hue. If an actual goblin went to speak with the queen, she would probably be terrified.

Tipp entered the throne room, carrying King Ummi's lunch. Tipp was King Ummi's biological son and Odie's brother. Odie tried to distract his puffin. Tipp was always sneaking the obese bird treats.

"Hi, Greg!" Tipp said, tossing a grape. Gregor caught it in his mouth and hopped after him.

"His name is Gregor the Destroyer," Odious said. "If you can't handle that, call him Gregor."

Tipp handed the king a platter and turned to Gregor. "Here you are, Greg," he said, tossing him another grape.

Odie glared at the goblin. "Stop feeding him. You're making him fat."

"A layer of fat never hurt anyone," Tipp said, rubbing his own round stomach. He pulled something from his tunic pocket and Gregor snatched it from his hand.

Odie glared at his goblin brother. "Father, make him stop."

King Ummi rubbed his pointed ear and frowned. "Tipp, stop feeding the blasted duck."

"But he likes it," Tipp protested.

Odie frowned. "Puffins aren't supposed to eat grapes. He only does because you've confused him. At least give him fish. That's what puffins should eat."

"It took me a long time to get him to like things besides fish. I can't carry fish in my pockets."

"You better run because I've taught Gregor something new."

Tipp crossed his arms and grinned. "Oh, let's see it then."

"Run or it won't work."

Tipp started to run and King Ummi let out a long sigh.

Odie raised his arms into the air. "Gregor the Destroyer! Attack!" He pointed at Tipp. Gregor took off. It was a clumsy run and not very fast, but Tipp's little legs weren't quick either.

Tipp ran in circles, laughing, and Gregor tried to follow and then tripped and did a few rolls.

"Nice trick," Tipp said, still grinning. "I don't believe he's coordinated enough."

"He would do better if you stopped feeding him every five seconds." Odie bent down and picked up a black feather. He always saved them to make capes. It took a lot of feathers to make one cape, so he had to collect crow feathers as well.

"We've had enough nonsense," Ummi said. "This is a waste of time."

"That reminds me," Tipp said. "Grubble said he saw a human that wasn't Odious walking around at the bottom of our mountain."

The king's mouth formed a tight line. "I know him. Tell the others not to concern themselves with him."

Odie was curious. He was the only human allowed up here. "Who is he?"

"I will tell you when I feel the time is right. For now, forget about him and stay out of his way. He can be dangerous."

Odie grabbed Gregor and bowed to his father. Trying to get his father to talk when he didn't want to was impossible, and he didn't feel like fighting with Tipp anymore. He had things to do. Once his inventions were all perfected, the goblins would stop thinking of him as a joke.

2

—·—

CHAPTER 2

Kaylee tapped her pencil on her desk and wondered if the new kid would ever stop staring at her. He wasn't exactly glaring, but it wasn't a friendly look either. Midterms were in two days and she didn't have time to be distracted. What was his problem with her, anyway? She'd never talked to him. He couldn't even speak English.

Mr. Dovin was giving a lecture on the periodic table and chemistry wasn't Kaylee's best subject. If she wasn't focused, she was going to fail the test on Friday. She tried not to let the boy bother her, but he wasn't giving anyone else strange looks.

Kaylee twisted a thin black braid around her finger and turned to glare at the boy. Two could play at this game. He narrowed his eyes and leaned back in his chair, folding his arms and not breaking eye contact. Kaylee's eyes stung, and she blinked hard. He grinned.

"Can I see you in the hallway for a moment, Kaylee?" Mr. Dovin asked, scaring her out of her thoughts. "I want the rest of you to copy the notes on the board."

She sighed and stood up. She was going to get a lecture on paying attention. Mr. Dovin wasn't just her teacher. He was also her tutor. Her mom paid him to tutor her for two hours every day, including weekends. It might be her imagination, but she thought he pushed her harder than the rest of the class.

She stomped into the hallway and turned to face him. "What did I do now?"

"Why were you glaring at Mateo? He's new to Missouri. He needs friends, not enemies."

She threw her arms in the air. "Why aren't you lecturing him? He won't stop staring at me."

Mr. Dovin sighed and ran a hand through his dark blond hair. "He's had some rough changes in his life. Can you please try to be kind to him? I was hoping I could count on you to befriend him."

"He only speaks Spanish."

"But he can understand English fairly well."

"I don't want him staring at me."

"I'll talk to him. He's staying at my house for a while and he needs some good influences. Why don't you invite him to eat lunch with you?"

"Fine," she growled. When Mr. Dovin asked you to do something, it was a waste of breath to say no. "Why is he staying with you?"

"His parents are friends of mine."

"I hope that doesn't mean he's going to be taking after-school lessons with us."

"He might be."

Kaylee sighed and made her way back to her seat. Mateo smirked at her. She sat down and copied the notes off the whiteboard. The notes were all online, but Mr. Dovin thought copying them by hand helped them remember better. She finished just as the bell rang. She shoved her notebook into her backpack and frowned when Mr. Dovin made eye contact with her and motioned at Mateo with his head.

She stood and turned to the boy, trying not to be intimidated by his height. "Do you want to eat lunch with me?" she asked through clenched teeth.

He just looked at her and walked away. Mr. Dovin's frown followed Mateo. Kaylee was relieved. It would have been awkward eating with him. He probably would have glared at her the entire time.

"That cute guy is looking at you," Kaylee's friend Mia said. Kaylee whipped around to see Mateo sitting at a round lunch table, watching her.

She turned back to Mia. "He's in my chemistry class and he won't stop staring at me. I don't know what his problem is. Dovin even asked me to invite him to eat with me."

Mia shook her head, her short, red hair bouncing. "And you didn't? He's so hot."

"Who cares? He's creeping me out." Kaylee bit into her sandwich and shook her head. "I know Dovin is going to make me hang out with him. He's from Mexico or somewhere like that, and he can't speak English. How are we supposed to communicate?"

"I don't know, but if you hang out, you need to invite me. Look at his arms! He must do weight training. And I love his hair. It must take him forever to make it look messy and neat at the same time."

Kaylee rolled her eyes. "I actually asked him if he wanted to eat with me and he walked away. I'm not asking him again."

"You will if Mr. Dovin asks you to," Mia said, sipping her soda. "You do everything he tells you to."

"I don't," she objected. Mia raised her brow and Kaylee sighed. "You know Dovin isn't just a teacher to me. He cares more about me than my stepfather and possibly more than my mom."

"That's not true," Mia said, putting her hand on Kaylee's arm. "Your parents love you."

"I know, but I also know who to go to when I'm in trouble or I need help. Not them. My mom shrugs me off and my stepdad doesn't even listen. Dovin's been there for me ever since he started tutoring me."

"Probably because your mom is paying him a ton of money. Teachers aren't rich, so he probably wants the money."

"I don't know why my mom had to marry a rich guy. Life was better before."

Mia cocked her head. "It must be hard to have all that money."

Kaylee took another bite and let Mia's comment slide. Mia didn't know what it was like to have your mom ignore you all the time. Kaylee's mom hadn't been around much since she'd hired Dovin. She was spending more and more time traveling with her husband, and the more she stayed away, the more Kaylee resented her.

Mateo was making enemies already. He watched Kaylee eat her lunch and wondered why he was always such an idiot. Too often, Mateo found himself glaring at something or someone when he was thinking. He tried not to do it, but it was hard to control. Today, when Kaylee turned and glared back, he'd realized what he was doing. He should have looked away or apologized instead of feeling defensive.

Perhaps his mom had been right. He never tried to be social, and he spent too much time thinking about things he couldn't control. If he'd been focused on the lecture, he wouldn't have been unintentionally glaring at her.

In this situation, he was glad his glare didn't convey what he was thinking. Kaylee was really pretty, with her flawless brown skin, little black braids, and her blue hoodie. Not that it mattered. If his glare wasn't enough, he'd walked away when she'd talked to him. He hadn't understood what she said, and instead of trying to find out, he'd run off.

"Hey, man, you new?" a boy with brown hair and a letterman's jacket asked. He sat across from him, placing his tray on the table.

Mateo nodded. Trying to speak would be a disaster. Mateo spoke two languages fluently, and English was not one of them. The language Mateo grew up speaking wasn't a lot different from English, but the accent was so strong it was hard for people to understand him. Understanding was a lot easier than speaking, as long as the person talking wasn't mumbling or going too fast. He'd grown up watching a lot of English TV, so he wasn't completely lost.

"I'm Chad," the boy said, grabbing an apple from his tray.

"Mateo. I speak Spanish," he said self-consciously.

"Oh," Chad said. "Can you understand me?"

"If you speak slowly."

"What?"

"Talk slow."

"Your accent doesn't sound Spanish. It's really weird."

Mateo shrugged. If he let his temper get the best of him, he would only end up in trouble. He didn't mind being the weird kid at school. That was how it had been when he was in Mexico. He wished he could go back to his childhood home. He would go there in a second if he could figure out how to get there. If only Dovin would take him…

"She's pretty, isn't she?" Chad asked, glancing over at Kaylee.

Mateo looked back at Chad. He'd been staring at her again. He nodded and kept eating his lunch.

Chad narrowed his eyes and then grinned. "I can teach you some things to say to girls. Things they like to hear."

Mateo shrugged again.

Chad spouted off a bunch of things he thought would impress girls, and Mateo tried to follow him. He was speaking too fast for him to understand most of it. Chad gave him a few lines and had Mateo repeat them back to him. They made little sense to him, but slang was hard to catch onto.

"I think you've got it," Chad said. "You're going to sound a little weird, but girls go for accents, right?"

Mateo just looked at him. It might be best if he didn't talk to anyone. If his accent was really as funny as Chad seemed to think it was, he didn't need people teasing him. Teasing would lead to fighting, and fighting would lead to being expelled. He'd already done that in his last school and his mom had been so upset she'd sent him here.

"Go say that to Kaylee," Chad said.

Mateo sighed and stood up. He'd never been shy, but not speaking the language well made him self-conscious. He moved toward Kaylee and almost turned around when her friend nudged her. Kaylee turned and frowned at him.

He flashed his best smile. "Chicken nuggets, bruh."

Her eyebrow rose and her friend giggled. He spun around to see Chad laughing behind him.

Chad slapped his knee and wiped his eyes. "That was priceless, man. I'm going to remember that forever."

Mateo took a step toward him and made a fist. Chad's eyes went wide, and he took a step back. He should have taken in their difference in size before he messed with him. Chad wasn't small, but Mateo could take him easily. He took another step and stopped when someone grabbed his arm. He turned, ready to fight, but Kaylee was looking up at him with a huge frown.

"Come with me," she ordered, pulling him across the cafeteria like he was a naughty little kid.

"Take him to the principal!" called Chad. "Tell him he threatened me."

Kaylee muttered something under her breath and dragged Mateo into the hallway. She grabbed a fistful of his shirt and lightly pushed him against the lockers. She turned and glared at him.

"What's your problem?" she asked, putting her hands on her hips.

He shrugged. Shrugging was becoming his signature move.

Kaylee tilted her head and studied him. "Fine, whatever. Just don't let Chad mess with you. Chad is a big jerk, and he thinks he's the greatest thing that happened to the school. If he thinks you're a threat, he's going to try to embarrass you and get you into trouble. Don't do anything he says. Do you understand what I'm saying?"

Mateo nodded. He didn't understand all of it, but he got the idea. He didn't want to say anything and have her make fun of him.

"What's going on?" Dovin asked, coming toward them. "Kaylee?"

Kaylee turned to him, hands still on her hips. "Don't blame me. It was Chad just being Chad, and I think Mateo was going to punch him."

Dovin blew out a breath. "Come with me."

Kaylee rushed back to the cafeteria and Mateo followed Dovin to his classroom. He sank into a chair and slumped down. He wasn't in the mood for a lecture.

"You can't get into fights," Dovin told him, thankfully in a language he understood. Dovin was the only person on Earth outside his family who was from his world. At least as far as he knew.

"I probably wouldn't have punched him."

"Chad can be difficult. Don't let him provoke you. I don't want to have to tell your mother if you get expelled."

"I don't know why she didn't send me back to Boztoll or at least to the Northern Kingdom. I hate Earth."

"She feels you are too young to go back yourself."

"She sent me here by myself. I'm sixteen. That's the same age my brother was when he went off on his own. I could stay with him."

"I'm sure your mother has her reasons. Can you try for her?"

He blew out a breath. "I guess. I hate it, though. This is worse than Mexico. I can only understand people if they talk slowly, then they look at me like I'm an idiot."

"It will come with patience. You also need to stop staring at Kaylee. It makes her uncomfortable. I hope the two of you can be friends."

"Why?"

"I have my reasons."

"I wish I could at least do magic."

"You mustn't do that. People here aren't ready for it."

"I know. My parents drilled that into me. It's not fair to keep me from being who I am."

"One day, you'll go back. Just be patient."

Mateo's mouth turned down. He hoped Dovin was right.

"Are you paying attention?" Dovin asked, holding out his twelve-inch whiteboard.

Kaylee yawned and leaned back on the brown leather sofa in her house. "I already know all this stuff. I don't know why I have to learn a dead language, anyway. If no one speaks it, what good does it do me?"

Dovin tapped his finger on his board. "Your mother wants you to learn it."

"Only because you convinced her it would be good for college. I've been learning it for years, and I can speak fluently to you. Isn't that good enough?" Kaylee's mom made her learn so many weird things. If Dovin told her something would make Kaylee stand out, her mom demanded she learn it.

Kaylee glared. "I did an internet search on Akkronese and nothing came up."

Dovin nodded. "That's because no one speaks it."

"So it's like old English? Why do I need to speak it? You're the only one I've ever heard of who speaks it. If it was really a thing, it should still pop up on the internet. It doesn't even seem like a unique language. It's only English with a really heavy accent. The spelling is almost the same. Anyone could read it even if they couldn't pronounce it."

"That's why you've been able to learn it so quickly."

"But what's the point?"

"Can you just trust me?"

Kaylee sighed. "That's what you said when I asked why you made my mom sign me up for martial arts and fencing. When am I ever going to be in a sword fight?"

Dovin scratched his head. "You never know when certain skills will be helpful."

"I wish you stopped giving my mom ideas."

Dovin sat on the sofa and turned to her. "I only tell your mom about things that I hope will help you someday."

"Why would speaking with an accent that no one understands help me?"

"Ask me again later. Right now, we have some chemistry to catch up on. All right?"

"Fine." Kaylee grabbed her chemistry book and flipped it open. It didn't matter how much she learned. Her mom would never be satisfied.

Kaylee hated Sunday dinner. It was the only meal she ate with her mom and her stepdad. She wished her mom hadn't ever married Kamal. He was a rich surgeon from India. As soon as they were married, Kaylee's mother had changed. With all the money she could ever dream of, she'd started trying to transform Kaylee.

Kaylee's grandfather on her mom's side had come from Africa, and her father had immigrated from Ireland. Neither family had much money, but from what Kaylee understood, her parents had been poor and happy. Once her father died, her mom changed. At least, that was her guess. She didn't remember her dad. She'd only heard stories. Her mother had still been decent to her until she became wealthy.

Having one tutor would have been bad enough, but her mom signed her up for three. She had one who taught her good grammar and spelling, one for math, and one for science. Her mom had also wanted her to go to a private school, but Kaylee had put her foot down on that one. She didn't want to lose her friends.

Once Dovin came into the picture, he was the only tutor, but she still had to take any extra activity Dovin suggested. Dovin knew how to convince her mom of anything, and her mother only seemed to care about appearance these days.

"Mom?" Kaylee asked after she swallowed some peas. "Do you think I can drop a couple of activities? I'm feeling overwhelmed."

"That's unacceptable, Kaylee," her mom said. "We have been blessed to have more than most people. That means you should be grateful and become the best version of yourself."

"Come on, Temperance," Kamal said. "She's doing more than most kids her age."

Kaylee looked hopefully at her mom. She hadn't expected Kamal to take her side.

Temperance ran a hand over her short black hair and sighed. "Life isn't supposed to be easy. The more you do, the better college you can attend, and the more money you will be able to make."

"I was happier when we didn't have money," Kaylee grumbled.

"That's a ridiculous thing to say," her mom said. "Everyone is happier with more money."

"I liked it better when I was allowed to make mistakes, and I miss Graham."

"We don't talk about Graham," Temperance growled.

"I know," Kaylee said, pushing away from the table. "I'm not hungry." She stomped up the stairs, sure she was going to be in trouble later. It wasn't fair that they couldn't talk about Graham. He'd been gone for six long years and it still made Kaylee want to cry.

Graham was Kaylee's cousin who had been raised with her. She had thought of him as a brother and fought with him like he was. She'd annoyed him as thoroughly as any real sister could annoy a brother. One day, he'd disappeared, only to return sometime later with a group of strange friends.

They were all wearing capes, of all things. She sometimes wondered if he'd joined a cult. It wasn't long before they left, giving Kaylee's mom a handful of gold and changing Kaylee's life forever. She was happy to know Graham was safe, but she hadn't heard from him since, and it hurt.

She threw herself on her bed and stared at the ceiling. She tried not to think about Graham too often. It always soured her mood. She wondered what he was doing and why he'd been dressed so funny. She also wondered what was so important he couldn't come visit.

Graham's relationship with Temperance had always been rocky. He called her 'Aunt Temper' when he didn't think anyone could hear him. Maybe Kaylee should try looking for him online.

A knock on her door caused her to roll her eyes. "Come in," she said reluctantly.

Dovin entered, and she rolled her eyes again. "My mom can't even punish me herself," she muttered, hugging herself.

"What's wrong?" Dovin asked her, taking a seat on her computer chair.

"Nothing," she said, sitting up. "I was just thinking about my cousin."

"Ah, Graham. I haven't seen him in ages."

Kaylee sat up. "You know Graham?"

Dovin's mouth formed a hard line. "Oh, um, yes. I taught him for a short time."

"I didn't think you were at the school when he was here."

He looked pointedly at her. "I wasn't."

3

CHAPTER 3

"Come here, little guy," Odie said, crawling on his hands and knees and looking under the bed.

"Just jump on the bed and he'll come out," Tipp said, running toward Odie's bed.

"No!" Odie yelled, jumping to his feet and catching his brother before he could land.

"Why did you do that?" Tipp asked, struggling until Odie let him go.

"If you scare him, he's going to spray. Do you really want to smell like rednax?"

Tipp straightened his tunic. "No, but he's never going to come out if you just sit there trying to talk to him."

Odie sighed and got back on the floor. He moved his comforter and stared at the small green animal. "Do you have any food?"

"I might have something," Tipp said, reaching into his pocket. "I have some cheese, but I'm saving it for Greg."

"Gregor isn't supposed to eat cheese. Give it to me."

Tipp handed him the cheese, and Odie held it out to the rednax. "Come get it."

The rednax came closer, its snout sniffing the air. When it got to Odie's hand, he moved back slightly. The rednax came out from under the bed and grabbed the cheese with his mouth.

Odie carefully lifted the animal and took it over to his table. Rednax needed to be handled carefully or everyone would regret it. They smelled worse than a skunk and the smell was harder to get rid of. They almost looked like a skunk, but they had a snout like a pig and they were green—at least until they sprayed. Once a rednax sprayed, they turned reddish brown with a yellow stripe going down their tail. They didn't turn back green until they could spray again. Odie tried to find the animals when they weren't able to spray, but that wasn't always possible.

"Hurry," Tipp said. "I don't want to do this all day."

"If you hurry when you're trying to get rednax venom, you'll be sorry." Odie rubbed the rednax's back to get him to calm down. Extracting their venom wasn't hard if you could gain their trust.

"Watch out for the fangs," Tipp said.

Odie kept petting him. "Rednax don't bite."

Tipp sat in a chair and stared up at the ceiling. Tipp wasn't big even by goblin standards and he looked like a child sitting there. "I don't know why you have to use their venom. If he sprays, Father will be angry."

"I'm not planning on him spraying. The venom can be used in so many things. Did you know if you rub rednax venom on someone, they can't do magic until they get it off? It works in lots of potions. I bet I could sell it for a lot because no one wants to extract it."

"I don't blame them."

"We should sell stuff like that for money instead of bothering Queen Claret."

Tipp rolled his eyes. "You have some weird thoughts when it comes to the queen. I bet you just hate talking to her because she's a girl and you don't know how to talk to girls."

Odie ground his teeth and kept petting the creature. "I talk to girls just fine."

"I've never seen you talk to any."

"How many humans do you see on the goblin mountain?"

"None."

"So how am I supposed to talk to them? It's not like you talk to girls."

Tipp shrugged. "I'm too busy for things like that."

The rednax lay on the table and made a small purring sound. Odie hated when Tipp was right. He didn't know how to talk to girls. He didn't really know how to talk to humans. Any girls he met would probably be repulsed by any goblin habits he might have. He didn't know how to act like people because he didn't spend time with them.

"Did you see the woman in the forest?" Tipp asked.

Odie shook his head. "Not this time. I was focused on catching the rednax, so I wasn't paying a lot of attention."

Odie had spent a lot of his life running around the forest. He'd noticed a woman watching him occasionally, ever since he was young. He didn't know who she was or what she wanted, but it had always made him nervous. If she ever noticed that he spotted her, she disappeared.

"This is so boring," Tipp said, standing on his chair. "Why don't you just scare the venom out?"

"That's not how it—"

Tipp jumped onto the table and growled. The rednax squealed and sprayed Tipp right in the chest.

"Oh, come on!" Tipp complained.

Odie wrinkled his nose as the smell entered his nostrils. "Good going, Tipp. Now my room is going to smell forever."

Tipp wiped at his chest. "It's not that bad."

"Not that bad? I think I might puke. Now I'm going to have to get him calm again." The rednax turned reddish brown. Odie sighed. It would be easier to work with now, but he couldn't stay here in this stink.

"Father is going to be angry. You know how he feels about bringing things like this into the castle."

"It would have been fine if you hadn't scared him."

Tipp grinned. "Perhaps, but I'm not the one who's going to get in trouble."

"How may I serve you, Your Highness?" Captain Nerman asked as he bowed to Queen Claret.

She shifted on her throne. "Is there any word on the Blade of the Phoenix?"

He rubbed his brown mustache. "No. We have soldiers out searching all the cities."

"I'm trying to understand what could have happened. There are five locks in Riviand, correct?"

"Yes."

"The Blade of the Phoenix is the key to holding down Riviand. Someone took the blade and stuck it in all the locks and turned them."

"It appears so, my queen."

"I'm just curious. Why were we only guarding one lock? Shouldn't we have soldiers watching all of them?"

He shifted. "The locks are inconveniently located. Guarding them would pose several problems."

"Isn't it a bigger problem to have them turned?"

"Yes."

Claret didn't want the captain to feel bad, but she couldn't understand how they had let this happen.

"I've never seen the locks, aside from the one in Tyran," he said. "I think they are hidden."

Claret nodded. "Someone obviously found them."

"It couldn't have been done without careful planning. The blade cannot be touched by anyone with magic, and as everyone has magic, it should have been impossible."

"Could it have been done by a giant or a troll?"

He nodded. "It's possible but unlikely. They have their own magic, and I'm not sure if they would be able to touch it."

"Goblins have magic," Claret said, trying to think. "Something tells me the goblins are behind it all."

"They have the most to gain."

"Will you look into it?"

"Of course."

Claret dismissed the captain and slumped back against the throne. She wasn't prepared for something this large.

They needed heroes like in the old stories. Someone strong and powerful who could fight against anything. She could only hope that some would appear. There was nothing in her that felt heroic. If it was left to her, Riviand might fall. She picked up an old book she'd been reading. It might have the answers.

The ground rumbled, and Claret grabbed the armrests of the throne. The earthquake only lasted a few moments, but it was enough to make her heart pound. It was a sign that the continent wasn't secure. Without the goblins, they might have drowned already. That had to be their plan. Make Riviand so dependent on them they could demand whatever they wanted.

Odious usually appeared after the earthquakes. She rubbed her lips together and thought, but she didn't know how to deal with the goblins or with Odious.

Odie groaned when he felt the castle shake. He was in the middle of an experiment. Every time his father raised the continent enough to shake things, he sent Odie to Tyran to deal with the queen. If he stopped working now, the mixture would go hard and he would have to start over. Gregor squawked and jumped around his ankles.

He left his room and went to the throne room. He was expected to come when there was an earthquake.

King Ummi sat on the throne, twisting a gold ring.

"What?" Odie asked. "I'm in the middle of something."

"I need you to go get gold from the queen."

"Why now? It feels like I was just there. She's going to get suspicious."

"We can't let them get too comfortable. They need to realize they depend on us."

"And it can't wait until tomorrow?"

Ummi glared. "I'm sure you can hold off on blowing up your room."

"I don't think this mixture is going to blow up."

"Do you usually?"

Odie took a breath through his nose. He did cause more than a normal amount of explosions. Still, he had made some really great things.

"I can't have Tipp take you. He still smells too much and might draw attention. I'll open a portal and send someone to get you later."

Odie nodded, and the king opened a portal. Odie jumped through and came out near the castle. He'd forgotten Gregor. He liked to have the puffin with him to add to his appearance. He walked to the castle, and the guards glared at him, but one led him to the throne room.

Queen Claret sat on the throne. She looked tired, but she had enough energy to glare at him. He swallowed. She knew. She knew, but she couldn't do anything about it.

"I suppose you need more gold?" she said as he bowed.

"Unless you've found the Blade of the Phoenix." He watched her watch him. Her emerald eyes narrowed. He wondered how long she had to brush her hair to make it shine the way it did.

"We haven't," she said. "Are you familiar with *The Serpent's Prophecies*?" she asked, holding up a worn leather book.

"No." He hated to admit he didn't know something, but lying would catch up to him and make him look worse.

"I hadn't until today. I've been reading them. They were written by one of the sorcerers who helped put Riviand under the ocean."

"Interesting." He didn't know what to say or what she was getting at.

"There is a prophecy that speaks of a time when Riviand would be in danger. It says that people from a different world would come and save the continent. I wonder if this could be that time."

Odie twisted his black ring. "I suppose, although no one can travel between worlds. We can't even go to the world above." Odie knew that wasn't true, but he would keep that to himself.

"If it is speaking of our time, I hope they come soon."

"That would be good," Odie lied.

Queen Claret sat the book next to her and stood. She had a small pouch in her hands. She tossed it and Odie caught it. "I hope this is the last time I see you."

Odie put the bag in his pocket and grabbed a glass vial. He threw it against the floor and fled as the room filled with smoke.

4

—·—

CHAPTER 4

Kaylee stood on the football field, waiting for Mrs. Jensen to assign her a partner. She hoped she was with Mia. Mrs. Jensen was a fun teacher who believed in hands-on experiences. She'd put together a treasure hunt for anyone who wanted to stay after school today.

"I want you to look at your clues and try to find your assigned object," said Mrs. Jensen. "You may dig but only in areas that are dirt. Everyone's items are in the orchard behind the school, so there is no reason to tear up school grounds. If everyone finds their 'treasure,' we will have a pizza party on Friday. If you find another team's treasure, it doesn't count."

Kaylee was ready.

"Now for partners. James and Tara, Mia and Matt, Rochelle and Anna, and Kaylee and Mateo."

Kaylee clenched her teeth and glanced at Mateo. He smirked and came toward her. Kaylee loved the challenges Mrs. Jensen came up with, but now she was going to lose because Mateo wouldn't be any help if he couldn't speak

English. She grabbed their envelope from Mrs. Jensen and started toward the orchard.

Mateo trailed after Kaylee. She did not look happy to be on his team. He wished they didn't have a language barrier. Then he could tell her he was going to make them win. Mateo had five brothers, and their favorite thing to do was compete.

She stopped and opened the envelope, unfolding the paper inside. "Find the treasure, pure as gold. You must dig deep, the story told. Purple is the color to find, climb up fast or fall behind. Find a tree and take ten steps, turn around and find the X." Kaylee scanned the area in front of them. "Great. There are tons of trees."

Mateo snatched the paper from her hand.

She rolled her eyes. "It's in English."

He ignored her. Reading English was almost the same as reading Akkronese. There was a short fence separating the schoolyard from the orchard. There was probably an opening somewhere, but finding it would waste time. Mateo sprinted toward the fence and jumped over. He turned and tried not to grin. His brothers always said he was a show-off. He would probably need to help Kaylee get over, unless she was good at climbing.

Kaylee raised a neatly shaped eyebrow and darted to the fence.

"No!" he yelled, sure she was going to hurt herself.

She sailed over the fence without a problem and landed in a squat. "They should make taller fences."

Mateo watched her walk into the orchard, his mouth hanging open. Her jump was more impressive than his because she was a head shorter. The other teams were all climbing over.

"How do we find something purple?" she asked.

Mateo looked at the trees. "Plums."

"What?"

"Plums."

"Plums? I don't see any fruit. I think it's the wrong time of year."

Mateo studied the trees. He'd spent the first part of his life on a farm and his family had a small section of fruit trees where they lived in Mexico. He was sure he could recognize a plum tree if he saw one. They walked around for a few minutes, and then he spotted one.

He pointed at a plum tree.

Kaylee studied it. She said something he didn't understand. He looked up into the tree but didn't see anything. All the trees in this section looked like plum trees. They all had the same dark brown bark and small leaves. They hurried around, peering into the branches of different trees.

"Here!" she called, pointing up into a medium-sized tree. Mateo ran over and scanned the leaves. Up in the branches was a shovel, with a purple sticky note on it. The tree wasn't big, and he worried about the branches breaking, but he scurried up and grabbed the shovel. He handed it down to Kaylee and then jumped.

"Nice," she said. "Now there should be an X ten steps away. You go that way," she said slowly so he would understand. He took ten quick steps but couldn't see anything. He circled around the tree, but no X. It had to be here somewhere. Kaylee didn't seem to be having any luck either.

"There's something over there," Kaylee said, pointing. "It's not an X, though." Mateo followed her to a spot on the ground. Something that appeared to be metal was poking out of the dirt. Kaylee kneeled down and tried to pry it from the earth.

"No X," Mateo said, leaving it to her. He walked around, searching the ground. Kaylee was trying to use the shovel to remove whatever she had found. Soft rain fell against his face. They needed to find it fast or the rain might wash the X away. One thing he had learned in his short time in Missouri was that when it rained, it poured.

"Wow," Kaylee said. Mateo turned. Kaylee was holding a sword in her hands. Why was there a sword in the middle of an orchard? It was probably fake. Mrs. Jensen must have hidden it there, and the X was just part of her poem.

Mateo came closer and studied the sword as Kaylee turned it in circles. It appeared to be real, but a teacher wouldn't bury a real sword. For being buried in the dirt, it was sure shiny. Kaylee was rubbing dirt off the hilt. The rain was coming down harder now and thunder boomed in the distance.

"We should go back!" Kaylee said over the sound of the storm. She held the sword out to him. When he reached out and took it, an orange flash shot from the sword, throwing him into the air. He crashed to the ground and grabbed his head. Pain racked his body, and he heard Kaylee scream from nearby.

He sat up as she reached him.

"What happened?" he asked, rubbing his temples. "It burned my hand."

Kaylee's eyes widened. "You speak Akkronese," she said in the same language. He hadn't realized he'd gone back to his native tongue.

"Yes."

"Are you all right?"

"My head is pounding and my hand hurts, but I think I'm fine."

"We need to get back to school. This storm is wild. I don't know what hit you, but it must have been some type of lightning."

"No, whatever it was came from that sword," he said, getting to his feet.

Kaylee looked at the blade. "That's impossible."

"I'm sure it was magic."

Kaylee let out a small chuckle. "Magic? You must have bumped your head. If you can run, we better run. The sky is looking green. We might have a tornado."

"I can run." They took off toward the school. Rain blew in Mateo's face and the ground was turning into a massive puddle. When they got to the fence, Mateo climbed over. He didn't want to slip and his hand was throbbing where he'd touched the sword.

"Here, hold the sword while I climb," Kaylee said, offering it to him. "It's really heavy." He could barely hear her over the storm.

"No, I'm not touching it again!"

Kaylee shook her head and dropped it over the fence. She was over and picking it back up in a flash. Kaylee screamed, and Mateo turned to see a short creature coming toward them. It was grayish, with enormous eyes and pointy teeth. It wore a tan tunic and had spiky brown hair.

"Goblin!" Mateo yelled. "Run!"

Kaylee ran and Mateo was on her heels. Another goblin popped up and chased behind them. The ground in front of them burst up, throwing dirt in all directions. They turned and ran diagonally. It was getting dark, and the sky was a swirl of gray and green. Goblins weren't fast runners, but they had magic.

They reached the school, and Mateo jerked open the door. Kaylee ran through, and Mateo slammed it behind them. There was no sign of Mrs. Jensen or the other students from their class. Kaylee kept running, so Mateo followed.

She ran into the gym and pointed to the bleachers. "Under there!" They went behind the bleachers and stopped. They were both breathing hard, and Kaylee was still clutching the sword.

"What were those things?" she whispered.

Mateo pushed his wet bangs out of his eyes. "Goblins."

"Goblins? Goblins aren't real."

"That's what you said about magic. I saw goblins once before. Not on Earth, though."

"What do you mean, not on Earth?"

"If you don't know about this stuff, how come you speak Akkronese?"

"Dovin taught me."

Mateo nodded. Dovin had told him he'd been teaching Kaylee a lot of stuff. He just hadn't said what. They both screamed when someone put a hand on their shoulders. Mateo spun around to face a tall Black man who was, at this moment, wearing a large frown.

"Coach Williams!" Kaylee breathed. "You scared me to death!"

"What's going on?" Coach Williams asked. "Why are you hiding under the bleachers, and why do you have a sword? Mrs. Jensen took the others down into the tornado shelter. I told her I'd find you."

They both just stared at him. Mateo wondered if Kaylee's heart was beating as fast as his.

Coach Williams cocked his head. "Kaylee, give me the sword."

"I wouldn't touch it if I were you," Kaylee said. "It shocked Mateo."

"Are those phoenix wings on the hilt?"

"I don't know," Kaylee said. "Someone needs to call the cops. There were some scary creatures chasing us outside."

"Creatures? Come out from under here," Coach Williams said, leading them out from under the bleachers. He stood staring at them.

"I can touch the sword," he said, holding out his hand. Kaylee hesitated and then handed it to him. Mateo was pretty sure this wasn't a man to be ignored. He was tall, with broad shoulders, and looked like he could bench-press elephants. He studied the hilt and ran his finger over it. "This is impossible. I thought it was only a legend."

"What?" Kaylee asked.

"The Blade of the Phoenix."

"I remember something about that," Mateo said, racking his memory. "My mom told me a story about it when I was young."

Coach Williams stuck out his arm, showing them a tattoo of a sword surrounded by fire on his forearm.

Mateo looked from the tattoo to the sword. "They don't look the same."

Coach Williams shrugged. "Of course they don't. I'd never seen the actual sword before, and I got this when I was young. I've regretted it many times."

"Why?"

"I was obsessed with legends as a boy. It seemed like a neat thing at the time. Tattoos are very permanent. Something you think is cool today might seem stupid tomorrow. Never mind that now. It seems impossible the sword would end up here. The Blade of the Phoenix is supposed to be in Riviand."

"Riviand isn't real," Mateo said. "It's only a legend."

"What's Riviand?" Kaylee asked.

"Let's save that for a time when we aren't worried about a tornado. We need to go to the shelter with the others. Come on."

They followed Coach Williams through the school. It took a minute for Mateo to realize he had understood everything the coach said. Coach Williams spoke Akkronese.

⸺⬦⬦⬦⸺

Before they could reach the tornado shelter, they rounded a corner and ran into Dovin. He was frowning and walking toward them.

"Why are you still at the school?" he asked.

"We were doing an activity with Mrs. Jensen," Kaylee said. "Why are you still here?"

"I'm a teacher. We don't get to go home when the rest of you do."

"We need to get into the shelter," Coach Williams said.

Dovin breathed through his nose and let it out slowly. "We aren't in danger."

Kaylee frowned. "It looks like we might get a tornado."

"It's not a tornado, and it's almost passed."

Coach Williams narrowed his eyes. "Then what is it, *Professor* Dovin?"

Dovin studied Coach Williams for a moment. "Professor?"

Coach Williams crossed his arms. "What's going on, man?"

Kaylee watched the two men in confusion. They were both staring suspiciously at each other.

"What is that?" Dovin asked, his eyes landing on the sword.

"You wanna look?" the coach asked, holding out the sword.

Dovin put his hands behind his back and took a step back. "Where did you get that?"

"We found it in the orchard," Kaylee said. "And why can everyone speak Akkronese all of a sudden?"

"Akkronese?" Coach Williams asked. "I've never heard anyone call it that before."

Dovin rubbed his chin. "Well, it didn't have a name, and I heard a girl call it Akkronese once. It's as good a name as any. Right now isn't the time to be concerned with that. We need to figure out why the Blade of the Phoenix is here and why there are goblins outside."

"Goblins?" Coach Williams asked. "Here?"

Mateo nodded. "They chased us when we were out there."

Dovin nodded. "They must be after the sword. We need to leave now. I can teleport us to my house."

Kaylee's forehead furrowed as she watched Mateo and Coach Williams nod. Was she the only one here who wasn't crazy? Mateo put one hand on Dovin's shoulder and Coach Williams put his hand on the other. They all looked expectantly at Kaylee.

"What?"

"I can't teleport you unless you're touching me," Dovin explained.

Kaylee raised her eyebrows and crossed her arms. "Is this all some sort of prank? It's not funny."

Coach Williams gave her a pointed look. "Kaylee, you've known me forever. You know I have no sense of humor. Now grab Mateo's hand."

"Ew, no."

Mateo winked at her and held out his hand. The sound of pattering feet caused them all to turn. A gray goblin was running toward them, baring his pointed teeth. Kaylee screamed, and Mateo grabbed her arm. Everything went black and Kaylee felt like an unnatural force whisked her around for a few seconds, and then everything was still.

When she opened her eyes, she was standing in an unfamiliar parlor. Everything in the room was brown, and the room was a mess. Clothing hung over furniture and crumpled paper blanketed a good portion of the room.

"That was awesome!" Coach Williams said, still clutching the sword. "When did you learn to teleport? I thought that was lost magic."

"My family passed the knowledge down for generations," Dovin said. "Kaylee, are you all right?"

Kaylee's legs were shaking, and she felt sick. She had no explanation for what had happened. All she knew was that one moment they were at the school and now they weren't. Mateo didn't appear rattled like she was.

Dovin looked at her with concern. "Kaylee?"

"What just happened?" she demanded.

"We teleported to my house."

"This isn't your house," Mateo said. "Not unless you have a hidden room I haven't seen since I came here."

"You've only seen my house on Earth."

"You're saying we aren't on Earth?" Kaylee asked, sinking to a couch.

"No, we aren't."

"Are you aliens?"

Mateo laughed. "Aliens don't exist."

"Of course they do," Dovin said. "It all just depends on your perspective. This world doesn't exist in your universe," he said, looking at Kaylee. "It's a different dimension."

"And you are all from this place?" Kaylee was having a hard time believing any of this was real, but what other explanation could there be?

"I lived here when I was young," Coach Williams said. "When I was a teenager, my family moved to Earth. Since I don't have magic, I prefer being on Earth."

"You must have attended my school," Dovin said. "That's why you called me Professor."

"I recognized you as soon as you started teaching," Coach Williams admitted. "I never had your class when I lived here, but I still knew who you were. Now what do we do about this?" He held up the sword.

"I'm not sure."

"What is its significance?" Kaylee asked.

Dovin moved the clutter from all the seats and invited Coach Williams and Mateo to sit, then he took a seat by Kaylee.

"In this world, there are two continents. They are both on the same side of the world. On the other side, there is nothing but ocean."

Kaylee blinked. Only two continents. It must be a small world.

"There is a legend about a third continent."

Mateo leaned forward, his elbows resting on his knees. "Riviand."

"Yes. Riviand was supposedly a large continent that was taken under the ocean."

"It sank?" Kaylee asked, feeling skeptical. "The entire continent."

"Yes, but it was done by magic. The people in Riviand were tired of the wars going on between the continents. A powerful group of wizards cast a spell on the continent. They put a protection over it and pulled it under the ocean. The Blade of the Phoenix acted as a key of sorts. It was supposed to keep the continent down."

Kaylee narrowed her eyes. "If the sword is out, wouldn't that mean the continent would come back up?"

Dovin rubbed his chin. "I'm not sure. There is a lot that is missing from the legend, since no one has ever been to Riviand. Most people don't believe it ever existed. It supposedly disappeared two thousand years ago. We live longer here than on Earth, but nowhere near that long."

"Do you believe it?" Mateo asked.

"I've always been skeptical, but I rule nothing out. That's the reason I'm so successful."

Kaylee would have grinned if she wasn't on the verge of a freak-out. Dovin was one of her favorite people, but his ego sometimes showed through. She scanned the room and felt confused. This room was immense. A house like this couldn't be purchased on a teacher's salary.

"Why are you on Earth teaching high school if you have a house like this?" she asked.

"I came to Earth for you. You and Mateo."

"Why?" Kaylee and Mateo asked together.

"I can see auras around people."

Kaylee rolled her eyes. "Sure you can."

"I'm not joking. Some years ago, I saw an aura around your cousin Graham. I knew without a doubt he was going to save our world."

"Graham's here?" A chill ran over her entire body.

"He lives in Akkron."

"He saved the world?"

"He and his friends did, yes."

Coach Williams leaned back in his chair. "That's good to hear. I've been wondering about him. He came to me for help a few years back. He was my star basketball player. We also found out we're related. I'm his cousin or uncle or something like that."

"Does that mean I'm related to you as well?" Kaylee asked.

"No. It's complicated."

"Can I visit Graham?" she asked hopefully.

Dovin's mouth turned down. "Perhaps, but not now. Years ago, I saw Kaylee when I was looking for Graham, and her aura was bright. I knew she would come to this world for an important reason, but I didn't know why. I saw something similar the first time I met Mateo."

"But I was already here," Mateo said.

"Yes, but I knew you would do something important."

"Can you see auras around everyone?" Mateo asked.

"No. It's very random. I can't always interpret them correctly either. I find it hard to believe the sword isn't tied to your destiny, though."

"Can I see it again?" Kaylee asked. Coach Williams handed it to her. "Why would we be linked to a sword?"

"According to the legend, the continent of Riviand needed this sword. If the sword is real, then I believe the legends are true. If the legends are true, then the people of Riviand may be in serious danger. It's possible you are meant to return the sword and save the people."

"Whoa," Kaylee said, shaking her head. "I am not the type of person to get chosen to save anyone, let alone an entire continent."

"We don't get to choose whether we are chosen. We get to choose if we accept the responsibility. Chosen is a funny word and auras are complicated. It might be that you are not chosen, but it was something you were going to do, anyway."

"Can't you help Riviand?" Mateo asked. "I remember when you came to Boztoll. You know a lot of weird magic that no one else does."

Dovin shook his head. "I can't touch the sword. When the sword was created, it was made to keep the continent down, and nobody with magic could touch it. Since everyone in Riviand had magic, no one should have been able to take it."

"I learned that the hard way," Mateo said, touching the burn on his hand.

"What's the deal with the goblins?" Coach Williams asked.

Dovin walked to a desk in the corner and opened a drawer. "That I am unsure of. Goblins are untrustworthy for the most part and greedy to a fault." He pulled a small bottle from the drawer and handed it to Mateo. "Rub some of that on the burn."

Mateo opened the bottle and squirted something on his hand and rubbed it around. "Goblins have magic. Can they touch it?"

"They shouldn't be able to."

"How did the sword get into the orchard?" Kaylee asked. There were still so many things that didn't make sense.

"It's strange, for sure," Dovin said. "There is no doubt you were meant to find it." He stood and sauntered over to a door in the corner. He opened it and pulled out a cloak and fastened it around himself. "I'm going to take you all home, and then I'm going to go see if there is anything strange going on in the ocean. Let's all meet in my classroom tomorrow after school."

"What about the sword?" she asked, holding it up.

"Keep it hidden. We can't have it falling into anyone else's hands."

Kaylee's mind felt almost as messy as Dovin's house. She wouldn't be shocked if she were to wake up in her own bed.

5

— · —

CHAPTER 5

Queen Claret stood on the roof of her castle and closed her eyes. The warm breeze blew her hair back, and she focused on feeling calm. Odious and the goblins were causing her to lose sleep. Knowing Riviand was in danger made her sick to her stomach.

Footsteps behind her caused her to turn. Her aunt came toward her. Durdessa didn't like it up here. She thought it was dangerous even though there was a small wall going around the roof. Claret loved it. She could see most of the city of Tyran from up here.

"What are you thinking?" Durdessa asked, tucking a strand of blond hair behind her ear.

"I'm just worrying about Odious."

Durdessa stayed back from the ledge but looked out at the road leading up to the castle. "Odious isn't the real threat. The goblins are. He only does their bidding."

"I know, but he's the one I deal with, and so he makes me unsettled."

"You've been spending a lot of time up here this past month."

"I shouldn't. Every spare moment I come here to see if Odious is walking down the road. How much will we have to pay the goblins? I can't prove the goblins are behind the Blade of the Phoenix being stolen, but I believe it was them. They know we have to pay them."

"Probably."

"So what do we do?"

Durdessa brushed off her long pink dress and sighed. "I don't know. For now, all we can do is pay them. We can't risk the continent rising."

"I suppose. I wonder what they are plotting."

"My guess is they figured it was a way to get more gold. Gold is one of the only things that motivates goblins."

"They don't want the continent to rise any more than the rest of us. What if I refuse to pay them?"

"Are you willing to risk Riviand?"

Claret's mouth turned down. "No. It makes me so mad. I imagine Odious sitting in the goblin castle surrounded by gold and counting it while mocking me."

"The goblin king isn't going to give gold to Odious. He commands and Odious obeys. I doubt Odious gets anything out of it."

"I wish I could see what he's up to. I bet it's nothing good."

"Do you have to put frog eggs in it?" Tipp asked Odie. Odie looked up from his mixture and frowned at his brother.

"I don't have to, but it might help."

"Help what?"

"The mixture."

Tipp rubbed his pointed ear. "Help it do what?"

Odie wanted to ban Tipp from his room, but then his father would get involved. "Could you just be quiet while I think? Don't you have somewhere better to be?"

Tipp shrugged. "No. And if I leave, you won't have anyone to experiment on."

He had a point.

"Besides," Tipp said, "this was my idea. If it works, we split the money fifty-fifty."

Odie let out a long breath through his nose. Odie was trying to make something that would grow facial hair on a goblin. None of the goblins could grow hair on their faces, and Tipp really wanted a beard. Odie was sure he would look more ridiculous than he already did, but if he could manage it, other goblins might pay for it.

Tipp picked up a glass jar and held it up to the light.

"Put that down," Odie commanded. "If that breaks, it will make a huge mess."

"I'm bored. Can you hurry?"

Odie poured in a small amount of purple liquid and stirred. He didn't think it would work. None of his experiments did the first time. He was fortunate Tipp didn't mind testing things.

"All right, rub some of this on your face."

Tipp looked into the bowl. "Why don't you try it too?"

Odie rubbed his chin. "I don't need to. I started shaving ages ago." By ages ago he meant two months, but Tipp didn't need to know that.

Tipp grabbed a handful of the purple foam and rubbed it across his cheeks.

"Don't forget your chin and under your nose."

"Nah," Tipp said. "I only want it to grow straight down from my cheeks. It will look better that way."

Odie shook his head. Goblins had a strange sense of fashion. Not that Odie was much better, but he knew a beard like that would be hideous.

"Is it supposed to burn?" Tipp asked, itching his face.

"I don't know, but don't scratch it. That might make it worse."

Tipp grabbed a rag from the table and wiped the foam from his face.

"If you wipe it off, it's not going to work," Odie told him.

"You did it wrong. Does it look bad?" Tipp asked, turning to Odie. Odie's eyes went wide. Tipp had large boils breaking out across his cheek. "I can tell it's bad from your face." He ran his hands over the bumps and smiled. "I bet this looks gross."

"Yep."

Tipp grinned. "I can't wait to show my friends. I bet it makes a fun sound when they pop."

Odie rolled his eyes. He'd lived his entire life with the goblins and he still found them disgusting.

"I should go negotiate with the queen next time. I bet she'd be horrified."

Odie didn't doubt it. Tipp looked disgusting. "We don't want her terrified. She's supposed to think we're on her side." Odie didn't want to think about the queen. His stomach churned every time he did. He could try to justify his actions until the end of time, but he would never stop feeling guilty.

"Hey, Kaylee," Chad said, catching up to her in the hallway.

She tried not to sigh. Chad drove her crazy. He'd had a crush on her for years, and he couldn't take a hint.

"Are you busy today?" he asked.

"Yep."

He scowled. "I'm starting to think you just don't want to hang out with me. How can you be busy every day?"

Kaylee kept walking. "I'm going to be late." She didn't want to be rude, but hanging out with Chad was one of the last things she wanted to do.

"Late for what?"

"Tutoring with Mr. Dovin."

"I'm sure you can skip one day. Come on. I'll take you to get ice cream."

"No, thanks."

"If you aren't interested, just say so."

She cocked her head. "I'm not interested. I thought I'd made that clear several times."

Chad grabbed her arm and pulled her to a stop. "Why? I know you aren't dating anyone. I asked Mia. Is it because my parents don't have as much money as yours? That seems a little shallow."

Kaylee rolled her eyes. "I don't care about that. I'm just not interested. Let go of my arm."

"Not until you give me a good reason. We would look great together. Why can't you see that? We would be a power couple. Any other girl in the school would love to date me."

"So go ask one of them."

"Give me a reason."

Kaylee tried to pull her arm away, but he had a good hold on her. "Me not being interested is a good enough reason. Let go of me." She knew plenty of self-defense moves, but that would be a last resort. She didn't want to draw more attention than they already had.

"Why aren't you interested?"

"I think you're obnoxious and stuck-up. Are those good enough reasons?"

Mateo popped up behind Chad and tapped him on his shoulder. Chad turned and Mateo punched him in the face. Chad dropped like a rock, and Kaylee covered her mouth.

"What do you think you're doing?" Chad demanded, wiping blood from his nose on his sleeve.

Mateo glared down at him. "Chicken nuggets, bruh."

Kaylee grabbed Mateo's arm and rushed him toward Dovin's classroom. They entered the room and Kaylee slammed the door.

"You can't punch people!"

Mateo shrugged. "He was being a jerk."

She put her hands on her hips. "That doesn't mean you have to be."

"He was bothering you."

"And I had it under control. You probably broke his nose!" Kaylee wasn't sure what she thought about Mateo, but someone needed to keep him out of trouble.

"You broke someone's nose?" Dovin asked from his desk.

Mateo grinned. "I doubt it's broken. It wasn't that hard."

"Chad wouldn't let go of my arm and Mateo punched him. And it *was* hard. His nose was bleeding."

Dovin sighed. "Mateo, your mother will be so upset."

Mateo gave a half smile. "Not if you don't tell her."

"No more fighting. All right?"

He shrugged. "Fine."

"You're going to be in trouble," Kaylee said. "I bet the principal is searching for you right now."

Coach Williams entered the room. "Hey, someone finally punched Chad in the face. That's been a long time coming."

"And it felt good," Mateo said.

"You did that?"

"Don't encourage him," Kaylee said. "Just because someone is a jerk doesn't mean you should be one back. If people could learn to control themselves, there would be a lot less trouble in the world."

Dovin nodded. "Kaylee is right. And we don't have time for trouble. I'm sure there is enough in Riviand. We need to go there."

"Go there?" Coach Williams asked. "People have been searching for that place for thousands of years."

"Yes, but I plan to succeed. I've handed in my resignation and I've talked to both of your parents. We can leave immediately. Coach Williams, are you coming with us?"

"I can't leave spur of the moment. If you need me, you can come back for me."

"My parents said I could go?" Kaylee asked. "To a magical world full of goblins?"

"I didn't tell them that, of course. I told them you had an opportunity to go study abroad. Your mother was thrilled. She and her husband have been wanting to go to the Bahamas, so I guess this is their chance."

"How long did you say I'd be gone?"

"Two months to a year."

Kaylee blinked. "A year! And she agreed to that?"

"Well, I'm excited," Mateo said. "I'm done with this world. My mom was okay with it?"

"Yes. I think she's hoping it might help reform you."

"I don't need reforming. I just need to get away from this place."

"You did just punch someone in the face," Kaylee reminded him.

"Yeah, well, that was necessary."

"It wasn't."

Dovin sighed. "We don't have time to argue. We might be Riviand's only chance. I want you both to go pack anything you might need. Any questions?"

Mateo raised his hand. "What is a chicken nugget?"

Mateo stood in Kaylee's entryway with Dovin. Just this area was as big as the kitchen in his house. The tan tiled floor was spotless. He wondered if he should remove his shoes. There were paintings on the walls that Mateo couldn't figure. They were all abstract and didn't look like anything he could make out. A grandfather clock chimed, and he studied the intricate patterns carved into the wood. Kaylee's family was definitely wealthy.

He hadn't been this excited in a long time. He was finally going home. Well, maybe not his home, but at least to a place where he wouldn't be the odd one. Maybe when they were done, he could go visit his brother, Sen. Sen visited Earth about once a month, but that was a long time to go without seeing your brother.

Kaylee bounced down the stairs, carrying a big black duffle bag in one hand and the sword in the other. "I don't know how to pack for something like this." Her little black braids were pulled back into a ponytail and she wore a red hoodie.

"We can buy anything you miss when we get there," Dovin assured her. "Say goodbye to your mother and we can leave."

"She's already gone," Kaylee muttered. "She doesn't have time for things like, well, me."

Mateo frowned. He wasn't as grateful as he should be. His mom had been ecstatic to see him when Dovin brought him to say goodbye. She'd hugged him at least four times, even though he'd only been gone for a week. It must be hard for Kaylee, having parents who weren't very involved.

"All right, let's go," Dovin said, grabbing hold of each of them. They teleported to Dovin's house. Mateo loved the feeling of getting jerked around and then appearing in a new place. Magic was the best.

Dovin turned to them. "Now we need to make a plan before it's too late for Riviand."

6

CHAPTER 6

Mateo's leg bounced up and down as he sat in the parlor at Dovin's house. He felt like a little kid who was too impatient to wait. Everyone always talked about his brother Sen and his adventures, and now it was Mateo's turn.

Kaylee poked her head into the room and grimaced. "No laughing, okay?"

Mateo gave her a thumbs-up and tried to look serious.

She walked into the room, wearing a blue tunic that went past her hips, a black cape, and knee-high boots. The Blade of the Phoenix hung securely on her back. "I look ridiculous."

A grin spread over Mateo's face. "You look great."

"Then why are you grinning like that?"

"Because you're dressed like everyone in this world. I've really missed it."

"When did you move to Mexico?"

"Six years ago. I never fit in, though. I can't tell you how happy I am to be back."

"If we're trying to find a continent that's under the ocean, and it's been under there for thousands of years, I doubt it will be the same as it is here."

"Probably not, but now I can do magic without getting into trouble."

Kaylee sat next to him. "What kind of magic can you do?"

Mateo held out his hand, and a ball of light sprang up in his palm.

Her eyes were as big as dinner plates. "Wow. That is so cool. I can't believe magic is real. I'm kinda glad I can't do it, though, because that means I get to hold the sword. Swords are cooler than magic."

Mateo let the light go out. He grinned and crossed his arms, leaning against the sofa. "If that makes you feel better." In reality, he didn't know a lot of magic. He had only been ten when his family left, and his mom hadn't taught him anything new since.

"At least I'm not the only one dressed like a weirdo," she said, taking in his outfit.

"Hey, I look good."

"When my cousin Graham came back with his friends, they were all dressed like this."

"Did you make fun of them, too?"

Kaylee smiled. "I don't remember. I was only ten or eleven. Thinking back about being that age makes me cringe. I was a huge brat, so I probably did."

"I met Graham once."

She leaned forward. "You did? Where?"

"You know how Dovin told you Graham helped save the world?"

"Yes."

"My brother was part of the group. They called themselves The Silver Eclipse. I met all of them before we went to Earth."

"Was it difficult for your family to learn Spanish?"

"No, I didn't actually have to learn it. We went to Mexico through a portal. Portals differ from teleporting. If you have magic and you go through a portal, you can speak whatever language the people in that place speak. It feels natural. My brothers who don't have magic had to learn it, but they picked it up pretty fast. We all knew a little because our dad taught us some."

"Interesting. I wonder how it would feel to just suddenly know an entire language. I bet my brain would explode."

He grinned. "It was kinda cool."

"Why didn't we go through a portal? That would be awesome."

"Portals are more difficult than teleporting. Only a handful of people can make them. They aren't very stable and sometimes you lose time, so most people prefer teleporting."

"Can you tell me more about Graham and his friends?"

Dovin entered the room. He was wearing a brown jerkin and cape. "Graham's story is extraordinary but will have to wait. The sooner we figure a way into Riviand, the better."

"Maybe we need a name, like The Silver Eclipse," Mateo said.

"Perhaps later," Dovin said. "We don't have time to brainstorm about things that don't matter."

"But I've already got one." He paused for effect. "The Dudes of Destiny."

Kaylee rolled her eyes. "I'm not a dude."

"The Dudes of Destiny and Kaylee."

Kaylee hid a smile. Mateo was a lot different from what she had first believed. He smiled a lot more and kept telling jokes. His glare had almost completely disappeared.

"We don't need a name," Dovin said. "We need a plan."

Kaylee tilted her head as she studied him. "I don't see how we can do this. From what I understand, people have been searching for this place for thousands of years. What makes you think we can find it?"

Dovin grinned. "Because *I* am searching for it."

Mateo snorted. "And you know better than everyone else?"

"Of course I do."

"So you never fail?"

Dovin stared at his hands and frowned. "I've failed so hard, I'll never completely get over it." His frown disappeared, and he flashed his white teeth. "I've never failed with something like this, though. If I put my mind to it, I'll succeed."

Kaylee believed it. Dovin was determined. He didn't even let her fail, even when she wanted to.

"I never tried to find Riviand because I never needed to. The people of Riviand disappeared for a reason, and I respect that. The only reason I believe we should do it now is because they need us."

"Is it as big of a thing as we think?" Kaylee asked. "I mean, all we need to do is give them the sword."

Dovin scratched his chin. "I'm sure there is more to it than that. The sword didn't get up here by itself. Then there were the goblins. Something is wrong, and we need to look into it."

Mateo ran a hand through his hair. "I remember someone saying they think Riviand was under Mermaid's Demise."

Kaylee raised an eyebrow. "Mermaid's Demise?"

Dovin nodded. "Mermaid's Demise is thought of the same way you think of the Bermuda Triangle. Ships stay away from the area because legend says that every ship to sail into the area sinks. It's always foggy, and it is said there is a large whirlpool that can easily take down a ship."

Mateo's eyes sparkled. "I hope you aren't going to throw us into a whirlpool."

Dovin rubbed a finger over his lip. "That would be a last resort."

Kaylee gave Dovin a look. "I'm not jumping into a whirlpool."

Dovin pulled a pack over his shoulder. "I think we should go talk to the goblins."

"The ones who chased us?"

"I doubt it, though I'm unsure. I'm assuming that the goblins who were after you are from Riviand."

"Are goblins mean?" Kaylee wasn't sure she wanted to meet with a goblin. The few she saw at the school had been terrifying.

Mateo laughed. "Of course they are. Goblins are always mean. My mom used to tell us stories. Goblins are mercenaries. They love gold and will do anything for it. One day, they'll fight on your side, then turn and fight for your enemies the next. They only care about who is offering them money."

Kaylee looked at Dovin for confirmation.

He nodded. "I would never trust a goblin, but I do have gold. They are fairly cooperative when bribed."

"Yay, let's go bribe some goblins," Kaylee said sarcastically.

"We can't teleport to the top of the goblin mountain. There are enchantments to prevent that. We can fly, however."

"You know how to fly?" Mateo asked. "I've never heard of anyone who can do that."

"I don't know how to fly, but my dragon does."

Kaylee's heart raced. "Dragons are real?"

"Yes. I have a few."

Kaylee squealed. "Now that is exciting!"

Dovin led them out to his backyard. It was more like an enormous field. Wild flowers and weeds grew everywhere. Four dragons rested in the shade of large trees. Kaylee felt her eyes pop out of her head. One was gold, two blue, and one orange.

"Can I touch one?" she asked, bouncing on her toes.

Dovin walked toward the golden dragon. "Yes. This is Magma. She's been with me since she was a hatchling." Magma lifted her head and watched them. She didn't seem concerned about seeing strangers walking toward her. Dovin rubbed her head. The dragon uncurled her slender, muscular body and her scales gleamed in the sunlight.

Kaylee gently touched the dragon and smiled. Her scales were hard and smooth. The dragon looked up at her with her large black eyes. Magma stretched out her long wings and yawned. "Wow. Why didn't you ever bring me here for one of our tutoring lessons?"

Dovin laughed. "I knew you were going to come here eventually, but I didn't know when or why. If I brought you here early, it could have caused problems."

The dragon leaned down and rubbed her head against Kaylee's face. This was the most exciting thing she had ever done. The dragon was beautiful.

"Most people who have never seen a dragon before are scared," he said, glancing over at Mateo.

"I'm not scared," Mateo protested. "I don't want to crowd her. Besides, I've seen dragons. Of course, they were a lot smaller."

Kaylee couldn't tell whether he was telling the truth. He seemed nervous to her. "Come pet her," she said when he didn't come closer. He swallowed hard and came nearer. "This is better than Christmas."

"Nothing's better than Christmas," Mateo said, patting Magma on the head.

"I can't believe we get to ride her."

Mateo gave her a half smile. "I hope I'm around the first time you see a unicorn."

"There are unicorns?" She would love to see a unicorn.

"And alicorns."

Magma had a large blue collar around her neck, and Dovin hooked a leather strap onto it. It connected to the collar and then to a band around the dragon's stomach. "It's to hold so you don't fall off," Dovin said.

"What's wrong?" Kaylee asked Mateo. He was holding his hand out, staring at it.

"I need some hand sanitizer."

Kaylee smirked. "Why? Because you touched a dragon?"

"I'm not scared of dragons. But I don't like to touch animals if I don't have a chance to wash my hands afterward."

"So germs bother you?"

"Only when they come from animals. And sometimes the grocery store. Nobody ever washes those carts, and I've seen kids do some pretty gross things to them."

Dovin smiled. "And you live on a farm."

"And I wash my hands a lot. Animals roll around in their own waste."

Kaylee cringed. When he put it that way...

"Are we ready to go?" Dovin asked.

"I'm ready," Kaylee said. She wanted to giggle. She was going to ride a dragon.

"Me too," said Mateo. "Do you think there will be somewhere to wash our hands when we get up there?"

Kaylee laughed. "When we get up to the goblin mountain? Well, maybe I shouldn't laugh. I suppose it's possible goblins wash their hands."

Dovin scurried up onto the gold dragon. "Climb up," he said.

Kaylee climbed up behind him, and Mateo was behind her.

"Hold on to the tether," Dovin commanded.

Kaylee grabbed hold and smiled. Her heart was pounding in her chest, but it was an excited kind of pounding.

"Take-off can be rough," Dovin warned, "but landing is worse. Make sure you're holding on tight at both times. Once we get going, it's fairly smooth."

Magma leaned backward and then sprang forward. Kaylee was ready for it, but she still screamed. It was faster than she ever would have believed a creature that large could go. They shot into the air like a rocket. Kaylee could feel her braids flapping behind her.

"This is awesome!" Mateo yelled. Once they got higher, the Dragon flew in a straight line and it wasn't so fast.

"How long will it take to get there?" Kaylee asked Dovin.

"No more than an hour! Dragons are fast."

Kaylee watched the scenery fly by below them. They didn't pass over any large cities or even villages, only the occasional house. She saw fields full of animals, but they were too high to make out what kind.

"We're almost there," Dovin yelled. "We are going to land on top of the mountain. Remember what I said about landing?"

Kaylee tightened her hold on the tether and prepared herself. Enormous mountains loomed ahead and the dragon flew toward them. The dragon dove, causing Kaylee and Mateo to scream, and Dovin to laugh.

Magma landed at the top of the mountain with the grace of a dancing hippo. Kaylee almost fell off, but she had her grip on the tether. She slid to the ground and pulled her cape around her. It was cold up here and her legs were a little wobbly from the ride. Mateo and Dovin stood to her side. There wasn't a lot to see. Just rocks and trees.

"Vork!" Dovin yelled. "Vork, can you hear me?"

Kaylee felt a small rumble, and the air in front of them seemed to rip open. A goblin stepped out and glared at them. He resembled the goblins they had seen at the school, but this one wasn't dressed the same. This one only had material going around his waist. He had the same grayish skin and large, intimidating eyes.

"You again?" Vork asked, looking at Dovin. "I had hoped to never see you again."

Dovin grinned. "Well, the feeling is mutual."

"I assume you are here for a reason? And I'm sure it's a reason I won't like."

"That's very possible," Dovin said.

"So why are you here?"

"We need to get to Riviand."

Vork's eyes widened, and he frowned. "Of course you do."

"Can you help us?"

"If I could go to Riviand, don't you think I would be there?"

"Legend says the goblins helped move the continent under the ocean."

Vork rolled his eyes. "How old do you think I am?"

"I'd say about three hundred and sixty," Mateo whispered to Kaylee. She smiled. He did look ancient.

Vork glared at Mateo, then turned his attention back to Dovin. "I don't even know whether Riviand exists."

"I'm sure it does," Dovin said, pulling a small bag of gold from his cloak.

"Oh, look. Gold," Vork said, his voice thick with sarcasm. "Now I suddenly know things."

"You have to know something."

"I don't."

"Can you ask the other goblins?"

"If I don't know something, they know less. It would be a waste of time. Riviand is supposed to be under Mermaid's Demise, correct? I would assume the way to get there is to jump in and let the whirlpool take you."

Mateo snorted. "Sure, jump in a whirlpool. That sounds like a great idea. I bet you just want us to go die."

"I wouldn't cry."

"And it is the correct way, Professor Dovin," said a high-pitched voice behind them.

Kaylee spun around to see a small blue... creature. She didn't know what else to call him. He was only about a foot tall and stood on webbed feet. His enormous nose hung over his mouth and he had one thick hair on the top of his head. Wings on his back appeared too small for his body, and he had short, thin arms. His round body made Kaylee think of a turtle.

"Padmire!" Dovin said, kneeling next to the creature. "I can't tell you how happy I am to see you again."

"I suppose I am dismissed?" Vork said.

Dovin glanced at the goblin. "Yes, thank you."

Vork turned and stalked away.

"I'm hurt you came to the goblins before me," Padmire said.

"I thought of you, but I didn't think you could leave your cave."

"I can leave the cave whenever I feel the need. I hadn't planned to come out again so soon but sensed something was wrong."

"Padmire, this is Kaylee. She's Graham's cousin," he said, grabbing Kaylee's arm and pulling her to her knees. Mateo kneeled next to her. "And this is Mateo, Sen's brother. Kaylee and Mateo, this is Padmire. He's a bungle from the Island of Meegore."

"Interesting," Padmire said, studying them. "And the three of you are going to Riviand?"

"If we can find it, yes."

The bungle frowned. "It was like you said before. You must jump into the whirlpool. It is the only way to get to Riviand. At least the only way I know."

"How do you know?" Mateo asked.

Padmire sniffed. "Are you doubting me? After all the trouble I took to get here?"

"How did you get here?" Dovin asked. "It would have taken forever for you to climb this mountain."

"I called in a favor from a friend."

"Padmire has been around for generations," Dovin told them. "He knows a lot."

"The girl has no magic," Padmire said. "Would you like me to open the cave for her?"

"What cave?" Kaylee asked.

Dovin turned to her. "Padmire is the protector of a very magical cave. Anyone who goes through it receives magic."

Kaylee tilted her head and thought for a moment. Having magic would be amazing, but if she had magic, she wouldn't be able to touch the sword, and they couldn't take it to Riviand.

"I better not," she said. "I need to carry the sword."

"Sword?" Padmire asked. He climbed up Kaylee's arm and looked over her shoulder.

"Hey, get off!" she protested.

The bungle jumped to the ground. He put his hands on his hips and shook his head. "Why do you have the Blade of the Phoenix? That must have been the trouble I was sensing."

"We found the sword," Kaylee said. "That's why we need to go to Riviand."

"The sooner the better," Padmire agreed. "Riviand cannot stay down long without it."

"So we really have to jump into a whirlpool?" Mateo asked.

"It's the only way. Riviand is not at the bottom of the ocean. It's under the bottom of the ocean."

Mateo wrinkled his forehead. "Huh?"

"It isn't that complicated. The whirlpool goes down to the very bottom of the ocean. Water from the whirlpool goes into the ground and comes out as a waterfall in Riviand. Anything or anyone that falls into the whirlpool ends up in a lake.”

“How do you know this if nobody goes down there?” Mateo asked skeptically.

“Because I am a bungle.”

“And what is a bungle?”

Padmire sighed. “I was created to protect the cave at Meegore. Several others were also created, but they didn’t survive. We were not created well, as you can see from my ridiculously useless wings to my webbed feet. They bungled us up, and that is why I am a bungle.”

“Makes sense.”

“I know more about everything than anyone could ever want to know.”

“Are we really going to jump in a whirlpool?” Mateo asked Dovin.

“I don’t believe we have any other choice.”

“You’re just going to trust this... guy?” Mateo asked, motioning at Padmire.

Padmire frowned. “You aren’t much like your brother. He was quiet.”

Mateo grinned. “With five brothers, you have to be fast to get a word in.”

“I trust Padmire,” Dovin said.

Padmire grinned, showing pointed teeth. “I’m going to come with you.”

“Wonderful,” Dovin said. “We don’t have time to waste. Everyone on the dragon.”

Kaylee sighed. She trusted Dovin, so she would trust the bungle and try to ignore his unsettling smile.

7

_— · —_

CHAPTER 7

T he ship rocked back and forth, and Mateo leaned against the railing and tried not to groan. He'd already lost his lunch over the side, but he still felt horrible. Sweat beaded up on his forehead and he wished for a cool breeze.

"Just breathe through your mouth," a man said, coming up from behind.

Mateo ignored him. Couldn't the man see he didn't want to talk?

"I'm the captain of this ship," he said. "I've seen a lot of sick tourists over the last few years. You can call me Oscar."

Mateo's head jerked up, and he studied the man. "Oscar? The pirate?"

The man rubbed his neatly trimmed black beard and frowned. "I had hoped people forgot about that."

"My dad is Rosendo. I saw you at my brother's wedding."

"Oh! Sen's brother. I should have noticed the resemblance. That Sen is a good kid. I suppose he's not a kid anymore."

Mateo nodded. He had never actually spoken to Oscar, but his father and Sen told him stories. Oscar had been friends with Mateo's dad when they were young and living in Mexico. They had ended up in this world and Mateo's dad had married Mateo's mom, and Oscar had tried his hand at being a pirate.

"I never caused a lot of trouble as a pirate. Now I take people around to visit all the islands. I don't have a lot of work this time of year, so I was happy to see you all needed a lift."

"I've never been on a ship before," Mateo admitted.

"Your little pal seems to be enjoying it," he said, pointing up to the crow's nest. Padmire sat inside, scanning the ocean.

Kaylee bounced over to them. She didn't look sick at all. "This beats school any day."

"I would take school," Mateo said, sinking down to the deck.

"You do look a little green."

"I have a solution that helps with the seasickness," Oscar said. "The trouble is, it gives some people a headache."

"I would take a headache over this."

"All right, I'll go get it." He scurried away, and Mateo wondered how he walked so confidently when the ship was swaying like it was.

Kaylee plopped down next to him. "I'm sorry you're sick, but this has been the best two days of my life."

"And you are excited to jump into a whirlpool?"

Kaylee shivered. "I'm trying not to think about that part."

"We're being awfully trusting of a weird blue turtle creature we only met yesterday."

"I don't think Padmire is a turtle."

Mateo closed his eyes and concentrated on not heaving. Sweat rolled down his face and back.

"Here ya are," Oscar said, handing him a vial. "Just a sip."

Mateo dumped some into his mouth and coughed. The cool liquid ran down his throat and he felt it hit his stomach. His eyes opened wide, and he sighed with relief. "That's so much better."

Kaylee raised one eyebrow. "That fast?"

Oscar shrugged. "It's magic."

Mateo stood, and Kaylee followed his example.

"Any headache?" Oscar asked.

"No."

"Good, good. Now you can enjoy the rest of the trip. Dovin said you want to see Mermaid's Demise. I usually avoid that area, but it won't hurt to go close enough to see the fog. You can't see the whirlpool, if it even exists, but the fog is interesting enough."

Mateo nodded. Dovin must not have told him they wanted to jump in.

"Why is it called Mermaid's Demise?" Kaylee asked, peering out at the ocean. "Are there really mermaids?"

"Not that I've ever seen," Oscar said. "Of course you hear rumors."

"Being a mermaid is not a natural thing," Dovin said, walking up to the railing.

"What does that mean?" Mateo asked.

Dovin leaned on the rail and frowned at the ocean. "Thousands of years ago, there was a powerful witch. She came up with a powder that could turn a person into a mermaid. The powder was turned into stones and placed into lockets, and whoever wore them could turn into a mermaid. She made forty or fifty of them and gave them to people she cared about."

"Wow," Kaylee said.

Dovin paused and shook his head. "She thought they were a gift, but really, they were a curse."

Oscar scratched his beard. "How so?"

"There is something addictive about being a mermaid. The longer they stayed in the ocean, the less they wanted to return to land. It might have been a gift to the people she gave them to, but it was a curse for those left behind."

Kaylee watched Dovin. "If that was thousands of years ago, they would have all died by now, right?"

"Yes. Some of them passed their lockets down, and I assume most were lost. If they died while under the water, it isn't likely they would be found."

Mateo's eyes searched the water. "Have you ever seen a mermaid?"

"Yes," Dovin said.

"So there's at least one out there?"

Dovin took a deep breath and let it out slowly. "Perhaps. It was a long time ago."

"I'm surprised I'd never heard about that before," Oscar said. "I've heard plenty of fish stories from the sailors I've hired over the years."

"I don't believe the people possessing the lockets wanted anyone to know about them. It might have put them in danger."

Mateo nodded. "From those wanting to hunt them?"

"Or steal the lockets."

"I'm going to watch the water more," said Oscar. "A mermaid would be an interesting sight to see."

Dovin nodded. "Indeed. I think I'll go talk to Padmire for a while."

Mateo watched him leave. "Did he seem sad?"

Kaylee nodded. "Maybe he knew a mermaid."

"I wouldn't mind seeing a mermaid, but I'm not sure I would want to talk to one. It just seems weird."

"No weirder than seeing a unicorn or a dragon."

"I grew up with stuff like that, but a mermaid is like part person, part fish. Something about that feels creepy."

"Yeah, I would prefer dragons to mermaids."

Oscar leaned over the rail. "I would love to see a mermaid. I'm a bit of a romantic."

Mateo wrinkled his nose. "I don't see anything romantic about a mermaid. Are you hoping to fall in love with one?"

Oscar threw his head back and laughed. "Me and a mermaid? That's the funniest image I've had in a while. Can you really imagine me with a mermaid?"

"Maybe a desperate one," Mateo teased.

Oscar laughed again. "I'm happily married. Married to an ex-queen, in fact."

"An ex-queen?" Kaylee asked.

"Yep."

Mateo grinned. "That's almost as hard to picture as you with a mermaid."

"Nah," he said. "If you met her, you wouldn't think that. Mermaids are magical creatures. My wife is as mean and ornery as they come. She has softened some since I met her."

Mateo already liked Oscar, even if he didn't believe everything he said.

Mateo smiled as he looked out at the ocean. Before his family had left for Mexico, he'd always been the funny brother. At least that was how he'd thought of himself. He wasn't sure anyone else did. The last few years, he spent being angry, but now he felt more like himself. He felt free here.

"What are you grinning about?" Kaylee asked.

"Nothing. I'm just glad to be back."

"Last one to the top has to rub my feet," Mateo said, flashing his white teeth.

Kaylee laughed. "It's going to be funny watching you rub your own feet."

Mateo just grinned. He was so unlike the way Kaylee had first perceived him. Maybe some people really did thrive in different places. She definitely felt like a different person here. It was the first time in six years her mom wasn't overscheduling her.

They had been on the ship for a couple days, and it was getting boring. They needed to find their own fun. Mateo was good at coming up with competitions. Oscar had a chess set, but Kaylee couldn't get into it.

"Ready, set, go!" Mateo called, and they both shot up the rigging.

Kaylee was fast, but so was Mateo. The rope was stiffer than she expected, which made it easier to climb.

"You two are going to break your necks!" Dovin called from below. They ignored him and kept going. Kaylee climbed faster, but she couldn't get ahead. She wasn't falling behind either. They were almost to the cable they agreed on as the finish line. Kaylee stretched her arm up, and before she could touch it, Mateo slapped it.

"Ha, ha! I win," he said, turning to her. He was breathing hard and smiling.

"That wasn't fair," Kaylee protested. "Your arms are longer."

"I can't help that," he said, leaning into the rigging. "I guess you get to rub my feet."

She wrinkled her nose. "That sounds disgusting."

"My feet aren't disgusting."

"Please. They've been inside those boots for days, and you haven't had a shower in at least that long."

"Yeah, I think we're all getting a little ripe. Still, you owe me."

"Can't I at least wait until we get to Riviand and you take a shower?"

"Fine, I'm not a monster. Don't your feet hurt? I'm not used to wearing boots anymore and mine are killing me."

"They are a little sore." That was an understatement. Kaylee's feet were covered in blisters. She'd tried walking around without boots, but whoever built this ship hadn't made it barefoot-friendly. After the third sliver, she put her boots back on.

"Mermaid's Demise ahead!" Padmire's shrill voice called, piercing their ears. He had spent the majority of the journey in the crow's nest.

Kaylee turned her head, making sure she still had a good grip on the rope. "Wow." A bluish-gray fog covered a large area of ocean. The fog swirled around itself even though Kaylee couldn't feel any wind.

"Race you down," Mateo said. Before he could give the signal, Kaylee started down as fast as her legs would move. When Kaylee had almost touched the ground, Mateo jumped the rest of the way.

She scowled as she stepped onto the deck. "You are such a show-off."

He just laughed and ran to the railing where Dovin, Oscar, and most of the crew were looking at the fog. Kaylee ran below deck and grabbed the sword. She put it on her back and joined everyone above. Dovin stuffed something in a bag and put it over his shoulder, fastening it at his waist.

"How secure is that sword?" Dovin asked her. She shrugged. It felt secure, but not if she was going to be thrown around in a whirlpool. Her stomach flopped now that they were about to go in. "Do you have a small piece of rope?" Dovin asked Oscar.

"Sure. Mel, get him some rope."

One of the crew members disappeared for a moment, then came back with a rope.

"I'm going to tie this around you and the sword," Dovin said.

Kaylee nodded and held up her arms. Dovin tied the rope around her waist and over both shoulders. She wanted to protest. This wouldn't make swimming easier.

"Are we ready?" Padmire asked from near her knee.

Oscar narrowed his eyes. "Ready for what?"

Mateo peered into the fog. "Can't you just teleport us down there?"

"You can only teleport to a place you know, and I don't know how magic works in Riviand."

"Oh no!" Oscar exclaimed. "I am not letting you jump into the ocean. Why didn't you tell me your plan?"

Dovin glanced at him. "Because you might have refused to take us."

"Of course I would have refused! It's suicide. Do you know how many people have tried to find Riviand over the years? A lot, and no one ever has. I won't take you any closer, and it's too far to swim."

Dovin squinted into the distance. "I can't teleport us to Riviand, but I can teleport us into the fog."

"I should have known this wasn't as innocent as it sounded," Oscar muttered. "I should have turned around the second I realized Mateo was Sen's brother."

"Why would that matter?" Mateo asked.

"Sen is always doing something dangerous."

Dovin looked from Mateo to Kaylee. "You're both good swimmers, yes?"

Kaylee cocked her head. "Isn't now a little late to be asking that?"

Mateo nodded. "I can swim."

"Then it's time to go." Dovin held out his arms, and Kaylee and Mateo grabbed hold. Padmire wrapped his arms around Dovin's leg. "Be prepared to hit the water and head for the whirlpool."

"You should rethink this," Oscar said. "What am I going to tell people when I come back without my passengers? Losing people is bad for business. And what will I tell Sen?"

"Don't tell him anything," Mateo said. "He doesn't have to know we ever met."

"Thanks for the ride, Oscar," Dovin said. "Don't worry about us. We're going to be fine."

The next thing Mateo knew, he was dropping through the air. He wasn't holding on to Dovin anymore and he couldn't tell how high he was. He plunged feet first into the ocean and held his breath. When he swam to the top, he scanned the water for the others. It was hard to see anything in the fog. Thankfully, the water was warm. There was a roaring sound behind him.

"Hello?" Kaylee yelled from somewhere on his right.

"Over here!" Mateo called back. He swam toward her and got to her just as Dovin did. Padmire was clutching Dovin's neck.

"This is so loud!" Kaylee hollered.

"Did you have to drop us from so high?" Mateo asked.

Dovin squinted at him. "What? It's too loud!"

Mateo just shook his head.

"Swim toward the sound!" Dovin called above the roaring of the whirlpool.

Mateo followed Dovin, Kaylee at his side. Padmire had a firm grip on Dovin's collar. Mateo was really regretting coming here. He'd been so excited to be back and on an adventure that he hadn't been thinking clearly. Now they were probably going to die. Why had he trusted Dovin so thoroughly?

Mateo was moving faster. Some mysterious force was pulling him. Well, not a mystery. He knew what was in front of him. He yelled as he felt himself drop. The speed of the whirlpool shocked him as he began moving with it. He knew it was supposed to be big, but this thing was enormous. It was so big he didn't even feel like he was going in a circle.

He looked around frantically, hoping to see Kaylee. It was too dark, and there was too much water flying around to make out anything specific. Water splashed over his head and he flailed around, trying to surface. His body flipped around and he wasn't sure if he was upside down or sideways. This was the end. He was going to drown.

8

_— · —_

CHAPTER 8

Queen Claret strolled through the rose garden, trying to relax. It wasn't an easy feat these days. She plucked a yellow rose and held it to her nose. Her frown deepened as she stared at the beautiful flower. She would never understand why anyone liked the smell. It always gave her a slight headache.

"Queen Claret!" A guard rushed toward her, pulling her from her thoughts.

"What is it?"

He looked distressed. "Some people fell in from the waterfall."

Claret's eyes widened. "People?"

"Yes. Well, three of them are. One is something I've never seen before. We just brought them in. They are all unconscious."

"A shipwreck?"

"There was no debris."

"Have you sent for the healer?"

"Yes, he is with them now."

Claret nodded. "Take me to them." She followed the man back into the castle. As if she didn't have enough to worry about. It was unusual for people to fall into Riviand. It happened occasionally, but there was usually a shipwreck to blame.

If these people had come of their own accord, then it was likely they were searching for Riviand. It wasn't common, but there had been a few in Claret's lifetime. Most came hoping to find a land full of gold or were looking for recognition. They were never happy to learn that Riviand had no more gold than the upper lands, and they could never return home.

The guard led her to a backroom in the castle. Four mattresses lined the floor, and on them lay a girl and a boy about her age, a middle-aged man, and a blue creature she didn't recognize.

"How are they?" she asked Adler.

The old healer peeked up at her and then went back to examining the man. "Alive. They all have strong heartbeats. The girl has a sword tied to her. I need to get that off so she can rest comfortably. I can't untie the rope with my old hands."

"I can get it," the guard said, pulling a small knife from somewhere. He sawed at the ropes that were around the girl and pulled them off. He unhooked the sheath, and it fell to the mattress.

"What should I do with it?" he asked her.

"Put it somewhere safe until we determine whether or not they are a threat."

"Yes, Your Majesty." The guard grabbed the hilt, and an orange flash blasted him across the room. The sword clanked to the ground, and the guard smashed into the wall and fell to the floor. Claret and Adler ran to him. Blood ran down his face from his head.

"I'm all right," he said as Adler examined his head.

"What was that?" Claret asked.

The guard pointed to the fallen sword. "It must be the Blade of the Phoenix."

Claret's eyes widened. Could it be? She ran to the sword and bent down. A pair of wings twinkled up at her from the hilt. She reached her hand toward it.

"Don't touch it!" the guard yelled. Claret pulled her hand back and stood. "I'm sorry I yelled."

"Don't be," Claret said, her face feeling warm. "I don't know what I was thinking."

The guard stood and walked up next to her. "How did someone outside of Riviand get the sword?"

"I'm not sure, but your head is still bleeding." She handed him a handkerchief from her pocket and held it to his head.

"I've had worse."

"What is your name?"

"Vigh, Your Majesty."

"How many people know about these people, Vigh?"

"There were five of us who found them."

"Do you suppose we can keep the finding of the sword quiet for now?"

"Yes, but what is the purpose?"

Claret stood tall to give off the appearance of confidence. "We don't know who stole the sword, and we don't know how they did it. The fewer people who know, the better."

"I won't tell."

"Nor will I," said Adler.

Claret trusted Adler, and she would have to trust Vigh. She didn't deal with most of the guards and so she didn't know him. He was probably new because she wouldn't have guessed him to be old enough to be in the guard.

Claret thought back to her book. Could these people be the ones prophesied to save Riviand?

The girl on the mattress groaned, and Adler rushed to her side. Her eyes popped open, and she hopped off the bed, then bent over, putting a hand to her head.

"Sit down," Adler commanded, pushing her gently to the mattress.

The girl looked up at them and started talking fast, her hands moving as she spoke. Claret couldn't understand a word she said. She stared at the girl, and she quit talking.

"Sorry, I forgot where I was," the girl said, her eyes falling to the sword. Her speech was strange, but so were all the people's accents who came from up above.

"I am Queen Claret. And who are you?"

The girl noticeably swallowed as her eyes fell on Claret's golden crown. "My name is Kaylee."

"Why are you here, and how did you come to have that sword? Did you steal it?"

The girl's eyes narrowed and then fell on her friends. She sucked in a breath. "Mateo? Dovin? What did you do to them?"

"We did nothing to them," said Vigh. "Well, we pulled you all from the water."

"They're all going to be fine," Adler said.

Claret tried to look commanding. "You didn't tell me how you came to have the sword."

The girl's eyes narrowed. "I found it."

"Where? On one of the upper continents?"

"I'm not sure how much I want to tell you. How do I know I can trust you?"

"We need the sword," Claret said. "Without it, we could all die."

"I believe you, but I don't know if I should hand it over." She turned to the boy next to her and shook him. "Mateo? Mateo?"

Claret tried to hide her impatience. It wasn't in her nature to be forceful, but Riviand's future depended on that sword.

The boy took a deep breath and opened his eyes. He looked at Kaylee and his eyebrows came together. "Where are we?"

"I don't know, but there's a queen. This adventure keeps getting more exciting," she said with no emotion. The boy sat up and his eyes scanned everyone in the room. He was handsome, with black hair and broad shoulders. Claret hoped she looked decent. It had been hours since she'd glanced in the mirror.

"Shouldn't I have a headache?"

"I feel fine," Kaylee said.

Claret nodded. "Every time someone falls into Riviand, they are unconscious. No one has ever drowned. When they wake up, they feel normal. We don't understand why. It must be part of the enchantment. I really need you to tell me where you found the sword. It is imperative that we fix the problems its disappearance has caused."

Mateo ran a hand through his hair. "We found it on Earth."

"I do not know Earth. Is it an upper continent?"

"No, it's a different world."

Claret blinked twice and looked at Vigh. He was frowning. Adler wasn't paying attention or was pretending not to. "How would the sword get to a different world? And how did you bring it here?"

"We don't know how it got there," Kaylee said. "It was near our school. As soon as we found it, goblins chased us. Our world doesn't have goblins."

"This is my world," Mateo said, "but I was on Earth. I'm from one of the upper continents, and so are Dovin and Padmire," he said, pointing at the still unconscious figures.

"Dovin can teleport, so we came to this world," Kaylee explained. "Well, the upper world."

Vigh snorted. "Teleport? Teleporting is a children's story."

Kaylee put her hands on her hips. "Then how do you suppose we got here?"

Vigh glared at her. "I don't believe you are as innocent as you say."

"We didn't say we were innocent. What are you accusing us of?"

Claret put up a hand. "Stop, Vigh. I believe them. The goblins must be behind this."

"Well, now that you have the sword, everything is fixed, right?" Kaylee asked.

Claret bit her lip and then forced herself to stop. A queen should never show weakness, and being nervous was a weakness.

"It is not as fixed as we might wish," she said.

"What do you mean?" the middle-aged man asked, sitting up.

"You're awake!" Kaylee exclaimed. "You scared me."

"I've been awake since they dumped me here."

Claret frowned. "Then why did you pretend to be unconscious?"

The man smiled. "It's sometimes easier to get information."

"Exactly," said the blue creature as he sat up.

Claret forced her anger down. How dare they pretend to be unconscious?

"We risked a lot to bring you that sword," the man said. "Now why isn't your problem fixed and what do we need to do?"

Claret was annoyed, but she trusted these people. They had brought the sword back to Riviand, after all, and there was the prophecy... "The sword is not just a sword. It is a key."

"Go on."

"When Riviand was first placed down here, there were five locks made. The sword fits into each of them. Whoever stole the sword unlocked all but one of them. It takes all five to keep the continent firmly down."

Mateo tilted his head. "Then how is it staying down?"

"The goblins have magic that is far superior to ours. They have been keeping it down, but they require large amounts of gold to do it. We have no choice but to pay."

"So now that you have the sword, you can lock it all up again," Kaylee said. "I don't see the problem."

"There are several problems," Claret said. "For one, none of us can touch the sword."

"Just find someone without magic."

"Everyone in Riviand has magic. No one should have been able to take the sword."

Dovin glanced at everyone. "Then I suppose we will stay and have Kaylee do it."

Kaylee nodded. "Sure." She stood and picked up the sword.

Claret felt her eyes widen. "You don't have magic? I've never seen anyone without magic before."

"So where are the keyholes?" Kaylee asked. "I can do it right now."

Claret glanced at the floor. "That's another problem."

"You don't know where they are?" the man guessed.

"No, I don't. The only one I know of is the one where the sword stays. It's here in Tyran, in the middle of the kingdom. All the locks must be turned and then the sword stays in that one. It's heavily guarded but was stolen regardless."

"Any ideas, Dovin?" Mateo asked.

Dovin rubbed his chin. "I don't know this place, so I can't begin to guess where they could be."

"There are hints as to where they are. We just never thought to look for them."

"How do you know they were all turned then?"

"We received a letter telling us from an anonymous source."

"I see."

Mateo frowned. "Why would you only have hints about where they are? It seems like important information."

Claret's mouth formed a tight line. "My father knew where they were, as I'm sure others do. He was planning on taking me to all of their locations, but he died before he could. When he was dying, he wrote a letter telling me where I could find them. He was very sick, and it is not as specific as it could be."

"Don't worry," the blue creature said. "We will deal with this."

Claret nodded. The creature made her slightly nervous.

"My aunt might know where they are, but she left just this morning to meet with some of the surrounding cities. She could be gone for quite some time."

"Riviand can't be too big," Mateo said. "Can we find her?"

Dovin shook his head. "Riviand was said to be the largest of the continents."

"My father used to tell me stories about a pyramid. I remember he said one of the keyholes was inside, but monsters guarded it. He told me about it when I was young, so

I'm not sure if it was true or just to entertain me. I have never seen a pyramid here, so it was likely untrue."

Vigh turned to her. "There is a pyramid, Your Majesty. It is in the southeast corner of Riviand."

"In the jungle?" Claret wanted to scream sometimes. Why hadn't her father told her about things like this? There were so many skills and so much knowledge she was lacking. "How will we find it?"

"I can take you."

"Shouldn't the queen stay here?" Kaylee asked. "Don't you need to rule the kingdom and stuff?"

Claret felt conflicted. She should stay here. Especially since Durdessa was gone. "We can discuss the details later. If you are all feeling well, I can take you to see the space from where the sword was stolen."

Kaylee looked down at her wet clothes and frowned.

Where were Claret's manners? "You can change your clothing first, of course, and I will have the servants draw you a bath."

The sun shone in Kaylee's eyes as they followed the queen across the village. She couldn't believe this place. How did it even have a sun? It was hard to believe they were under the ocean. When she studied the sky, it looked the same as a regular sky. There was dirt on the ground and flowers and trees aplenty. It could pass as anywhere on Earth. Well, on a medieval Earth.

The clothing the people wore was definitely different. Their clothing was closer to what Mateo and Dovin were wearing than something she was used to seeing. Most of the women they passed wore dresses with long sleeves that hung too low to seem practical.

The queen had given them all clothing and Kaylee had gotten a few funny stares when she asked to have a tunic and pants like the men. Adventures were messy, and a dress would only get in the way.

Several shops lined the streets. They were all made of brick or stone and had sloped roofs. The houses they saw were the same, except smaller, and some were made of logs. People hurried down the dusty streets, barely sparing them a look as they passed.

Kaylee had to pay close attention to understand what the queen was saying. Her accent was strong. She hoped the queen didn't want to come looking for the locks with them. Kaylee didn't like the way Queen Claret kept glancing at Mateo. Not that Kaylee was interested in him or anything.

"This is crazy," Mateo said, pointing up at the sky. "I thought we would look up and see fish or something."

"Well, Padmire did say it was under the ground. I don't get how they have a sun."

"Magic used to be a lot stronger. I doubt there is a person alive who could pull this off in our day."

"Here it is," the queen said, pointing at a small glass structure. Guards surrounded it, even though the sword wasn't there. When the queen went closer, one guard opened a glass door, and they followed her in.

At the center of the structure was a small fence surrounding a marble square. In the middle of the square was a slit, just big enough for a sword to fit inside.

"Should I put the sword in?" Kaylee asked.

"No," said the queen. "This is the only one that is still locked. You can return the sword here once the other locks have been turned."

"Do all the locks look like this?" Mateo asked, pointing at the marble.

"I am not sure. I hope so. If they don't, they might be more difficult to find."

"I can take you all to the pyramid," Vigh said. "Most of the guards know where it is."

Dovin studied the lock. "Perhaps I should go with Vigh and Kaylee, and the rest of you should stay here and try to figure out where the other locks are."

"Did you hear?" Kaylee said. "There might be monsters."

Dovin cocked his head. "And?"

"You should probably stay here. The mentor always dies. It's like a rule or something."

"That's ridiculous. I've mentored plenty over the years and I've never died."

Mateo grinned. "But should you really be risking it?"

"I'm not going to stay here while you all throw yourselves in danger."

"But you would be better at figuring out where the other locks are than we would," Kaylee said. "Why don't you stay here with the queen, and Mateo and I will go with Vigh?"

"I'll stay here as well," said Padmire. "I can't get around fast."

Dovin's eyes darted back and forth between them. "I might agree to stay, but only because I've waited on children figuring out hints before."

Queen Claret tapped her lip. "We have a large library. I'm sure there is information about the locks in some of the books. We can ask around the castle as well. Just because I don't know doesn't mean others don't."

Dovin grimaced. "Very well. By the time you return, I will probably have the other three locks figured out."

"What is the world above called?" the queen asked. "We have nothing about it recorded and no one who has come down wants to talk about it."

Mateo smirked. "It didn't have a name until recently. We call it Basura."

Dovin frowned and shook his head. "The name caught on before it could be stopped."

"What's wrong with Basura?" Claret asked.

Mateo grinned. "It means garbage in Spanish. My dad didn't like the world, so that's what he called it. We thought that was its name. My brother ended up... I don't know, famous or something, and so the name caught on because people heard him use it."

Kaylee shook her head. Mateo seemed proud to be from a place called garbage.

"Can you teleport us to the jungle?" she asked Dovin. She was always up for an adventure, but walking might waste time.

"Of course," Dovin said. "I'll need a map so I can picture it in my head."

"I still find it hard to believe you can teleport," Vigh said. Kaylee wondered what he looked like without his helmet. He must be older than he looked because he didn't look a day over twenty. He had a handsome face, with a strong chin and bright blue eyes.

"I won't be surprised by anything anymore," Kaylee said. "I didn't even know magic existed until last week."

Queen Claret's eyes widened. "Your world has no magic?"

"None that I know of."

"How odd. No magic and no goblins."

"There is more we need to find than just the locks," said Dovin. "We also need to figure out who stole the sword. If we don't, what is to stop them from doing it again?"

"I have never heard of a person in Riviand who couldn't do magic," said Vigh. "We make rounds by the waterfall every day, but it's possible we missed someone coming in."

Dovin was still staring at the lock. "I can't imagine someone sneaking in from above to steal the sword. Most people think Riviand is only a legend."

"And how did they get the sword out?" Vigh asked. "No one has ever been able to leave Riviand. There's no way out."

"Maybe they could teleport," said Kaylee.

Dovin rubbed his chin. "I doubt a person can teleport out. When Riviand was placed here, it was to get away from the rest of the world. I would assume they made it so no one could teleport in or out."

Kaylee scowled at Dovin. He could have mentioned that earlier. What if they couldn't get out? She would worry about that later.

"Besides," Dovin said, "the person who took the sword couldn't have possessed magic, so they couldn't teleport."

Kaylee nodded. "Right."

"How often do people fall into Riviand?" Dovin asked.

"Not often," said Vigh. "In all the time I've worked here, you are the only ones I am aware of."

Kaylee wasn't sure that was impressive. How long could someone his age have worked here?

"There are a handful of people who live among us who fell in," said the queen. "As far as I am aware, they all had magic. The only one I know personally is my aunt."

"Your aunt isn't from Riviand?" Mateo asked. "How does that work?"

"Well, she's not really my aunt. When she came through, she ended up at the castle. It was a long time ago. I don't remember a time when she wasn't here. She became close friends with my father and mother and helped counsel them."

"And she has magic?" Dovin asked.

"Yes. She's a good person. I would never suspect her."

"Could someone pick the sword up with another object?" Vigh asked.

"I'm not sure," Kaylee said.

Dovin shook his head. "I wouldn't try it. I had Kaylee try different sheaths until she found one that fit the sword, but I didn't dare touch the sheath once the sword was inside."

"Should we try?" Mateo asked, grinning. "Any volunteers?"

Vigh touched the bump on his head. "Not me."

"Yeah, me neither. It already blasted me."

"Let's stop wasting time," Dovin said. "Are you ready?"

9

CHAPTER 9

Odie measured two teaspoons of hods bark oil and a drop of rednax venom into his bubbly green mixture. It was going to work this time. He was sure of it. He stirred quickly and watched the mixture harden.

"No, no, no," he muttered. He grabbed the dropper of rednax venom and put in two more drops. He stirred vigorously and hoped the bubbling mixture wouldn't erupt and make a mess in his room. "There we go!" He smiled and looked at Gregor. "I think it finally worked."

The door burst open, and Tipp entered. "Father is raising the continent a bit more. He wanted me to warn everyone, so there isn't a panic like last time."

Odie looked around his room. He needed to secure some things. Even though the goblins only raised the continent less than a fraction of an inch, it would cause an earthquake, and the obsidian floor was unforgiving when Odie's vials fell. He grabbed some of his more breakable things and placed them on his bed. He glanced at his shelves and sighed. There wasn't room for everything on his bed.

"Does that mean he wants me to go ask for more money again?"

"Probably. He thinks it's better to have everyone deal with a human. They don't trust goblins."

Odie went back to stirring. "With good reason."

"What are you making? Are you going to blow everything up again?"

Odie looked down at his goblin brother. "I haven't blown anything up in ages. Look what I made." He held the pot down so Tipp could see.

"You invented goo."

"It's not goo. If I've done it correctly, it's a sleeping potion."

Tipp grinned. "Really? How does it work?"

"You light it on fire. Should we try?"

"Yeah. If it works, can I borrow some?"

"Depends on what for."

Tipp made a ball of fire appear in his hand and threw it into the bowl. Green smoke blasted into the air.

Tipp yawned. "How will we know if it works?"

Odie's eyes felt heavy. "Oh, no!" He grabbed a stack of papers and fanned the smoke away from them.

"What... is... it?" Tipp asked, right before he fell to the ground.

"I guess it works," Odie said, then everything went dark.

"That was amazing," Queen Claret said after Dovin teleported them all into the jungle. Kaylee smiled, noticing the queen's hands were trembling. She was glad Dovin had a skill that these people weren't used to, so they had some sort of advantage. The queen wasn't going to go in the pyramid, but she wanted to see it.

"Teleporting can be very useful," Dovin said.

Mateo nodded. "You should teach it to me. You taught my brother."

"Perhaps someday."

Kaylee reached back to touch the sword. She had to assure herself it was still there.

"So where is the pyramid?" Mateo asked.

Vigh scanned the jungle. "It's hard to determine. That way must be north," he said, pointing. "We want to go southeast. Follow me."

"What do you think it will be like?" Kaylee asked, walking behind Vigh and the queen, with Mateo at her side.

Mateo grinned. "It's probably got trap doors that drop you into pits of snakes and booby traps that shoot arrows. Possibly mummies. There have to be mummies."

"I think you watch too much TV."

"I know I watch too much. Still, it's good to know what we're in for."

"Movies aren't going to prepare us for something real."

"You never know."

Queen Claret glanced behind her. "Do you really think any of those things will be in there? I do not wish to send you all into danger."

"Aren't you the one who said it had monsters inside?" Kaylee asked.

The queen nodded. "That's what my father said, but it might just be a story."

"What do you think, Dovin?" Mateo asked, looking over his shoulder.

"It sounds like nonsense to me," Dovin said. "Probably just stories to scare children."

Kaylee shivered. "Well, I'm going to be careful. I've learned that lots of things are real that I wouldn't have expected."

They entered a clearing, and fifty feet off stood an enormous pyramid. It wasn't like any pyramid Kaylee had ever seen. The sun shone on it, reflecting a rainbow of colors, making it hard to look directly at.

Queen Claret sped up. "It's beautiful!" she exclaimed. "I cannot believe my father never brought me to see this. It looks like it's made of crystal. Why don't more people talk about it?"

Vigh coughed. "People talk about it quite a lot. We study it in school."

"Oh." Queen Claret was the first one to the pyramid. She ran a hand over it. "It's smooth and so tall. How do you suppose it was built?"

Mateo put his hands in front of his face and moved them apart as if framing a headline. "Aliens."

Kaylee snorted. "Aliens? Really?"

"Do you have a better guess?"

"If people here have magic, I imagine they can build things in ways I can't dream of."

"It is said the wizards who sent Riviand here built it," Vigh said. "Some people think giants made it. No one knows for sure. There is a lot of speculation."

Queen Claret frowned. "When I have a moment, I'm going to research this place. I hate being ignorant about things like this."

Kaylee couldn't believe the queen didn't know about something so magnificent in her own kingdom. She must not get out much.

Mateo studied the structure. "How do you suppose we get in? I don't see any glowing signs that say enter."

"I'll leave you to figure that out," Dovin said. "I'll come back here every hour. Just wait for me here. Now that I know exactly where it is, I'll be able to come directly to it. Are you ready, Your Majesty?"

"Yes," Queen Claret said, touching the pyramid one more time. She reached for Dovin's arm, and the two of them disappeared.

Vigh scanned the high wall. "I've never heard of anyone going inside."

"A door would have to be down low," Mateo said, running his hand over a wall. "The sides are too smooth and slippery to climb."

"Maybe there isn't a door," Kaylee said. "I thought pyramids were built to keep people out. And if there is a door, it could be high, since there is magic involved. We should have made Dovin teleport us inside."

"You have to know where you are teleporting. If he tried to get us inside, we could end up in a wall or something."

Vigh pointed to Kaylee's back. "The sword is glowing."

Kaylee pulled it from its sheath. The sword was shining bright blue.

"Wow," Mateo said. "I wonder if it does that when it gets close to a lock."

"It didn't do that when it was near the lock by the castle."

"Maybe that was because it was already locked?"

"It almost feels like it's pulling." Kaylee held the sword up and let it lead her. She felt ridiculous but kept walking. Vigh and Mateo followed her around the pyramid. When they reached the back, a piece of the pyramid began glowing the same color as the sword. They walked closer and the glowing portion slid open.

Mateo grinned. "This is awesome. Ladies first," he said, motioning toward the opening.

Kaylee raised her eyebrow. "Thank you." She held back a smile when Mateo frowned. He probably thought she would try to get him to go first. She stepped past him and into the dark area.

Mateo and Vigh followed. Vigh had his sword out, and Mateo was holding an orb of light. They probably didn't need it because the sword was glowing brightly. The opening behind them closed, and Kaylee took a deep breath. She hoped it would open for them when they came back.

The walls inside the pyramid matched the outside. They were slick and looked like crystal. The floor was hard gray stone and she couldn't see the ceiling.

"I should go in front," Vigh said. "I'm a soldier and I have had extensive training."

"I should be in front," Kaylee protested. "You won't be able to see without a light."

"I have a light, so I should be in front," Mateo said.

Kaylee shook her head. "My light can stab something if it needs to." She giggled nervously. "That is a sentence I never thought I would say."

"The hallway is large enough we could all be in front," Vigh pointed out.

Mateo tilted his head. "Yeah, but if one of us falls into a pit, that's better than all of us."

"Let's just walk," Kaylee said, holding up the sword to light the path. "It might not have any traps or anything. Maybe the only way to get in is with the sword, so they didn't need any other protection."

"Obviously, someone else got through here before us," Mateo said as they began walking.

"But they had the sword or they couldn't have turned the lock."

"What if nobody turned the lock? Maybe it was just a lie to freak everyone out."

Kaylee frowned. That was possible. She hoped there would be a way to know if it was locked or not. She didn't want to be the one to actually unlock it. The light from the sword caused eerie shadows to bounce around as they walked. Kaylee tried to think of something to say. Talking kept things light. Walking in silence felt spooky.

"Stop!" Mateo commanded, holding his arms in front of Kaylee and Vigh. "It's a hole."

Kaylee sucked in a breath. Two feet in front of them, the ground disappeared. She hadn't been paying close enough attention. She watched Mateo squat down and try to shine his light into the space.

He glanced up at her. "There's a ladder."

She nodded. "So it's not a trap, just a way down."

"I wouldn't count on that," Vigh said. "There could be something at the bottom."

"Like what?"

Mateo shivered. "Maybe it's full of snakes."

Kaylee grinned. "That would be so cool. I love snakes. I've been trying to get my mom to get me one forever. That would be my dream."

"Funny," Mateo said. "Your dreams and my nightmares are the same thing."

Kaylee giggled. "Are you scared of snakes?"

"Who isn't? They're slimy and have huge teeth. And venom."

"Snakes aren't slimy, and only about ten to fifteen percent are venomous. Well, at least on Earth. I don't know about this place."

"Ten to fifteen percent is plenty. And if someone is going to put them at the bottom of the pit, they will probably find a poison kind."

"Not poison, venom."

"Same thing."

"It's not. Venom is injected, while poison is ingested, inhaled, or absorbed through touch."

Vigh rolled his eyes. "Are we going to argue about snakes or go down the ladder?"

"I'll go first so Mateo doesn't get eaten by a snake." Kaylee sheathed the sword and took a step forward.

"Let me go first," Vigh said. "I can go down and make sure it's safe. I'm trained for things like this."

"I'm fine with that," Mateo said.

Vigh sheathed his sword and pulled up a ball of light. He started down the ladder, carefully balancing the orb.

"Snakes are misunderstood," Kaylee told Mateo. "I wish I had my phone so I could show you some cute ones."

"There is no such thing as a cute snake."

"You're just saying that because you've never seen a blue beauty."

"I can't believe there's a snake with beauty in its name."

"I want to get a DeKay's brownsnake, but they don't do great in captivity. Even you would have to admit they're cute. Google it when you get home."

"I'm never going to admit a snake is cute and I'm not googling it. It would mess up my search history." Mateo looked down the hole. "It must be deep. So what if we go down there and we are trapped in a pit full of rattlesnakes?"

"Then hold still and sit down."

"Why? Will that make them leave us alone?"

"No."

"Then why sit?"

"Because if you stand too long, you'll get tired."

Vigh was surely taking his time getting to the bottom. Mateo glanced down and couldn't see anything. "Hey, Vigh!" he called. "Can you hear me?"

"Is he down?" Kaylee asked.

"I don't know. I can't see his light anymore."

She grinned. "Maybe the snakes ate him."

"Ha-ha. You aren't as funny as you think you are," Mateo said. He wouldn't admit it out loud, but he did find Kaylee funny.

"So what do we do?" she asked. "Do we wait or go down?"

Mateo took a minute to think. If something had happened to Vigh, it might be too dangerous to go down. But if Vigh was in trouble, they should try to help him.

"I'm going down," Kaylee said when he didn't answer. "He might be in trouble." She started down the ladder, and Mateo followed. She was going fast since both of her hands were free. Mateo was only using one hand so he could keep his light going.

"Everything seems safe down here!" Vigh called up. "You should have waited for me to tell you to come."

"You didn't answer when Mateo called," Kaylee said, hopping off the ladder. Mateo wasn't too far behind.

Mateo stepped down and glanced around a small room. "Wow." The walls looked the same as up above, but blue gems covered the floor. Some were piled in large heaps.

Kaylee picked one up. "Not as cool as snakes but still neat."

Mateo grinned when Kaylee handed it to him. "I would take this over a snake any day. Are they sapphires?"

"I don't know. Probably."

"Why would someone dump a bunch of gems down here?"

"Who knows? In all the pyramids I've ever heard of, there was someone buried in it. They were usually buried with treasures."

"I do not believe anyone was buried here," Vigh said. "I think it was built to be a beautiful structure to house one of the locks. That is just my opinion, of course."

"So if we take some, do we get cursed?" Mateo teased. "Isn't that always a thing?"

"I'm not taking any," Kaylee said. Mateo was tempted, but he wasn't going to chance it. He doubted Kaylee was tempted. Her house was huge, so he assumed her family had money.

"Why would you be cursed?" Vigh asked.

"For taking treasure from a pyramid," Mateo said. "It happens in all the movies."

"What is a movie?"

Mateo ran his fingers through his hair. He didn't know how to describe a movie. "Have you ever seen a play? Where people act out a story?"

"Yes."

"It's like that."

Kaylee ran her hands over the walls. "What do we do now? There isn't a place to stick the sword, so I'm guessing we need to keep looking."

Mateo glanced down at his boots. "Gross," he said. "There's something coming up through the floor."

"What is it?" Kaylee asked, raising her foot and studying the purplish slime.

Vigh frowned. "It's getting higher, so we should probably go back up."

"Where did the ladder go?" Kaylee asked.

Mateo swallowed hard. "It must be a booby trap."

"I can levitate everyone up one at a time," Vigh offered.

"That won't work," Kaylee said, staring up into the hole. "It's blocked."

Mateo's heart raced in his chest. "We have to find the way out." The slime was covering his foot. "I refuse to die in a pit of purple slime." He touched the wall, but it all felt the same.

Vigh hit the wall with the hilt of his sword, but it didn't even cause a dent. He kneeled down in the goop, pushed gems aside, and felt the floor. Mateo got down and copied him. Kaylee kept searching the walls. There had to be a way out. The only light was coming from the sword.

Kaylee pulled it from her back and held it up. The wall lit up just like it had when they were outside, and it opened. They ran through and stopped.

"That wasn't too bad," Mateo said, shaking the purple goop from his hands. He brought up a light. "I say we try the sword first next time we need to get out of a room."

"What is happening?" Kaylee shrieked, pointing down. She turned and ran down a hallway. Mateo looked down and saw spiders crawling out of the cracks in the ground. He jogged after Kaylee.

"Kaylee, wait!" he called.

"Are they gone?" she asked, turning.

"I don't see any over here."

She shivered. "Those were so gross."

"You like snakes, but you're scared of spiders?"

"Spiders are creepy, and those were huge!"

"They weren't that big."

"Spiders are the things of nightmares."

"You can easily step on one."

Kaylee shook her head. "It might jump up and bite."

"You think a spider is fast enough to jump on your leg and bite you before you can step on it?"

"You never know."

Mateo laughed. "Well, I think we outran them."

"The farther we get from them, the better."

Mateo looked around. "Hey, where's Vigh?"

"I don't see him."

"Vigh!" Mateo called. There was no answer. "Why does he keep doing this? Did he get out of the place with the gems?"

"I don't know. I was too busy being terrified of the spiders to notice."

"Do we go back?"

"I'm not going back."

Mateo squinted, trying to see down the hall. The only light was his orb and the sword. They weren't bright enough to see very far. He didn't want to leave Vigh behind. The ground rumbled and something pushed Mateo to the floor. He heard Kaylee scream, and he found himself rolling at an incline. His light was out, and he could only see flashes of blue from the sword. How had the hall turned into a slope? He tried to stop himself, but it was too steep. When he wondered if he would ever stop, he slammed into a wall.

10

— · —

CHAPTER 10

C laret grabbed hold of the doorframe as the castle shook. Fear filled her heart as she realized Riviand was rising again. How long would the goblins be able to hold them down? She hoped it wouldn't take long to turn all the locks and secure the continent.

The earthquake was brief, and Claret rushed through the halls to make sure everyone was all right. Several things had fallen to the ground, and the chandeliers were swinging, but nothing looked too damaged.

Dovin came striding toward her. "Are you all right, Your Majesty?"

"Yes, thank you."

"Are earthquakes common here?"

Claret shook her head. "We never had any until the sword went missing. Now we have one every time Riviand rises."

"With luck, the others will get to the locks soon. I just teleported to the pyramid and they aren't out yet."

"I hope nothing bad has happened," Claret said, wringing her hands.

"I'm sure they're fine. I didn't expect them to be out yet."

"Odious will be here soon. I hate dealing with him."

Dovin tilted his head. "Who is Odious?"

"He is a human who lives with the goblins. Their spokesman. Every time the earth shakes, he comes and asks for more gold."

"Is he threatening Riviand?"

"No. The goblins do some type of magic to hold the continent down. According to Odious, it takes a lot of expensive ingredients to make the magic work. He claims they don't have enough gold to do it without our help."

Dovin rubbed his chin. "Right, you said something like that earlier. That sounds like typical goblins. Do you trust them? Do you trust this Odious?"

Claret took a deep breath. "The goblins haven't caused a lot of trouble in the past, but they are greedy and self-serving. I have wondered if they are behind all of this. I feel even stronger about it since you said there were goblins on that other world chasing Kaylee and Mateo."

"What is Odious like? Why does he live with the goblins?"

"I believe the goblins raised him. I am not sure of the details. He is probably around my age. I always feel nervous when I talk to him. I don't feel like he would harm me, but he is quite strange. He wears a cloak of black feathers and he always has a puffin with him."

"A puffin? Like the bird?"

"Yes."

"What magic does he have?"

Claret thought for a moment. "I'm not sure. He's never done magic around me. He appears rather quickly after the earthquakes. I've wondered if he teleports or perhaps has an alicorn."

"You have alicorns here?"

"Yes."

"It's amazing the way Riviand has thrived for so long down here. I didn't expect it to look so much like the upper continents."

"Does it? That is good to know." Claret often wondered what it was like above. If it wasn't any different, there was no reason to wish she could see it.

"It seems a bit more old-fashioned, with fewer conveniences, but it is thriving."

"Your Majesty?" a serving woman said, walking toward them. She bowed.

"Yes?"

"There is a boy in the throne room to see you."

Claret sighed. "Does he have a bird?"

"Yes."

"Tell him I will be in shortly."

"Yes, Your Majesty." The woman bowed again and disappeared.

Claret looked at Dovin. She had known this man for less than twenty-four hours and she trusted him completely. Something about him made her feel safe. "Should I keep paying the goblins?"

Dovin nodded. "Do it this time. We don't want them to know we have the sword. If they do, they might try to keep us from the locks and we don't need anything standing in the way."

"But if there were goblins on that other world, and they were trying to find the sword, wouldn't they already suspect it was here?"

"I don't believe so. They saw two young people with the sword. They likely didn't know that they would end up here."

"All right."

"Do you mind if I come with you? I'm curious about this Odious."

"I would appreciate that. I don't like to meet with him on my own. My aunt usually comes with me."

Odie straightened when Queen Claret entered the throne room. A man he had never seen before followed the queen. That made him nervous. Odie didn't like change. The man was well dressed and held himself confidently. He must be a new advisor. The queen sat on her throne and the man stood at her side. Odie held on to Gregor and bowed.

"Odious," Queen Claret said. "I assume you are here because of the earthquake?"

"Yes, my queen."

"It seems the goblins' magic is not holding us down for very long."

"It is unfortunate. We do the best we can. If you were to triple the amount of gold, we could make a larger amount of spell and hold it down longer." Odie cringed at his wording. He'd actually said a larger amount of spell. That didn't sound believable at all.

"Triple? What is going to happen when we run out of gold?"

"Hopefully, the Blade of the Phoenix will be returned before that happens. Or perhaps the goblins will figure out a way to keep us down permanently, without the sword."

The man by the queen narrowed his eyes. "Are the goblins capable of that much magic?"

Odie forced himself to stay calm. He couldn't let this man intimidate him. "They have a lot of magic. I am sure they will think of something."

"I wonder who stole the sword," the man said, his eyes burning into Odie. "I would hate to be whoever it is when they are caught."

Odie swallowed and ignored the sweat running down his back. "I agree. If I ever find out who did it, I'll send Gregor after them."

"Who is Gregor?"

"His puffin," Queen Claret said.

"Ah. I see," the man said.

Odie wasn't sure, but he thought the man was hiding a smile. Everyone who made fun of Odie and Gregor would be sorry once Gregor was fully trained. Puffins could bite hard if provoked.

An older woman came in and the queen whispered something in her ear. The woman nodded and disappeared.

"I have sent for the gold," the queen said. "I hope this is the last time."

Odie nodded. "It's hard to say."

The man turned to the queen. "Perhaps it would work out better if Odious gave you a list of the items the goblins need for their spell. We might be able to get them at a better price, and instead of giving them gold, you could give them the ingredients."

Queen Claret nodded. "That sounds like an excellent idea."

Odie frowned. King Ummi wouldn't like that. "Some ingredients are very rare. They would be difficult for you to come by."

"Send me the list as soon as you can and I will try to have the ingredients for you next time."

"Of course," Odie said. He couldn't think of any way to refuse without sounding suspicious. The woman came back and handed the queen a bag. It was bigger than last time. Odie tried not to look too eager. That gold would make his father happy. Hopefully happy enough not to punish Odie for allowing the queen to make demands.

The queen stood and brought him the gold. He took it and placed it in his pocket.

"Odious is an interesting name," the man said.

Odie nodded. "When my goblin parents took me in, I was only three. I was dirty and smelled bad. They said the first thing they thought of when they saw me was Odious, and it stuck." Odie hated his name, but there were goblins named far worse. Gregor squawked. That was their sign to leave.

"Well, thanks for helping us save Riviand," he said. He pulled a glass vial from his pocket and threw it at the ground. Green smoke filled the room and Odie ran from the castle. He loved it when people thought he had powers no one else did. He wished he could see people's faces when they thought he could disappear.

"Does he always leave like that?" Dovin asked.

Claret smiled. "Every time."

"Hmm. He needs a little more smoke if he wants people to think he's teleporting or opening a portal."

"His exits are always amusing. He makes me nervous, but today I couldn't help feeling for him. It must have been hard being raised by goblins."

Dovin nodded. "And being called Odious."

"It's no wonder he has so many strange behaviors."

"I wonder if I could talk to him sometime. Maybe get him to leave the goblins and have a chance at a normal life."

Claret tilted her head. "There are times I wonder what a normal life is."

Dovin rubbed his chin. "That is a good point. I suppose we all have our own normal. Now I better go check on the others."

Claret nodded, and Dovin teleported away.

It was strange seeing someone teleport. One second, they were there and the next, gone. She wondered if Dovin would teach her. That was a skill that would be extremely helpful. She could travel around the kingdom without losing time.

Claret sat back on the throne and yawned. She had been tired ever since she took the crown. She'd never imagined how much effort it took to rule a kingdom. There was always someone who wanted her advice or help with something.

She wished she had gone with the others. Seeing inside the pyramid would have been interesting. Being the queen made her miss out on a lot of things other people her age were doing. They were probably having a wonderful time while she had been stuck here talking to Odious.

"Are you okay?" Mateo asked. Kaylee nodded, even though she was sore and dizzy from falling down that slope. Mateo probably didn't feel any better than she did.

Kaylee had kept a hold of the sword on her way down. It was a miracle she hadn't hurt herself any more than she had. Mateo had rolled, but she had slid, which probably helped. She held the sword in front of herself and peered up at the place they had come from.

"That's too steep to climb," Mateo said, standing by her side. "I hope Vigh is okay."

"He has all that armor and his sword," Kaylee said. "He's also trained to fight, so he's likely better off than we are."

"You're probably right."

The sword was tugging toward the left. "Does it seem odd to you that we've only gone down since we came into the pyramid?"

Mateo nodded. "We must be under the pyramid. Or maybe even under the ground near the pyramid."

"The sword wants us to go left." Kaylee followed where the sword led. "I wonder if Dovin's worried about us yet."

"I doubt it. It hasn't been very long."

"Oh good, stairs," Kaylee said after they turned a corner. "I'm glad they don't go down."

Mateo grinned. He looked a bit freaky with the blue light bouncing off of him. "Wanna race to the top?"

"I don't think that would be safe. We should probably go slow."

"You weren't going very slow when you saw the spiders."

Kaylee shivered. She was embarrassed about the way she had reacted to them, but she had always hated spiders. She knew it was as silly as Mateo's fear of snakes, but she couldn't help it.

Kaylee started up the stairs as fast as she dared. She didn't want to fall into a pit or spring a trap. She didn't know enough about pyramids to know if traps really existed in them or if that was all Hollywood. If she remembered correctly, some pyramids had curses for people who stole treasure. She didn't believe in curses, but she hadn't believed in magic until just recently, either.

"Run," Mateo suddenly said from behind her.

Kaylee could tell he wasn't joking from the tone of his voice. She didn't pause to ask why, just ran. Kaylee tried not to panic when she heard something running behind them. She sprinted up the remaining stairs and down another hallway. This place was full of hallways.

Kaylee rounded a corner, took a few steps, and slammed into a wall. Mateo smashed into the back of her. They spun around and Kaylee covered her mouth to hold in a scream. Three green creatures with large, pointed teeth walked toward them. They were three feet tall, with pointed ears and long snouts that resembled alligators.

"I told you it was aliens," Mateo muttered.

Kaylee grabbed the sword in both hands and pointed it at the creatures. A blast of orange lightning shot from the sword and smashed one of them in the chest. Kaylee almost fell down in the process. The other two creatures turned and ran.

"Get them!" Mateo yelled, jumping over the fallen creature.

Kaylee followed him, rolling her eyes. "Mateo, come back. We don't have time to chase them."

"Just blast them," he said, coming to a stop.

"But they're running away."

"Yeah, and they might find us later."

"I don't even know how I did that."

"Well, what are we going to do? It's a dead end, and we can't go back the way we came."

"Maybe the sword will open something for us again." She turned and made her way back. The fallen creature was nowhere to be seen. "The monster is gone."

"Weird. Where do you think it went?"

Kaylee glanced around nervously. "I'm not sure."

"We should've made Dovin come with us. He needs to teach us some of his tricks. I never got to learn enough magic. If I could levitate things better, I could take us back up the slope and we could find Vigh.”

Kaylee held the sword up. “I hope he didn’t get stuck in the slime.”

Mateo felt the wall. “The sword isn’t opening anything.”

Kaylee looked up at the wall and frowned. “I bet we have to climb.” She couldn’t see any openings above, but there were hand and foot holds going up just like on a climbing wall, and this wall wasn’t made of crystal like every other place they had seen. She touched one handhold. “I think it’s made of stone.”

“How are you at climbing?” he asked. “I think I see a ledge up there.”

“All right. I’ve taken a few climbing classes, thanks to Dovin. I won’t be able to climb and hold the sword, so it might be hard to see.”

Mateo squinted up. “I can levitate my light, but I’m not sure if I can levitate it and climb at the same time.”

“What if you levitate it and I climb and then when I get to the top, I can hold the sword down toward you? It might give enough light to help you climb.”

“Okay. Let’s do it.”

Kaylee sheathed the sword and grabbed a handhold. They were close enough together that it wasn’t difficult. She tried not to think about what would happen if she got to the top and there wasn’t an opening. Mateo’s light followed her. They should have sent the light up before she went to see what was there.

As soon as she had the thought, the ledge came into view. With luck, it was big enough to stand on and it led somewhere. Up was fine, but going back down would be harder. She pulled herself up and put her leg over the ledge.

"That wasn't as high as I thought it would be," Mateo said.

"No, and it was easy." Kaylee got to her feet and pulled out the sword. She held it down so he could see, then he made it up in record time.

"If we had raced, I would have totally beat you," he said with a smirk.

"That's what you think," Kaylee said. "I had to go slower because we didn't know what to expect."

"You know, if someone had told me a week ago that we would be walking through a pyramid together, I wouldn't have believed it."

Kaylee grinned. "Yeah, me neither. It's strange what can happen in a week."

"It looks like we go up again," Mateo said, pointing behind her. Kaylee turned to see another wall with handholds.

"This is weird. We went down so far just to climb up. Can you make your orb go up so we can see how high it is?"

Mateo nodded and held his hand in the air, causing his light to float up.

This area was higher, and it took a lot of concentration for Kaylee to get up. Without safety ropes, she was one misstep away from getting seriously hurt. When she reached the top, she was sweating. She held the sword down so Mateo could see.

"We must be near the top," Mateo said when he got himself all the way up.

"Oh no," Kaylee said once she turned. There was nothing up here except a small platform and a three-foot-wide tunnel in the ground. It was perfectly round and went straight down. "How deep do you suppose that is?"

Mateo looked down and sent an orb of light into the opening. He lowered it slowly. Kaylee watched it go down for what felt like a really long time. When it finally reached the bottom, she sighed.

Mateo glanced at her. "One hundred bucks says the lock is down there."

"So what do we do? Can you levitate yourself down there?"

"No. I've never levitated myself. I could climb down, but I can't touch the sword."

She sighed. "I'm going to have to do it."

"It's too high."

"If I press my back against one side and my legs on the other, I can lower myself by walking my legs down."

Mateo frowned. "I don't know. It doesn't sound safe. How will you get the sword down with you? You can't keep it on your back if you do that."

"I can put it on my lap."

"It might fall."

"Do you have a better idea?"

Mateo thought for a moment. "I could levitate the sword down before you go."

"What if somebody takes it?"

He took a deep breath. "You could go first, then I could lower the sword."

"Are you sure you can levitate it?"

He shook his head. "It's heavy, and heavy stuff makes me nervous."

"I'll manage the sword."

"I could go down first. Just to make sure it's safe, then I could stand underneath in case you fall."

Kaylee bit her lip. "No, you should stay up here. If something happens, you can go for help."

Mateo didn't look happy, but he nodded.

Kaylee removed the sheath from her back and made it hang at her side. "This might work. It throws off my balance a little, but it should be fine." Sitting on the ground, she carefully slid herself over the hole. She pressed her back against one side and her legs on the other. She pushed hard so she wouldn't fall.

Mateo shook his head. "I don't like this."

"Neither do I."

Mateo kept a light moving near Kaylee. One wrong move and she could fall to her death. He shouldn't have let her do this. He had to admit she was making good progress, though.

He wouldn't tell Kaylee, but he was really glad that of all the people he could be on this quest with, it was her. She was brave and a lot more fun than most people he knew. Their time on the ship would have been boring if she hadn't been willing to hang out with him. He knew the little crush he had on her only went one way, but that was okay for now.

"I did it!" she called from below. She shouted something else that he didn't understand, but it sounded like she said he should come down. He thought she wanted him to stay here, but she must have changed her mind. He positioned himself the way she had and made his way down the tunnel. The sides were smooth but not slippery. His guess was that it was made of stone.

Mateo brought up an orb of light and rested it on his lap. He would need to be careful and not let himself fall while he was trying to keep the light going. The dark didn't scare him, but being stuck in a dark creepy tunnel might. This was harder than it looked. Kaylee made it look effortless and smooth, but Mateo had to concentrate to keep his legs from going higher than the rest of him. He slipped a few times and barely caught himself.

The bottom didn't come a second too soon. The drop from the hole to the floor was farther than he'd expected, but he landed on his feet. Kaylee was glaring at him. He smiled like it was nothing.

"What are you doing?" she asked. "I thought you were going to stay up there?"

"I thought you said come down."

"I said, 'I'm down.'"

"Oh. Well, too late now." He inspected the area. The cavern was about twenty feet and matched the outside of the pyramid. Rainbow colors reflected on the walls and floor even though there was no natural light. In the center was a square of marble, with a slit in it.

"We found it," Kaylee said. She held up the sword and glanced at Mateo. "What if it's really locked? How will I know?"

"It is not locked," said a voice from a dark area of the cavern.

Mateo jumped, and Kaylee turned toward the voice, sword at the ready. One of the green creatures from earlier came cautiously forward.

"Blast it!" Mateo commanded.

"Please don't," the creature said. "If you resort to that again, I am going to have to use magic against you."

"Who are you?" Kaylee asked.

"I am Lort, one guardian of the pyramid. I believe you *blasted* me earlier."

"Sorry about that."

Mateo shook his head. "Don't apologize to it. Don't you remember? They were chasing us."

"Not chasing you," said Lort. "We were trying to help you, but you ran. We tossed your companion out. He did not have the sword and did not seem useful."

"So you guard the lock?" Mateo asked suspiciously.

"Not the lock. We guard the pyramid. The lock just happens to be in here."

"Did you see who unlocked it?" Kaylee asked.

Lort shook his green head. "Unfortunately not. When the sword turned, there was a bright flash, but we never detected anyone. They must have been invisible."

Mateo's eyes went wide. "I didn't know anyone had that type of magic."

"You may proceed with the sword," said Lort. "When the lock is secure, I will let you out. You came through in a most unique way. If you had come through the front door, you would not have needed to go through so much trouble."

"In our defense, the doors weren't labeled," said Mateo. "Or visible, for that matter."

Kaylee stood above the lock and lifted the sword above her head with both hands.

"You need not stab it," said Lort. "Just stick it in and give it a turn."

Kaylee nodded. She stuck the sword into the lock and turned it. A flash of blue light lit up the cavern and a hard breeze blew against Mateo. He closed his eyes for a second, and then everything was still. A crackling sound followed, and the sword burst into golden flames. Kaylee jumped back, and they watched as the flames reached the ceiling and then slowly burned out. If Mateo wasn't imagining things, the sword was sparkling brighter than before.

"So that is that," said Lort. He turned to the wall and pushed. A door opened to the outside. "Please do not return, unless absolutely necessary."

Kaylee tapped the sword quickly and pulled away. She repeated the motion. "Wow, it's not hot," she said, taking the sword from the lock. "I think it's shinier."

Lort nodded. "It only makes sense."

Mateo wished he could touch the sword. He couldn't believe it wasn't scorched.

Lort tapped his foot. "Are you going to admire the blade all day or leave?"

Mateo grinned. "We'll leave."

They stepped out into the warm sun, and the door slammed behind them. They had to shade their eyes after being in the dim pyramid for so long.

"I can't believe we could have gone right in," Mateo said, looking at the place the door had been. There was no crack or line to show it was any different from the rest of the pyramid walls.

Kaylee smiled. "Yeah, but now we have a good story. And look. There's Vigh." She pointed to the guard, who was jogging toward them. He had purple goo going up to his knees, and his pack appeared to be full of rocks.

"Hey, Vigh," Mateo said. "I'm glad you aren't dead."

"Thanks." Vigh smiled. "I'm glad you aren't dead either. That would have been hard to tell the queen. A green monster grabbed me and threw me out. I couldn't get back in."

Kaylee ran her hand over the pyramid. "I don't think anyone can get in without the sword. At least, not the way we got in."

Mateo nodded. "It's probably just as well. Lort might not have been the scary monster we thought he was, but he doesn't take me as the type to entertain guests. You would think he would have been excited to talk to someone from out here."

"Lort?" Vigh asked.

"He was one of the green monsters. He helped us get out."

Vigh rubbed his side. "Hopefully in a gentler way than they did with me."

11

CHAPTER 11

T he library in the castle was the biggest one Mateo had ever seen. Shelves reached up as tall as a three-story building, and they were all bursting with ancient leather-bound books. It was probably mostly for show. Some books were so high up, he didn't see any way a person could reach them. There were ladders, but they didn't go to the top. A long table in the center of the library was covered in books and two old maps. When they had returned to the castle, it was to find Queen Claret hovering over the materials.

Dovin had gone straight to the table and begun leafing through a brittle page in a book. "I'm happy the two of you were so fast."

Kaylee nodded. "It wasn't bad. If all the keys are this easy, we should have everything back to normal in less than a week."

Mateo glanced at her. "Don't make it sound that easy. We did have to deal with those aliens, getting thrown down that slope, spiders, and hypothetical snakes."

Dovin paused and looked up. "Hypothetical snakes?"

Kaylee smiled. "There were some scary things. Not the hypothetical snakes, since they were, you know. Hypothetical."

"You both look like you could use a nice bath and a clean pair of clothing."

Mateo nodded. "I wouldn't say no to that. I'm going to be sore tomorrow from all the climbing and falling."

Kaylee walked to the table. "Did you find anything about the other locks?"

Queen Claret nodded. "We found some books with drawings and we've been trying to figure out where they are on these maps."

She held up a book and Kaylee leaned in. "Are those giants?"

"Yes."

Mateo joined them and looked at the book. It showed a sword coming out of the ground. It was surrounded by trees and three large giants. "Friendly giants?"

Claret nodded. "Are there any other kinds?"

Dovin moved one map closer. "In my experience, giants are usually friendly. If I'm not mistaken, they should be here." He pointed at a spot on the map.

Claret peeked over his shoulder. "Yes, that is a spot with giants. There are two areas that they live in and that is one, and then there is another in the west," she said, pointing at the map. "The giants are welcoming, but they prefer to keep their distance."

Kaylee glanced at her. "Have you ever met them? How big are they?"

Claret turned pink. "I've never actually talked to any of them. Or seen them."

"I've seen a giant before," Mateo said. "He was probably ten feet."

Kaylee shrugged. "Hmm. That's not big enough to step on us or anything. Is that our next destination?"

Dovin rubbed his chin. "Perhaps. If they live in two areas, it might be hard to guess the best spot to try first."

Mateo was feeling their last adventure. "I might need a few days to recover. I bet I wake up and find all sorts of bruises tomorrow."

Kaylee's mouth turned down. "Do we have time? What if we wait and the continent rises?"

"Shouldn't it be more secure now that another lock is secured?"

They both looked at Dovin.

He let out a breath. "I'm not sure. It's all a guess. I would assume two locks would be stronger than one."

Claret frowned. "I wonder how secure anything is. If the goblins are behind everything, I'm sure they have a plan. I don't think they would really let the continent rise. It would kill them along with everyone else."

Dovin nodded. "That's true. We probably aren't in as much danger as the goblins want us to think we are. If they are behind it, that is."

"I try not to think of what diabolical things Odious and the goblins are up to," Claret admitted. "It makes me nervous."

"You better run!" Odie yelled at Tipp. Tipp ran up the only long street in the goblin village. The street went down the mountain, and small, thatched houses lined both sides. Goblins lived all over in these mountains, but this was the only paved area.

Odie ran after his brother, a homemade stink bomb in his hand. Tipp was going up the mountain and Odie was confident he could catch up to his brother with no problem. Tipp's legs were short, and he wasn't in shape. Odie ran up and down this road every day, so he had the advantage.

Tipp glanced over his shoulder and laughed. "If you can catch me, I'll give you my dessert tonight!"

Odie flung the stink bomb. It didn't go far enough and splattered on the path in front of him. Tipp laughed and kept running. Odie ran through the horrible-smelling mess and pulled out another. He threw it, hitting Tipp in the back of the head.

"Hey!" Tipp yelled. "That wasn't fair! I'm telling Father."

Before Odie could protest, Tipp disappeared through a portal. Odie stopped running and frowned. Great. Now he was going to get in trouble. He couldn't get to the castle fast enough to even give his side of the story. He wished Tipp didn't know how to make portals.

He passed a house where a goblin was hammering something on the side of his house. He waved, and the goblin frowned and refused to meet his eyes. It didn't bother Odie. That was how most of the goblins treated him. He continued walking. There was no use putting off his punishment. He would get in trouble for the stink bomb and for failing with Queen Claret. He patted the large bag of gold in his tunic pocket. At least there was that.

He might have made it back without incident if Tipp hadn't met him and started bothering him. He'd told Tipp about his conversation with the queen, and Tipp had accused him of being soft. Odie would love to see Tipp do better. Tipp feared everything and he would cower under Queen Claret's gaze.

His father's large, black castle was getting closer. He tried to come up with something to say to his father, but he kept getting distracted when Claret popped into his mind. It really was unfair what they were doing to her and her kingdom.

He rushed up the black steps to the castle and two guards opened the doors to let him in. He ran down the black hall and into the throne room. Sometimes his eyes got tired from looking at so much obsidian. King Ummi sat on the throne and Tipp sat on the steps going up to the throne with a smug look on his face.

Odie took the bag of gold from his pocket and tossed it to his father. Ummi caught it, his stern expression unchanging.

"I know what you're going to say," Odie started.

Ummi frowned. "One of the locks has been secured."

Odie blinked twice. He was wrong. That was the last thing he'd expected to hear. "Secured? But how?"

Ummi opened the bag and pulled out a piece of gold. "I don't know, but the continent is more secure than it was this morning."

"That's impossible," he muttered. "For that to happen, it would mean—"

"That someone has the Blade of the Phoenix," the king finished.

Odie narrowed his eyes. "No way. The sword isn't even in Riviand anymore. It's not even in this world."

"Then what is your explanation?"

Odie rubbed his temples. "I don't have one." He scrunched his nose. The smell coming from Tipp was bad.

"I trusted you to get that sword to a place no one would ever find it."

"No one could have found it. Someone must have figured out another way to lock them."

"I can't trust you to do a simple thing."

Odie's mouth formed a tight line. "No one else could have done what I did, and it wasn't simple. Without me, we never could have taken the sword."

Tipp snickered. "You act like you did it all on your own. Without Father making you invisible, you wouldn't have gotten anywhere."

"Yes, and without me, being invisible wouldn't have mattered. I am the only one who could touch the sword."

Tipp shrugged. "Yeah, but you obviously failed if someone found it."

Odie frowned. He couldn't be blamed for that. "I wasn't the one who chose where to hide the sword. You know I can't leave Riviand without help. The goblins you sent with me should have been guarding it on that other world. They should get the blame if it was found. Have you questioned them?"

"They haven't returned."

Odie nodded. He wasn't surprised. If they knew the sword had been found, they wouldn't dare come back and tell the king. There were harsh punishments for failure.

King Ummi pointed a long, thin finger at him. "I will deal with them when they return. For now, figure out who has the sword and don't let them lock any more. If they lock them all, they won't let the sword out of their sight again. I'm too old to be making up new strategies."

Odie gritted his teeth and bowed slightly. He turned and stormed from the room. His frown deepened when he realized he didn't have Gregor. He must have fallen off when he'd taken off after Tipp. He rushed from the castle and started running down the road. It didn't take him long to find Gregor bothering bugs on the side of the road.

"There you are," Odie said, bending down and scooping up the bird. "Sorry about that. Are you up for anything more today? It looks like Father is sending us on another mission." He cradled the puffin in his arms and continued his descent. "It really isn't fair. Everyone here treats me like garbage, but where would they be without me? They all act like I'm a thorn in their side, but as soon as they need something, who do they go to? Me."

"Hey, wait for me!" Tipp yelled from behind.

Odie kept walking. The last thing he needed was Tipp and his rotten egg smell tagging along.

"If you don't wait for me, then you have to walk!"

Odie sighed and stopped. Not being able to open his own portal limited him.

12

CHAPTER 12

Claret pulled her purple cloak tighter and adjusted her hood. "There sure are a lot of trees."

Mateo grinned. "I suppose that's why they call it a forest."

Claret felt her cheeks heat. "I suppose I should get out more."

"You've never been in a forest?" Kaylee asked.

"I have, just not very often. My aunt is the one who travels around and I stay at the castle. It might be harder to find the giants than I thought. Who knew how dense trees could be?"

Kaylee scanned the forest. "It's probably not easy to hide a giant, let alone a village of them."

Dovin nodded. "We aren't looking for a village of houses, though. Giants don't build structures. They live on the land and only use natural things. We won't see too many signs of where they have been unless we watch closely."

Claret tilted her head. "That's not true. Giants live in houses just like anyone."

Dovin raised his brow. "Really? That's different from Basura."

"Their villages resemble human villages, but they're in the forest. At least that's what I've been told." Claret hoped she was right. She would feel silly if Dovin knew more about the giants than she did. She had studied a lot but seen little in her life.

Dovin smiled. "That will be interesting to see. I should keep a journal about the differences between the continents."

"I hope your friend Padmire will be all right at the castle." Claret had secretly been glad when the bungle stayed behind. She knew he wasn't dangerous, but he was still a little frightening. When he smiled with his pointed teeth, it made a chill run down her spine every time.

"He'll be fine," Dovin said. "Treks like this are hard on him. His feet weren't meant for traveling long distances."

"He's kind of creepy," Mateo said. "I thought he might be less so when he smiled, but his smile is worse than his frown."

"Yes!" Claret agreed. "I was just thinking the same thing."

Dovin chuckled. "Padmire is harmless."

Kaylee pointed ahead. "I see smoke."

Claret followed her finger, and relief flooded her. That must be the giants. She'd worried they wouldn't find them and would waste time wandering all over the forest.

Mateo picked up the pace and everyone hurried to keep up. "Do we ask the first giant we see if they know where the lock is?"

"I'm not sure," Dovin said. "We will have to see what the giants are like and play it by ear."

Claret frowned. "Play it by ear? I don't understand."

"It means we will just do our best depending on what we find."

"Oh. Is that an expression from Basura?"

"It's actually from Earth. I've spent a lot of time there."

Mateo stopped. "There's a building up there."

Claret looked at the structure in the distance. Gray and white stones made up the outer walls and the four windows on the back were square, with no glass. They must have some way to cover them or it would be a disaster during bad weather. Smoke was billowing from one of two chimneys on the roof.

Kaylee walked past Mateo. "No reason to stop. Let's go."

Claret wished she had Kaylee's confidence. They walked around the structure and a village came into view. There were other buildings slightly smaller but similar to this one. They turned and faced a large wooden door. Claret guessed it to be at least thirteen feet high. A carved sign above the door read *Kinton Library*. Mateo pushed the door and it creaked open.

Claret was the last one in. She squinted as her gaze swept the room. The lighting wasn't very good because most of it came from the deep windows. There was a fireplace in one corner that gave some light, but it was still dim after being out in the bright sun. Stone slab tables occupied the majority of the room. They were in neat rows and all had about ten books on each surface. The books were all leather-bound, just like at the castle. There weren't any shelves.

"May I help you?" a deep voice asked.

Claret's eyes jumped to the back of the room and landed on a giant. He stood behind a desk, towering over it. His long black hair was pulled back into a tight braid and his beard hung down to his chest. He wore small, round spectacles that appeared out of place on his face. She would guess his age to be somewhere in his thirties, but she didn't know how giants aged.

Claret stepped forward. "I am Queen Claret. We have come from Tyran to speak with the giants."

"Queen Claret?" he mumbled, coming out from behind the desk. He dropped to one knee and bowed his head.

"You run the library?" she asked.

"Yes. My name is Hundo. How may I serve you?"

Claret swallowed and glanced at Dovin. *Playing things by ear* was not her favorite thing.

Dovin stepped up next to her. "Hello, Hundo. My name is Dovin. There have been some troubles in Tyran and we were wondering if any of those problems have occurred here as well."

Hundo frowned and stood. He rubbed his beard and glanced at the floor. "Trouble like how?"

"Earthquakes? People sneaking around that shouldn't be."

The giant let out a long sigh. "There have been earthquakes. They haven't been large enough to do any damage. As for anyone sneaking around... that is all speculation. I try not to dwell on things I cannot change."

"We have reason to believe the goblins are behind it."

Hundo rubbed the back of his neck. "Goblins? I don't know if I would think it was goblins."

Dovin leaned forward. "The Blade of the Phoenix has been stolen. Most of the locks were turned. We are doing our best to make sure the continent doesn't rise."

Hundo's frown grew even deeper. "I was afraid it might be something like that."

Claret forced herself to keep her eyes on the giant. She didn't want to appear weak. "Do you know anything that can help us?"

He shrugged. "I do not believe so."

"Is there anyone who might?"

"Hmm." He glanced up at the ceiling and tapped his chin. "No one comes to mind."

"Well, thank you for your help," Dovin said, turning to leave. "I saw some other buildings. We can try those."

"Yes, of course," Hundo said, rushing past them and holding open the front door. They exited and Hundo took off toward the closest building, his long legs getting there quickly.

Kaylee frowned as he disappeared into the structure. "That was odd."

"Should we go in there?" Mateo asked. "It looks like a bakery."

Claret tilted her head. A sign with a carving of a loaf of bread swung in the breeze in front of the building. "Do you think he is warning whoever is inside?"

"Perhaps," Dovin said, leading them toward the bakery. "If he is, we might as well go there next. It's difficult to know what he thought about us." When he opened the front door, a bell jingled, alerting anyone inside of their arrival.

A counter with a few desserts on top met them. Claret was hungry, but the desserts didn't look appetizing. The icing on the rolls had a green tint, and the muffins were black around the edges. Behind the counter stood Hundo. He had removed his glasses and was wearing a tan apron.

"Can I help you?" he asked.

Mateo grinned. "You work at the library and the bakery?"

Hundo cleared his throat and rubbed his arm. "Someone has to do it."

Dovin peered around the room. "Is there anyone else here?"

"No, just me."

"What other shops are in the village?"

"Well, there is a clothing shop, feed shop, blacksmith... I hope you don't need the blacksmith. I haven't quite got the hang of that one."

Mateo arched his brow. "You're the blacksmith?"

Hundo's shoulders dropped, and he let out a sigh. "I am everything these days."

Claret frowned. "Are there no other giants?"

"Not anymore."

"Where are they?"

He shrugged. "I cannot be sure. Everyone got nervous when the earthquakes started. They decided the giants should all be together, so they left to find our other village. I don't know if they found it or not. Our groups are different and we don't communicate with each other."

Kaylee's eyes narrowed. "Why didn't you go with them?"

"Someone had to stay behind. We couldn't let the village fall to pieces. We had a vote, and I... won. It's my job to take care of everything so it will not become run-down when the others return."

That explained the desserts. Hundo must not be a baker.

Dovin's eyes connected with Hundo's. "Do you know where the lock is?"

"What lock?"

Dovin rolled his eyes. "The lock to hold down the continent. We have reason to believe it is around here."

"Oh, hmm," he said, fiddling with his apron. "I don't know why that would be around here."

"We need to find it, or we could all end up dead."

Hundo flinched. "There isn't much anyone can do, even if they find it."

Kaylee pulled the Blade of the Phoenix from her back. "There is when we have this."

Hundo's eyes widened.

"We need to find the lock so we can secure it."

He gazed at the floor. "Well, I might know where it is, but how do I know you are going to fix it and not make it worse? I thought the other human was here to help."

Claret leaned forward. "What other human?"

"A boy. He came looking for the lock. He said it needed to be tightened, but I fear he unlocked it. I should have known better than to trust him."

"It's already unlocked," Kaylee said. "There isn't anything we could do to make it worse."

"How do I know you won't destroy it so it can't be fixed?"

Claret stepped forward. "As the Queen of Riviand, it is my responsibility to keep my people safe. I would do nothing that would hurt our world."

Hundo nodded. "I believe you, but you have to understand. I was left to protect things, and I failed."

Kaylee frowned. "I thought the earthquakes didn't happen until all the locks were turned. Why had your people already left the village?"

"There were small earthquakes before," Claret said. "Probably right after each lock was turned. Don't blame yourself, Hundo. Anyone could make that mistake. Can you tell us what the boy looked like? We thought goblins were behind it."

"There was no mistake. He was human. He was young. Dressed all in black. He had a feathered cape. There was a bird with him."

"Odious," Claret muttered. "That's as good as the goblins. He works with them. Now we know for sure."

"Goblins are devious creatures," Hundo said, shaking his head.

Kaylee held up the sword. "We have secured one lock already. If you can take us to the next one, the world will be on its way to being safe. You will have saved your village."

Hundo smiled. "You think so?"

"Yes."

"All right. I will lead you there."

Claret's heart sped up. It wasn't often she got to be part of something like this. Few would get to see what it looked like when the sword turned in the lock.

Kaylee grinned when the giant pointed out the keyhole. It was hidden under a rock that Hundo pushed off of it. They never would have found it without Hundo's help. This one was preferable to the one in the pyramid. They hadn't been in any danger and they only had to walk a short distance. If the other two were this easy, they would have Riviand saved in a snap.

She held the sword in her hand and pushed it into the lock. She turned it and a flash of blue shot out from the sword and then burst into flames, just like before. They all watched until the fire went out.

"Wow," Claret said, moving closer. "That was amazing. So it's locked?"

"I think so," Kaylee said, pulling the sword out. "I felt the click."

"It's not fair Kaylee gets to do the cool stuff," Mateo said, smiling at her. "All we get to do is tag along."

Kaylee laughed. "All I do is turn the sword. I don't think it's going to go down in the history books."

Dovin tilted his head. "I wouldn't count on that. Just because something isn't difficult doesn't mean it's not important."

"Yes," Hundo's voice boomed. "Sometimes the smallest acts make the most difference."

Something hit the ground near Kaylee's feet and shattered, and she turned as green smoke burst from the ground. She heard more glass breaking and before anyone could react, the area was blanketed in smoke and Kaylee couldn't see anything else. She coughed as the smoke entered her lungs. The smoke was thick.

She screeched when something plowed her to the ground. The sword fell from her hands and she scrambled on her hands and knees to grab it. As soon as she wrapped her hands around the hilt, someone grabbed her hand and tried to pry the sword from her. She gripped it hard and pulled backward. Someone fell into her and continued trying to take the blade.

"Kaylee, where are you?" Mateo asked.

She gritted her teeth and kicked the person. In the moment it took him to be surprised, Kaylee rolled as fast as she could, the sword held above her head. With luck, he couldn't see any better than she could. She jumped to her feet and held the sword in front of her.

Taking slow steps backward, she listened for the sound of anyone moving. She bumped into someone and clenched her teeth to keep herself from yelling out.

"It's me," Mateo whispered, putting his hand against her back.

She turned and nodded. The smoke was getting thinner and she could make out his face. "Someone tried to take the sword," she whispered.

Claret screamed. Mateo grabbed Kaylee's hand and pulled her toward the sound.

"Claret!" Dovin called out. "Where are you?"

There was no answer. A hard wind smacked across Kaylee's face, almost knocking her over. The green smoke disappeared into the trees. Dovin stood with his hands out, staring intently after it.

"Did you blow the smoke away?" Mateo asked. "That was amazing."

Kaylee's eyes swept across the clearing in time to see a boy in black run behind a tree. Claret was nowhere in sight.

Dovin frowned and pulled back his arm and threw it forward. A ball of fire the size of a baseball leaped from his hand and blasted the tree in front of them. The boy ran out and went deeper into the trees.

"Split up!" Dovin commanded. "Find Claret. She wasn't with the boy."

"It's no use," Hundo said. "I saw a goblin grab her and jump through a portal."

13

CHAPTER 13

Mateo glanced around the forest and breathed deeply. He bent over and put his hands on his knees as he tried to catch his breath. The boy in the feathered cape was fast. Mateo had been sure he would catch him, but he had changed directions and zigzagged so many times he had eventually lost sight of him.

"Did you lose him?" Kaylee asked, coming into the small clearing.

"Yeah," he said, standing straight. He didn't want Kaylee to think he was winded. She was breathing hard and looking around. "I didn't realize you were behind me."

"We changed directions a lot. Do you think you can find the way back? It all looks the same to me."

Mateo's mouth turned down as he scanned the trees again. "No chance. I wasn't paying attention to the way I came. I was just trying to stop that guy. We should probably go that way," he said, pointing behind her. "We know we came from that direction at some point."

She nodded, and they started walking. "My back hurts from carrying the sword. It's a lot heavier than the ones I use when I'm fencing."

"I would take it for you if I could."

"It's not a huge deal. I just wonder if there's an easier way to carry it."

"Any ideas on what we do next? If a goblin took Queen Claret, should we be trying to save her? Or should we try to get to the other two locks?"

She moved her mouth from side to side. "Hmm. I'm not sure. If goblins captured me, I would hope you came for me. But if we don't get all the locks secured, everyone is in danger."

"We don't know where the other locks are, though."

"True," she said, jumping over a large tree root. "But we don't know where the goblins are either."

He nodded and tried to keep up with her fast pace. For being a head shorter, she walked fast. "It's probably easy to find them. If they have a city or village or whatever, people can probably point us in the right direction."

"But even if we find them, what are the two of us going to be able to do? I think we need to get to Claret's castle and tell Vigh what happened. If the goblins kidnapped the queen, the guards might be best for that job."

Mateo hadn't thought of that. This could cause a war between the goblins and the rest of Riviand. "Who's in charge when the queen is missing?"

She shrugged. "I have no idea. I'm sure it isn't Vigh, but he must know who is."

"We should have brought him with us. He's probably good to have around in a situation like this."

Kaylee stopped. "I don't know. He didn't seem overly useful at the pyramid. I wonder if we should stay where we are. If we keep walking around, we might end up more lost. There was a hiking club I did one summer, and they told us you should stay in one place if you get lost."

Mateo narrowed his eyes. "I can see how that would be a good thing if people know you're lost. There's a good chance no one is going to miss us or know we're out here."

"Dovin and the giant know."

"I guess, but we don't know where they went or what they're doing. I wish Dovin would teach me to teleport. That would solve a lot of problems."

Kaylee pointed to the ground ahead. "What's that?"

Mateo looked at where she was pointing and saw something red sparkling on a pile of fallen leaves. They walked cautiously over to it.

Kaylee squatted down next to it. "It looks like a glowing bouncy ball." She reached out to pick it up, and Mateo grabbed her arm.

"Don't touch it!"

She pulled her arm back. "Why not?"

"It looks like magic. We don't know what it is, so it might be dangerous."

"It doesn't look dangerous."

Mateo tilted his head and grinned. "Famous last words."

She stood and shoved him playfully in the shoulder. "So we just leave it there?"

"I think so. Better to leave it and not risk anything." He took a step closer, and the ground gave out beneath him. He let out a shout as he fell. Kaylee grabbed his arm, and the weight of him pulled them both down. He closed his eyes as leaves and dirt smacked his face. He crashed down and Kaylee fell on top of him.

"Oof," she said when she landed. She jumped to her feet and peered up.

Mateo was lying on his back, staring up at the opening to the hole. They were about ten feet down. The sun shone in his eyes. He rubbed his ribs where Kaylee's sword had smacked into him. The sword had shocked him, but it was sheathed, or he would be dealing with more than a little pain.

"Are you all right?" she asked, offering her hand.

He took it and stood. "Yeah. I can't believe we fell for that. Literally."

"Now what? It isn't super high."

Mateo rubbed his back. "It's high enough."

Kaylee ran her hand over the dirt wall. The soil fell over her hand and onto her arm. "It's not as solid as it could be. If we try to climb, we're just going to get covered in dirt."

"We can try yelling. Dovin might hear us."

"So might whoever dug this pit."

"Who digs traps like this? I would guess it was someone trying to hunt or something. They might let us go."

She raised her eyebrow. "And they might not."

"If you sit on my shoulders, do you think you could reach the top?"

They both stared up.

"Probably not. Maybe if I stood on your shoulders, but I'm no acrobat."

Mateo didn't know what an acrobat was, but he got the gist. "I wish I could levitate better. All the things my mom wouldn't let me learn would come in handy right about now."

"What can you do?"

"Besides making a light, not much. I used to levitate small things to throw at my brothers, but nothing big. I wasn't old enough to learn to summon anything, but I guess I could try."

"What would be the best thing that could help us?"

He rubbed some dirt from his hair. "I don't know. If I remember right, you have to know where the object you want to summon is. I don't know where many things in this world are. I'm not sure if I can bring things from other worlds."

Kaylee pulled the sword from its sheath. "What if I use this to make holes in the dirt? Then we could step in them."

He looked up. "Wouldn't hurt to try."

Wrapping both hands around the sword's hilt, she pulled it back and then thrust it forward, stabbing the dirt wall. The sword only went in a few inches. Dirt fell from above, covering part of the sword. She wiggled the sword around, trying to make a hole. When she pulled it out, more dirt fell into the slit she made.

"I don't think it's going to work," he said. "On the plus side, you killed the wall."

"Ha-ha. Why is the dirt so loose? It seems like it should be packed hard."

"Maybe things are different in Riviand. It is under the ocean, after all."

"But the ground is solid when we walk on it."

Mateo pushed his hand into the space Kaylee stabbed. His fingers went in easily, then stopped. "The dirt is pretty hard after a few inches. It might just be loose because it's at the edges where someone dug."

"Maybe I could push my feet and hands into it far enough that I could pack it with my foot and climb that way. I am good at climbing, thanks to Dovin."

"Pack it?"

"Yeah, with the bottom of my foot."

Mateo raised his eyebrow. "It doesn't make sense to me, but if you want to try it, go ahead."

She awkwardly put the Blade of the Phoenix back into its sheath. "Okay, here goes nothing." Kaylee reached high and stuck her fingers as far into the dirt as she could. Dirt fell down her arms. "Gross, it's in my sleeves." She lifted one leg and kicked her foot in. It only went in far enough to cover the toe of her boots. She pushed her foot down a few times. "See, now it's hard under my heel?" She pulled herself up and kicked her other foot in a little higher, and she fell backward.

Mateo figured something like that would happen, so he was ready and caught her underneath her arms, the sword smashing into his body. The hilt smacked him in the nose, shocking him. He grunted and took a few steps back.

"Sorry," Kaylee said, turning to face him. "I thought that would work."

Touching his nose, he pulled his fingers away to see blood. "Ouch. I don't suppose you have a tissue?" His eyes were watering and his entire face was throbbing.

"I doubt they have tissues here," she said, pulling a small square of flowery pink material from her pocket. "Queen Claret gave me a handful of these back at the castle. I'm not sure what they're actually for."

He grabbed it and pushed it to his nose.

Kaylee frowned and pulled another square from her pocket. "I hope it isn't broken."

"It's fine. Don't worry about it. Barely hurts," he lied.

She pushed down on his shoulders. "Maybe you should lie down, or at least sit down and put your head back."

Mateo let her push him to the earth. He sat cross-legged and tilted his head back. She handed him the other square of material and he replaced the old, bloody one.

"I'm going to yell for Dovin," she said. Turning, she cupped her hands around her mouth. "Dovin! Dovin!" She paused for a moment. "Dovin!"

They were both quiet as they listened for a response. Nothing.

"The bleeding stopped," he said, rubbing the material under his nose to make sure he got any blood. The last thing he wanted was to have Kaylee thinking he looked gross.

She glanced down at him and tossed him another square. "You might want to spit on it or something to get that."

He scowled and licked the material before rubbing it above his lip.

"You got it," she said. "Dovin!" she called again.

"The sword hit me and didn't blast me into the wall. It only shocked me a bit."

Kaylee shrugged. "Maybe it figured a smack in the face was enough."

Mateo didn't know what to do with the bloody cloth, so he tossed it to the ground and stood. A quick glance at his tunic showed a trail of blood going down the front. That was just great. He hoped Kaylee appreciated him. He could have let her fall.

"Sorry I fell on you. Twice," she said as if she'd heard what he was thinking.

He gave her a half grin and a small chuckle. "Glad I could be there."

She arched her brow. "Really?" She touched a sore spot on his head that he hadn't noticed before. "You look a little beat up."

Mateo swallowed. What was it his brother Miguel had told him about girls? Something about them finding reasons to touch you if they liked you. Now her eyes were narrowed as she brushed dirt from his hair. Mateo liked to talk big and act confident, but sometimes he felt like a huge wimp inside.

"How did you even get this much dirt on your hair?" she asked, letting her hand drop.

He laughed. "You should see yours. I'm sure it's just as bad."

She put a hand to her hair and brushed it off. "Gross. That's going to take forever to wash out." She bent her neck and rubbed her hands through her braids, a steady stream of dirt falling. "It takes forever to take these braids out." She flipped her head up, almost whipping him in the face.

"Is my head bleeding?" he asked, touching the spot she had pointed out earlier. He looked at his fingers. They were clean. Well, not clean, but they weren't covered in blood.

"No, but you might end up with a goose egg."

His eyebrows came together. "Goose egg?"

"A bump. It's funny you spent so much time on Earth and you still don't know what everything is."

He crossed his arms. "I'm pretty sure things are different from one country to another. Besides, I was living in a small village, so that probably makes things different as well."

She grinned. "I wasn't trying to insult you. I just think it's interesting."

He sighed and looked up. "I think I'm going to have to throw you."

Her grin slipped away. "Throw me? Are you serious?"

"I know it's risky, but I don't think we have a lot of options. We don't know who dug this hole or when they might come back. I can lock my fingers, you step in my hands, and I'll fling you up. If anyone gets hurt, it will probably be me because you might land on me again."

Kaylee rubbed her lips together as she looked from Mateo to the top of the hole. "It might not be as bad, but it still doesn't feel great falling on you."

"Do you have a better idea?"

"No."

"As soon as I throw you, I'll try to levitate you at the same time."

She tilted her head. "I thought you weren't good at that."

"I'm not, but I can try to at least push you in the right direction."

"And what happens when I get up there?"

He shrugged. "Lower a branch?"

"I don't know what kind of body-building woman you think I am, but there is no way I'm going to be able to pull you out of here with a branch."

"I thought you were into exercise and sports."

"That doesn't make me superwoman. The most likely scenario is you pull me back in. You have to outweigh me by fifty pounds."

He drummed his fingers against his leg. "Hmm. You could look for a rope."

"A rope? In the middle of the forest?" Right as she said it, a rope fell into the hole, whipping Mateo in the face.

He put a hand to his cheek. "Dovin?" he called up. No one answered. "What do we do?"

Kaylee grabbed the rope and pulled on it. "It feels sturdy."

"But we don't know who's up there."

"So you wanna stay here?"

He sighed. Even if they didn't climb, there was no guessing what the person up above would do, and it might be better to meet them when they weren't at a disadvantage. "All right. You want to go first?"

14

CHAPTER 14

Kaylee rolled over against the dirt when she reached the top of the hole. She had never been this dirty in her entire life. The rope had helped with the climb, but it didn't stop the dirt from slipping under her feet. Pride and determination had kept her going to the top. She was great at rock climbing, but slippery dirt was a whole different story. She pushed up onto her elbows and looked around. She couldn't see anyone.

She got on her hands and knees and looked into the hole. Mateo was already on his way up. "There's no one up here."

He nodded but didn't say anything. She sat back and waited until he got over the top. He was wearing a lot more dirt than he had been before.

"Well, that was fun," he said sarcastically. "Let's try to avoid any shiny objects."

She would ignore that comment. "Now what? Someone lowered that rope and tied it to a tree. It didn't happen on its own."

He stood and brushed the dirt from his clothes. "I was hoping it was Dovin."

"He wouldn't have run off, though."

"No. I don't see any reason to hang around, waiting for anyone to show up. Let's get out of here." He grabbed her hand and pulled her to her feet so hard she almost fell the other way.

"Thanks," she mumbled, righting herself.

"What are we looking for?" Mateo asked. "Dovin, Claret, or the way to the castle?"

"Any of those would be good." She started walking, and Mateo followed.

"What if we don't find our way out of here? I don't know about you, but I've never had to survive in the outdoors before."

"I'm sure we'll get out. I bet Dovin is looking for us."

"Unless he went after Claret."

They walked in silence for a while. Kaylee tried to come up with a plan that didn't only involve walking, but she couldn't seem to think. She was tired and walking wasn't helping.

"Soooo," Mateo said, breaking the silence. "You and Chad?"

Kaylee cringed. "Gross! No."

Mateo laughed. "I think he likes you."

"Yeah, and I think he's a freak."

"Well, I probably broke his nose."

Kaylee side-eyed him. "Don't say that like it's a badge of honor. Being a jerk to a jerk still makes you a jerk."

Mateo shrugged. "He was bothering you."

"He's always bothering me. I would have dealt with it. I always do."

"But he keeps bothering you, so however you're dealing with it isn't working. My way works. He hasn't bothered you since."

"I haven't seen him since."

"See? It worked perfectly."

Kaylee laughed softly. "Sure. So what about you? You have a girlfriend back in Mexico?"

"Nah. Everyone stays away from me. I have an attitude problem."

"You sure seemed to when you came to school. You aren't like that here."

"Yeah, that's because I'm home here. Well, not exactly here, but it's my kind of place. Sorry, I know I wasn't pleasant." He gave her a mischievous smile. "You didn't have to go telling on me to Dovin, though."

Kaylee stopped and faced him. She placed her hands on her hips. "I did not tell on you."

"Oh yeah?" he asked, crossing his arms and smiling. "Then why did Dovin tell me to stop looking at you?"

She smiled. "Okay. I guess I did, but only because Dovin gave me a lecture about being nice to you. I don't know why I was getting the lecture since you were the one glaring at me all the time."

"I wasn't glaring at you on purpose. I was thinking, and you just happened to be the person I was staring at when I spaced out."

"So you just happened to space out every time you looked at me?"

Mateo grinned. "If I'm going to space out, I might as well be looking at something majestic."

Kaylee snorted and waved her hand dismissively. She started walking again. Her cheeks felt hot, but she wouldn't let him know. "That is the worst line I've ever heard, and I've heard some bad ones."

Mateo chuckled. "It really was. Let's go find Claret."

Odie stomped into the throne room, sure he would find King Ummi. He was amazed at how long his father could sit on his hard obsidian throne. He spent almost all of his time there. The king admired one of his rings.

"Father?"

The king glanced up. "Ah, Odious. I'm glad to see you made it back."

"I would have been back sooner, but Tipp left me out there!"

"He went back for you."

"Yes, but he shouldn't have left me in the first place. I almost got captured!"

"Sometimes we have to sacrifice for the greater good."

Odie glared up at the king. "Sacrifice? What are you talking about?"

A smile flooded King Ummi's face. "Tipp brought the queen back."

Odie's eyes went wide. "Queen Claret?"

"Of course Queen Claret. Do you know of any other queens?"

"Why would he do that? Do you want to start a war?"

"If we must. Someone is securing the locks. I see you haven't managed to get the sword. Once there is no longer a threat to Riviand, we will have no power over the queen anymore."

Gregor jumped around near Odie's feet, but he barely noticed. He rubbed his sore ribs where that girl had kicked him. "What is your plan?"

The king rolled his beady eyes. "To ransom her, of course."

Odie narrowed his eyes. "How does that work? She's the one with the power and the money. She can't pay her own ransom."

"Maybe not, but she can tell someone who can. I'll have her write a letter and send it to the castle."

Odie moved his jaw from side to side. He hadn't wanted it to come to this. There was no way he would believe this was a move to reclaim what the goblins thought they were owed. The king was being greedy. There was nothing else to it.

The king twisted one of his rings. "You will deal with her. She is more likely to cooperate with another human. You will spend all your time making sure she isn't plotting anything."

"Ridiculous," he muttered under his breath.

"What was that?"

"Nothing," Odie mumbled.

"That's what I thought. She's in the dungeons. Why don't you go check on her?"

"You put her in the dungeons? She's not a criminal. Give her a room."

"No one can perform magic in the dungeon. If I move her to a room, there is no telling what she might do."

Odie spun and stormed from the room. Gregor hopped behind him. "Go home," he told the bird. Gregor went in the opposite direction. He would go to Odie's room and probably tear it apart. It was his favorite thing to do, second only to eating.

Odie rushed down the black stone hallway and stopped in front of a door leading down to the dungeon. Two goblin guards stood by the door. One smirked when he came near.

"Ready to spend some quality time in the dungeon?" the smirking goblin asked. "Sounds like you get the privilege of seeing what it's like to be a guard."

Odie rolled his eyes. "I don't have to stay down there. This job is obviously too important for the two of you."

The goblins both frowned and one opened the door. Odie hurried through and began the long descent. He used to count the stairs when he was young. There were two hundred and seventy-five. Nothing to sniff at. He took them two at a time and paused at the bottom.

The dungeon wasn't a place they liked to keep people. It was humid and the smell was horrid. Smells didn't bother goblins, but King Ummi didn't like to make the trek down all the steps if he didn't have to. There was a smaller prison in the village that was used most of the time. The king had probably put Claret down here so no one could come save her.

There were twenty cells going down one long hallway, with ten on each side. Each cell was over forty paces across. It seemed like a lot of wasted space to him. They could use it for something amazing since there were rarely prisoners down here. He would love to turn some of the space into a lab. Of course, something would need to be done about the cold. It was freezing down here all year long.

Odie's steps echoed and the candles lighting the hall made ominous shadows on the walls and floor. There were no windows in the dungeon, so there was no natural light. When Odie was young, he and Tipp would dare each other to come down here and walk to the end of the hall. It had taken Odie until he was twelve to actually make it all the way and Tipp even longer.

Odie walked down the hall with confidence, even though there was a constant chill running down his back. He glanced in each cell he passed, surprised the queen wasn't in any of them. If he were to make a wager, he would bet that Tipp had put her in the cell at the very back, just to make sure Odie had to walk all the way down each time.

When he got to the two last cells, he saw her. His eyebrows rose in surprise. There was a nice bed with a dark blue blanket and fluffy pillows. His father must not want to mistreat the queen... ignoring the fact that she was his prisoner. Claret sat at the foot of the bed. Her long hair fell over her shoulder and her green dress flowed down to her black boots. She was still wearing her black cloak, and she was glaring at him.

Odie held up his hands. "I had nothing to do with this."

Claret's mouth formed a tight line.

He stepped forward and gripped the bars with both hands. "Really, I had no idea the king would do something like this."

"It's a waste of his time," she said. "He's not getting any money for me."

"Unfortunately, he probably will."

She crossed her arms. "No. Our kingdom will not pay ransom. Everyone knows that. If we pay ransom once, it will never stop."

"You really think your people will allow you to stay here?"

"It is our policy."

"King Ummi will find a way."

"I suspected you were the ones who stole the Blade of the Phoenix. It was stupid of me to pay you."

"You know humans are not as innocent as they would like to believe. They pushed the goblins farther and farther toward the mountain until they lost almost everything. If you think of it that way, you owe the goblins for taking their land."

Queen Claret's pretty green eyes narrowed. "Who told you that? Maybe you should study things a bit more before you run off doing the goblins' bidding."

"What do you mean?"

"When Riviand was first taken under the ocean, the goblins claimed the mountain. They actually have more land now than they did originally because they spread to the area around the mountain. You can find that in any history book."

Odie's mouth turned down at the corners. Could that be true? Claret didn't look like she was lying, and what would be the point? If it was in the books, then it had to be true. The history books were written by some of the best scholars of their time, or so he had been told. Odie had never been enthused about history. It was too dry for him.

"I'm sorry you're here," he said honestly. "Don't waste your time trying to escape. There is only one way out and it's carefully guarded. It would seem I've been chosen to keep watch over you down here. Don't think you can knock me out to escape because you won't be able to get past the guards above."

"So you are what, just going to stand there all day?" she asked.

He rubbed a hand over his chin and sighed. "I might need to have a chair brought down."

"So if I need something, I ask you?"

"Yes. Do you need something?"

"There's a ridiculous number of spiders and other crawling things in here. There's no way I will ever relax like this."

"Don't worry. I'm on it."

Claret was tired. She's had a busy morning, and now she was in the goblins' dungeon. It smelled like vomit. Still, she was forcing herself to hide a smile as she watched Odious move around her cell with a rolled up piece of parchment, smashing bugs. Bugs didn't bother Claret in moderation, but it was ridiculous down here. She couldn't look anywhere without seeing some creepy crawling thing.

Her cell was wide open as Odious tried to rid it of the bugs. She believed him when he said there was no reason to try to escape. If she left the cell and ran into goblins, they would lock her up even better. She didn't enjoy Odious's company, but given the choice between him and the goblin who brought her here, she chose him. At least he didn't smell like rotten eggs.

"This is ridiculous," Odious said just as a goblin with string brown hair appeared with dinner. It was the first female goblin Claret had seen. "Hey, Vivi," he said to the goblin. "I need you to have someone bring me everything from my room."

"Placing yourself in the dungeon, are you?" Vivi asked, entering Claret's cell. She placed a tray with two plates of food on a small table. She straightened her blue dress and glared at him.

"Just do it," he said. "Please."

Vivi nodded and left. Odious grabbed a plate of food and handed it to her.

"Thanks," she said, staring down at the heaping plate of mashed potatoes and chicken.

"Eat it fast before the bugs get it." He took the other plate and began eating.

This was all so strange. Claret would have thought being in a dungeon meant meager rations and uncomfortable conditions. She would never finish this much food. So far, the goblins were trying to keep her happy. At least if you ignored the part where she was in a smelly dungeon. The chicken was temporarily helping with the smell. There might have been a bit of dirt in the potatoes, but she didn't look too closely.

"I have an idea for the bugs," Odious said. "Once they bring me my things, I'll be able to have them cleared out."

Claret didn't answer. She just ate.

"I can probably do something about the smell as well. It might take a few tries. It's pretty gross down here."

Before they finished eating, lines of goblins began bringing things over and placing them in the hall outside her cell.

"What are you doing?" Odious protested when they brought a bed over and began assembling it.

One goblin grinned, his sharp teeth showing a tint of orange. "You said to bring everything in your room."

"Yes, but I didn't mean... oh, never mind."

Claret put a napkin over her mouth to hide her smile.

She didn't realize how fast goblins could be. It didn't take long before the hall in front of them was transformed into what must look like Odious's bedroom. There was a bed, a wardrobe, a big shelf, and a long table. On the table and shelf were glass vials and jars full of things Claret couldn't quite see well enough to identify.

"That's everything, Odie," a goblin said. "I hope your father doesn't decide he likes you down here. It's probably easier to clean when you blow things up."

All the goblins laughed as they left.

Claret tilted her head. "What did he mean?"

Odious frowned. "Don't worry about it."

15

—·—

CHAPTER 15

Kaylee groaned as her eyes opened, and she realized her face was on the hard dirt. Last night was horrible. After they realized they weren't finding their way back to the giant village, they had decided to get comfortable for the night. That was easier said than done because they didn't have any supplies. They had slept on their capes. If someone had told Kaylee a year ago that she would be wearing a cape, she would have laughed, but she was grateful she had one.

She had kept the sword strapped to her back, which hadn't helped her sleep well. They couldn't risk someone coming and taking it now that she knew there was someone besides her who could touch it. She had tried to sleep all night on her side so the sword wouldn't be pushing into her back, so now she was stiff.

Mateo was next to her, sitting with his back to her. He had his hands stretched out. Kaylee pushed herself up and watched him. He was probably trying to do some type of magic, but nothing was happening.

"What are you doing?" she finally asked.

He jumped and turned. "You scared me! I was trying to move a log over by that tree. It isn't going so well."

"You levitated the light in the cave."

"That's easy. Light doesn't weigh anything. According to Dovin, the weight shouldn't matter, so it's all in my head."

"Should we go? I'm starving. Yesterday's breakfast feels like it was weeks ago."

"I found some berries," he said, placing his cape in front of her. On it were some red and purple berries she'd never seen before.

"Are you sure they're safe?"

"Yeah, we used to grow them when I was little. You can eat all of them. I already had some."

She picked one up and put it in her mouth. She forced herself to ignore the fact that they weren't washed and they were on Mateo's dirty cape. "They're good. It almost tastes like a raspberry. How long have you been awake? You probably shouldn't have gone off looking for food. What if you couldn't find your way back?"

Mateo grinned. "Are you saying you would miss me?"

She rolled her eyes. "I don't want to be lost out here by myself. When do we start panicking?"

"Panicking?"

"Yeah. We can't stay out here forever, living off of berries. We need to find water and better shelter if we are going to be here for long. I should have studied the maps closer. Then we might know how big this forest is."

"I only glanced at the map. I figured Dovin knew what he was doing."

"I hope Claret's okay."

"I doubt the goblins would hurt her. They probably want to ransom her or something like that."

Kaylee finished the berries. There had been more than enough to fill her up, but she worried she might get a stomachache later. They were going to need to find more than just berries. She heard a sound in the forest and her head swerved to the side.

"Did you hear that?" she whispered.

Mateo cocked his head. "It sounds like a horse."

Kaylee jumped up and walked carefully toward the sound. If it was a horse, she didn't want to scare it. Mateo followed. He didn't look as eager as she felt. A horse would probably have a rider who could point them in the right direction. If not, Kaylee was a decent rider. Of course, if the horse was wild, that wouldn't do them much good.

They rounded a tree, and Kaylee's mouth fell open. Standing in front of them was a solid black alicorn. Her wings rested against her and she was chewing something. "Oh my goodness," she whispered. "She's beautiful." The alicorn looked at them and bent over to eat grass. She didn't seem to care that they were staring at her.

"She's big," Mateo said. "Too bad we don't know how to ride one."

"Do you think she would let us?"

"If she lives in the forest, she's probably wild. I've only ridden one once, and I was behind someone."

"I bet it's about the same as riding a horse."

"I don't know how to ride a horse."

"I do."

"I'm not getting on a wild animal."

"You want to stay lost in the forest for the rest of your life? If we can get her to take us, it will be so much faster. And if we can get her to fly…"

"No flying," Mateo said. "You might know how to ride a horse, but that isn't the same as flying."

"Even if we can't control her, she might fly us somewhere. Anywhere that has people would be okay."

Mateo shook his head. "There isn't anything to hold on to. It's too dangerous."

Kaylee walked to the beautiful animal and stuck out her hand. The alicorn sniffed it and let Kaylee rub her nose. "Hello, my name's Kaylee. My friend and I need a ride. Do you think you can take us out of this forest?"

The alicorn rubbed its nose into her, and she giggled. "You are so sweet. Come on, Mateo."

He crossed his arms. "No way."

"Fine. I'll go. If I ever find Dovin or anyone, I'll send out a search party."

He cringed. "How are you going to get on? That thing is the size of a dinosaur."

"Can you lean down so I can climb up?" she asked, rubbing her neck.

"Alicorns don't speak people."

"Don't speak people? Really?"

The alicorn dropped her head and bent her front legs. Kaylee flashed a triumphant smile at Mateo and climbed on her back. "Are you coming?"

He frowned but came forward and climbed on behind her. "Just for the record, I think this is a stupid idea." The alicorn stood, and she smiled when she heard Mateo suck in a breath. His arms tightened around her.

Kaylee nudged the alicorn gently with her foot, and she started walking.

"It almost seemed like she understood you."

"Are you saying she didn't?"

"Why would she? She's an animal."

"This is a magical place, so I figured it was worth a try."

"I think she must be trained, and she just understood that's what you wanted her to do."

Kaylee shrugged. It really didn't matter. What mattered was that they were making better time, and they didn't have to walk.

Mateo could admit when he was wrong. The alicorn was a lot faster than they were, and with luck, she would take them somewhere that wasn't in this forest. Plus, there was the bonus of getting to put his arms around Kaylee. If he told her he thought that was a bonus, she would probably throw him off and make him walk. He had to be careful so the sword wouldn't hit him in the face or shock him. Kaylee had angled it sideways so it wouldn't poke the alicorn.

There was the chance the alicorn would just trot around the forest, and they would stay lost. He hoped she would take them to water. If he remembered correctly, alicorns drank a lot of water.

Kaylee leaned forward and turned her head. "I'm going to see if I can get her to run."

Mateo thought about arguing, but when had that done him any good? Instead, he held on tighter and gritted his teeth when the alicorn began running through the trees. He wished there was a saddle. They entered a clearing, and the alicorn sprang into the air and flew upward. Mateo held in a scream.

"Why did you make her do that?" he asked, the wind slapping him in the face.

"I didn't! I am totally freaking out!"

He leaned in closer to be heard over the wind. "If we just hold on, she'll have to stop eventually!"

Kaylee didn't answer. They rose higher and Mateo focused on the back of Kaylee's head. If he looked down, he might panic. Or cry. That was one thing he did not want to do in front of Kaylee. He would never live that down.

After about ten minutes, his heart started to beat normally. He was still holding on tighter than was probably necessary, but he wasn't taking any chances.

"Where do you think she's taking us?"

Kaylee didn't turn. "No idea. I see a village up ahead. I hope she goes down there."

It was almost like the alicorn heard her. She began flying down, and Mateo stiffened. He closed his eyes because he knew Kaylee couldn't see him. After what felt like forever but was probably only a few minutes, he felt the jolt of hitting the ground. His eyes opened, and the scenery was flying by. It looked the same as the forest had before. They must have missed the village.

The alicorn went through a cluster of trees and when she stepped out, there was a lake.

Kaylee leaned forward. "Wow. Look how blue the water is." The alicorn walked up to the water and bent her knees, allowing them to slide down.

Mateo's legs felt shaky. He wouldn't let Kaylee see. They hadn't been riding for that long. He didn't know if the shaking was from riding or from being terrified. The alicorn began drinking the water and Kaylee dropped to her knees. She scooped up a handful and drank it.

"Aren't you worried it might make you sick?" he asked.

"Yes, but I am so thirsty. It tastes so fresh."

Mateo squatted down beside her and tried to scrub his hands, then he cupped them. He brought some water up to his mouth and drank it. She was right. It was the best water he had ever tasted. If they got sick, he supposed they could throw up together. He shook his head at the thought.

"We missed the village."

Kaylee grinned. "Did you have your eyes closed?"

"What are you talking about?"

"We didn't miss the village. It should be over that way," she said, pointing.

He scooped up more water. If he was going to get sick, he might as well make the most of it.

She glanced at the alicorn. "What should we call her?"

"The alicorn? We can't keep her."

"Why not?" she asked, standing.

"For one thing, she's a wild animal. She probably doesn't want to stay with us. And how would we take care of her?" Great. Now he sounded like his mom.

"I think she can take care of herself. I think I'll call her Willow."

"That doesn't sound like an alicorn name."

"Well, what does?"

Mateo scratched his head. "Cindy?"

Kaylee rolled her eyes. "Come on, Willow," she said, turning and walking away. The alicorn followed her.

Mateo grinned and made up the caboose. "Are you sure you're going in the right direction?"

"Positive. You really were closing your eyes, weren't you?"

"You can't ever prove it."

Kaylee laughed. "I would have closed my eyes, but that seems even scarier to me. I want to know where I'm going."

They rounded a corner, and the village came into view. Mateo sped up. Now that he'd had water, he felt a lot more energetic.

"I wonder who lives there," Kaylee said, also picking up her pace. "I hope they can point us toward the castle."

Mateo's mouth turned down. "I'm worried about Dovin. I always think of him as being able to do anything. He should have found us by now."

"He might have gone after Claret."

Mateo hoped so, but he really thought Dovin would tell them first, or at least point them in some direction.

They came to a narrow dirt road that led into the village. All the houses they could see were small and poorly constructed. They were made of logs, but they weren't neat and they didn't fit together well. The roofs were all covered with tree branches and none of the houses looked big enough for more than a few people to fit inside.

They walked up to the closest house, and Kaylee rapped on the door. They waited a few minutes, but no one answered. She turned to him. "Do you know the story of the three pigs?"

"Yeah."

She knocked again. "That's what this place reminds me of. It's like the second little pig built this entire village."

Mateo nodded. "It does look like a sneeze might blow the whole thing down."

A squeaking a few houses down drew their gazes. A large head with thick quill-like hair poked out, and wide eyes stared at them.

Kaylee squinted ahead. "What is that?" she asked under her breath.

"Troll." Mateo hadn't seen a lot of trolls, but they were hard to forget.

The troll looked from side to side, then motioned them forward.

"Are trolls good or bad?" Kaylee whispered.

"Depends on the troll."

"Do we go?"

"We don't have a lot of options. I say we go."

Kaylee nodded, and they walked toward the troll. Willow seemed content to stay where she was munching on some weeds.

The troll was motioning faster. "Hurry," he said in a low voice. "Try not to let anyone see you." He moved from the doorway and let them enter. Once they were inside the dark house, the troll pushed the door shut and barred it.

16

CHAPTER 16

Claret pushed her bed into the farthest corner of her cell. The farther from Odious and his experiments she was, the better. He had already caused two small explosions and set his cape on fire. He sat at his table, mixing things together and muttering to himself. The smell in the dungeon had changed. Now instead of the smell of vomit, it had the smell of fire and burned feathers. She preferred it, though neither was good.

"Odious? Perhaps you should stop. It would be bad if you burned down the entire place."

Odious looked up, then he scanned the dungeon. "I don't think I could burn this place down if I tried. It's all metal and stone. You can call me Odie."

Claret nodded. She would go by Odie if her name were Odious. "I can smash the bugs. It's not that important."

"What else am I going to do down here? I think I've almost got it." He took a jar of green powder and measured out a few spoonfuls and dropped it into his glass vial. Next, he added a reddish-brown liquid. He grabbed a few hairs from a bag and tossed them in. She had been watching him do things like this for hours.

Claret wanted to pace, but that would make her appear anxious. Her father always taught her to keep her composure and not let anyone know her inner turmoil. If the ruler was nervous, it made everyone nervous. If Odie weren't here, she would climb into bed and go to sleep. She had no idea what time it was. It could be the middle of the night or day.

Odie glanced up from his work. "I think I know what to do, but it's going to smell."

"It already smells."

"Yes, but I think I need a few drops of rednax venom."

Claret wrinkled her nose. Rednax were cute little animals that smelled awful. It was the kind of stink that could give a person a headache. "Will it smell?"

"Rednax stink when they spray. The venom itself doesn't."

"That's good."

"Yeah, but it smells when it's mixed with some of the other stuff I put in here. Sorry."

Odie took out a dropper and dipped it into a container. He placed two drops into the vial, covered the top with a lid, and shook it. It bubbled and Claret stood back against the far wall and held her breath. When nothing exploded, she sighed with relief.

"I think this might work," he said. "Could it really be that easy, though?"

"Easy? You've been working for hours."

"I never get anything right in a few hours. It can take days or even months to make something work right." He poured the concoction into a small round glass ball and put in a stopper. He shook it vigorously. "Are you ready?"

Her eyebrows rose. "For what?"

He held up the container. "For whatever is going to happen when I break this."

She swallowed. "I suppose."

Odie stepped away from the table and threw the glass ball against the floor. Claret cringed at the sound of breaking glass. Green smoke rose from the ground. It was almost like the smoke Odie used when he was trying to make it look like he disappeared, but it was spreading to cover everything.

Claret pressed herself against the wall as the smoke moved toward her. When it hit her, she almost vomited. The smell from the rednax insulted her innocent nose. She cupped her hands over her face, but it didn't shield her from the smell. Her eyes watered and she heard Odie cough.

All she could see was green. She hoped it wasn't doing something bad to her lungs. They felt like they were on fire. Something fell onto her arm and then her cheek. She brushed at it and focused on breathing.

The smoke began to clear, and Claret screamed. Dead bugs were pelting her from above and there weren't only a few. She screamed again as the bugs rained down. She batted at her arms.

"Sorry!" Odie called from under his table. "I should have known that would happen. There have been hundreds of years of cockroaches living down here unbothered."

As soon as Odie said cockroaches, Claret felt lightheaded. She wasn't scared of one bug on the wall, but this was like a nightmare. The bugs stopped falling and Claret shivered. She frantically brushed them from her hair and jumped up and down to make any on her clothing fall. With every jump, she heard the squishing of the bugs. She had nowhere to go to get away from them. Her bed was covered, as was every surface.

Claret's heart had never beat like this in her life. Tears began running down her cheeks, and she couldn't even think clearly enough to try to get them to stop. She was shaking like a scared little girl. She ran across the cell and jumped, grabbed onto the bars, and held herself away from the bugs. If anyone had ever told her she could hold her body weight up like this, she would have thought they were lying, but it was amazing what fear could do.

Odie rushed out from under the table and over to her bed. She could feel her hands slipping. Odie's eyes were wide, and he had an enormous frown on his face. Grabbing the blanket from the bed, he snapped it, causing bugs to fall to the floor. He brushed off the few that had fallen onto the mattress and put the blanket back down. He hurried over to Claret and she practically threw herself at him. He stumbled but caught her.

She wrapped her arms around his neck and sobbed. Odie rushed her across the crunchy corpses and tried to place her on the bed. She couldn't seem to release her hold. What a queen she was turning out to be.

Odie didn't know what to do. He was sitting on Claret's bed with his arms around her while she sobbed on his shoulder. Odie had never had to comfort anyone before, so he wasn't sure what to do. He had also never been this close to a girl, and it made him nervous. If King Ummi ever let Claret free, she was going to have her people tear apart the goblins for sure. As soon as she pulled herself together, she would realize Odie was behind her tears and she would go from sobbing on him to trying to kill him.

"What did you do, Odie?" Tipp said, running toward the cell. When he saw Odie and Claret, his eyes went wide. Claret was not crying quietly.

"What do you mean, what did I do?"

Tipp shook his head. "The entire castle filled up with green smoke and then dead bugs started falling from the ceiling. Nothing like down here, though," he said as he stepped on the dead bugs. "I kind of like the crunch."

Claret shivered and then went quiet. She must be getting her wits back because she moved away from him and crawled over the bed and pulled the blanket over her entire body.

Odie turned and placed his hands on his hips. "Go get all the servants and have them come clean this up."

Tipp laughed. "There is no way. They are all going to be cleaning the castle, not the dungeon."

"Then go get me a broom."

"I'm not your servant."

"If you go get one, I'll give you a stink bomb."

Tipp's beady eyes narrowed as he thought. "That's not worth the stairs. Give me two and I'll do it."

"Fine."

Tipp retreated back the way he had come. Odie glanced at the bump in the bed and frowned. From the way the blanket was rising and falling, he could tell Claret was still upset. He couldn't think of anything to do or say, so he went to his table and found a rag. He whipped it around to get all the bugs off, then started wiping all the dead bugs from the table. Next, he went to his shelf and cleaned it.

Tipp didn't return, but a guard appeared with a broom in his hand. The goblin passed it to Odie and left. He sighed as he started sweeping. He couldn't blame Claret for reacting the way she had. Odie was used to living with bugs and it had still terrified him.

Claret had fallen asleep to the sound of Odie sweeping the dungeon floor. When she woke up, everything was quiet. She knew she should come out from under the blanket, but she couldn't seem to make herself move. She was also embarrassed. Crying on the sleeve of your worst enemy was not the best way to conduct one's self. She would give herself five minutes, and then she would come out and act as if nothing had happened.

The smell of rednax still filled her nose, but it was mellow compared to what it had been. Her eyes felt heavy, and she was almost sure she could go back to sleep if she tried.

She could hear a small sound, like someone was writing. She sighed and sat up, pulling the blanket from her head.

Odie sat at his table, scribbling onto parchment. He looked different. It must be his hair. He usually wore it slicked back, but now it looked like he had rolled around on his head. It must have happened when he brushed the bugs out. She shivered at the memory. He looked a lot more normal and vulnerable sitting there.

He glanced up at her and froze. She must look a fright. His eyes widened, and he looked back down at his paper. She glanced around her cell. There wasn't a bug to be seen. Odie was not the person he wanted people to think he was. What kind of captor cleaned out their prisoner's cell just so they wouldn't be scared?

"What are you doing?" she asked.

His eyes jumped to her, then back down. "I know that was a terrifying experience, but I'm writing everything I did. People would pay for something that would get rid of bugs so thoroughly."

Claret nodded. She wouldn't mind someone getting rid of the bugs in her castle, but she would prefer not to be inside when it happened. Of course it wouldn't be as terrifying because her castle was clean. There was also the smell to consider.

"Is there a way to make it smell better?" she asked. "I'm not sure anyone would want their home to smell like rednax."

He frowned. "I'm not sure. The rednax was what made it work in the end, and there aren't a lot of smells that are more potent. Mixing two powerful smells might even make a worse smell."

"Are you an alchemist?"

"Um, I like to think so."

"You make things because you don't have magic?"

Odie twitched and glanced at her. "Who says I can't do magic?"

Claret arched her brow. "You stole the Blade of the Phoenix. Only someone without magic can touch it."

He laughed nervously. "Me? What makes you think I stole it?"

"I won't reveal my sources." Claret didn't have any sources, and she wasn't completely sure Odie was behind it, but she would almost wager on it.

He ran a hand through his already mussed hair. "You've seen me use magic."

"I don't believe so."

"What about all the times I disappeared after our meetings at the castle?"

"You mean all the times you shattered a glass vial on my floors and filled my castle with smoke so you could run away? Your smoke wasn't thick enough and I could see you."

Odie clenched and unclenched his fists.

"It doesn't matter if a person has magic or not. It doesn't make the things you create any less impressive. I think it's more impressive that everything comes from your head."

His features softened. "Everyone doesn't feel that way."

"How did you get the blade out of Riviand? People have tried to leave and have never been able to."

He shook his head. "I don't want to talk about any of that."

Claret wanted to press for more information, but she was tired. She wondered if Odie could be an ally if she worked on him enough.

"How long have I been down here?" she asked.

"I'm losing track of time. Probably close to a day and a half."

That wasn't very long. She wondered if Riviand knew she was missing. She didn't even know if Dovin and the others had seen the goblin grab her.

Mateo and Kaylee would probably come for her if they knew. They were both brave and ready for anything. Claret could probably learn a lot from being around them. She wanted to be strong, but more often than not, she felt confused and lost.

Odie was having a hard time making eye contact with her. He had always been good at it before. She wondered if she had scared him when she was sobbing on him. She doubted many boys their age would know how to handle that.

"I'm sorry I was so upset over the bugs," she said, watching him closely.

He shrugged. "It was my fault. Sorry it scared you so much."

"Do you think King Ummi will ever let me go?"

He frowned. "Not without a ransom."

She climbed off the bed and walked to the table. He hadn't bothered closing her cell. It wasn't like she could get away anyhow.

"You know the goblins are wrong. Why do you do what they say?"

Odie bit the inside of his cheek, and he refused to look up from his paper.

"Do you really want Riviand to go to war?" She placed her hand on his shoulder and he jumped up.

A goblin came walking toward them, and Odie rushed to him.

The goblin gave a slight bow. "Your father would like a word."

"Excellent," Odie said. He rushed off after the goblin.

Claret watched him leave. She had never been good at manipulating people, and she'd never wanted to. Still, there was a place for everything, and if she played it right, she might get Odie to help her.

Odie entered the throne room and scowled. A man stood next to the throne, smirking at him. The man had blond hair and the strangest eyes Odie had ever seen. He noticed them as soon as he saw him, even though he was a distance from the man. When he turned his head, they looked almost orange. He wore a leather jerkin and black pants and boots. His cape was black, with some type of white embroidery around the edges. A sword sat at his waist and he was touching the hilt. He appeared to be in his thirties. The thing that unsettled Odie the most was that the man was here at all. Humans did not belong here.

"Odie!" King Ummi said from his throne.

"Sorry about the bugs," he muttered.

"We will talk about that later. I want you to meet Garin. Garin, this is my son Odious."

"Pleasure," Garin said with a smile Odie didn't like. Odie didn't know why he was here, but nothing good could come from it.

"Garin has been working with me for the past few months."

Odie's eyes narrowed. "Oh?"

"Garin has some good ideas. With his help, I believe we will get the gold we want from Queen Claret's people."

He crossed his arms. "How much do we really need?"King Ummi's eyes locked on his. "We will not argue about this again. Tipp told me something interesting. He said the queen was, uh, er, I mean..."

Odie rolled his eyes. Goblins didn't show affection, and they never talked about it. "She was crying on my shoulder?"

"Crying?" The king rubbed his gray chin. "He didn't say anything about that. Still, if we have her rattled enough to cry, that could be to our advantage. Isn't that right?" he asked, looking at Garin.

Garin nodded. "That could be very good."

"She wasn't crying because she's here," Odie clarified. "It was the raining bugs."

"Well, Tipp said there was some sort of... a... hugging going on."

Garin turned to the king. "If your son can get the queen to think he is sympathetic to her, he might be able to control her."

Odie clenched his fists. He wouldn't admit that he actually was feeling sympathetic to her.

"If she comes to trust him, that could be beneficial. We may be able to take over her kingdom at some point."

King Ummi shook his head. "I don't want her kingdom. What would I do with it? I only want her gold."

Garin looked like he wanted to argue but changed his mind.

King Ummi cleared his throat. "What are the chances of the queen seeing you as a friend?"

Odie shrugged. "I don't see it happening. The bugs made her overly anxious. That's the only reason Tipp saw what he did."

"We can talk about it later," King Ummi decided. "A man was found sneaking around the mountain. He was captured. I want you to look at him and see if you know who he is. BRING IN THE HUMAN!" he yelled, causing Garin and Odie to flinch.

The doors opened, and two guards pushed a man through the doors. He was the same man who had been with Claret at her castle and he had been with her when Tipp caught her in the forest. The man looked up at Odie with a blank expression.

"Do you recognize this man?"

Odie swallowed hard. "Perhaps."

"Perhaps?"

"I think he might be one of Queen Claret's advisors."

The man's mouth twitched slightly.

"I think he should be placed in the dungeon with the queen," Odie said. If Claret had a friend here, she might not be as worried.

"Is it smart to put the two of them together?" Garin asked.

Odie nodded. "If she sees we can capture her advisor, she might be scared."

King Ummi smiled. "Good idea, Odious. Take the man to the cell across from the queen."

The man's eyes flashed with something Odie couldn't interpret. All Odie knew was that it wasn't anger or fear. The man had gotten himself captured on purpose.

17

CHAPTER 17

Kaylee took in all the details of the troll's small hovel. It was smaller than her bathroom back home. There was a pile of blankets in one corner, two cupboards that looked like they had been thrown together in a hurry, a three-legged stool, and a hard-packed dirt floor. Light shone in through the cracks in the walls. Mateo was scanning the room, his eyes flickering from place to place as if he expected something to pop out and grab him.

"Please sit," the troll said, motioning to the floor. "You may call me Zute."

Kaylee and Mateo sat on the ground and watched the troll peek nervously out a small gap in the wall. Kaylee always pictured trolls as small, but this one wasn't. He was as tall as she was. He had a large nose and big eyes. Whatever was on his head resembled hair but looked more like black and gray porcupine quills. They reached down past his shoulder. His tunic and trousers looked similar to what Mateo was wearing.

"I wish you hadn't come to our village." He held up his hand when Kaylee opened her mouth to speak. "I am not blaming you. It is only unfortunate."

Kaylee tilted her head and frowned. "Why? We didn't come here to cause any problems. We're only looking for directions."

Zute pointed to Kaylee. "I see you have the Blade of the Phoenix."

Mateo looked from Kaylee to the troll. "How did you know that?"

"I didn't until now. I was only guessing."

Mateo frowned.

"I do not wish to trick you, but we trolls are worried about the things to come, and we were warned to avoid you." He grabbed a loaf of bread from the cupboard and handed it to Kaylee.

Kaylee's eyes narrowed. "Warned?"

"That is why no one roams the village. My people are scared." He handed another loaf to Mateo.

Mateo chuckled. "Of us?"

"No. Of the man who came to our village. He told us there were some people who might come and ask for our help and they might carry the Blade of the Phoenix. He said that if we were to help them, he would count us as his enemies and come against us with an army."

"When was this?" Kaylee asked.

"Last night. We left our village and came here."

"This isn't your village?"

He snorted. "Of course not. Trolls are great builders. We have a beautiful city. This place is something we threw together a few years ago when we sensed the goblins might be causing trouble. We only come here when we fear for our safety."

"Who was the man?" Mateo asked.

"He did not give his name, but he filled us all with dread. When the light caught his eyes, they glowed with fire."

Kaylee leaned forward. "Like literal fire?"

"I cannot say. It is hard to describe what we saw. Now my people worry. We cannot have that man causing trouble for us. Do you not know who he is? He was looking for you."

Mateo shook his head. "I have no idea. I've never met anyone like that."

Zute's eyes were fixed on them. "Beware him. I believe he wishes to keep you from using the sword to secure Riviand. I assume that is what you are doing."

Kaylee glanced at Mateo. "Why would he care? Is he working with the goblins?"

Zute hissed, and Kaylee shivered. "Do not speak of goblins!"

Mateo stood. "But we think they are the ones who stole the sword to begin with. Well, they had a human helping them. It's possible he is the one who spoke to you. I didn't see his eyes."

"He was our age," Kaylee broke in, getting to her feet. "He wore a black feathered cape."

The troll rubbed his arms. "The man who spoke to us was older."

"We need to find the last two locks and then make sure the blade is hidden," Kaylee said.

"Which ones have you secured?" Zute asked.

Mateo shifted. "At the pyramid and near the giants."

"Then you must go to the one in Colter's Lake—"

"Did you say 'in?'" Mateo asked.

"Yes. In."

"That's just great," he muttered.

Kaylee didn't say anything, but she wasn't any more excited about that than he was. She was good at swimming, but finding a keyhole on the bottom of a lake sounded difficult.

"The last is in the goblin mountains."

Mateo threw his head back and blew out a breath. "Dang. I guess we won't get any help there."

Zute frowned. "The goblins and the trolls have never been friendly with one another. I wish you the best. Please do not tell anyone you were here. We do not want to be on the wrong side of this."

"Of course," Kaylee said. "Thanks for the bread. Now can you please give us directions to Colter's Lake?"

Mateo wanted to complain, but Kaylee was walking just as much as he was, and she hadn't complained once. The troll told them the lake was only a bit of a walk to the northwest, but they had been walking for more than what he would call a bit. They had tried to find Willow, but the alicorn was nowhere to be seen. There weren't many trees this way, just enormous weeds. They had to avoid the pokey ones. Some were as big as they were.

"Do you think we're going to be stuck in Riviand forever?" Kaylee asked.

Mateo frowned. He'd wondered the same thing a time or two. "I hope not."

"If no one here knows how to leave—"

"Someone does. That boy who tried to take the sword. He must have left, or how did the sword end up in the orchard?"

"I guess. What if we are stuck, though?"

Mateo watched her as they walked. Her face didn't show any emotion. "I dunno."

"I keep trying not to think about it, but it creeps up on me when we aren't doing anything."

Mateo nodded. "I hope we aren't stuck, but honestly, I'd rather be stuck here than on Earth."

She pulled her braids back and secured them in a ponytail. "I don't know how I feel. If we're gone for a long time, we're going to miss a lot of school. Making it up won't be very fun."

Mateo laughed softly. "I don't really care about school."

She side-eyed him. "School isn't my favorite thing, but it's important. Without an education, what are you going to do with your life?"

"I don't plan on staying on Earth for most of my life. If we go back, I won't stay. I want to live in Basura."

"Don't they have school there?"

"Yeah, but it's not the same. Once you decide what you want to do with your life, you find a mentor and they teach you everything you need to know."

They both gazed up at the sky when they heard a honking sound. "Geese. Come on," he said, picking up the pace. "I bet the lake is close. Geese stay near the water."

"There," Kaylee said, pointing ahead. "I can see it."

Mateo squinted. He could see some blue up ahead, but it was still going to take a while to get there. "What are we going to do when we get there? I bet the lock isn't easy to find, and I don't know about you, but I can't breathe underwater."

"I have no idea. I'm dreading this one even more than the one near the goblins."

"I guess we'll have to jump in and keep going up and down until we find it."

She let out a frustrated sigh. "It could take forever. What if the water is murky? I can't imagine finding something so small in a lake. You don't know any magic that can help?"

"No. Sorry." Mateo knew he wasn't the greatest at magic, but he hadn't realized just how much he didn't know until he'd come here. "You need to help me convince Dovin to teach me to teleport. That would make all of this easier."

"Are there sea monsters or anything like that in this world?"

He laughed. "Not that I know of."

"Hey, don't laugh at me. There are all sorts of creatures here that I've never seen, so I'm just making sure."

He arched his eyebrow. "You want to race to the lake?"

Kaylee grinned. "You wanna lose?"

Kaylee put a hand to her side and ignored Mateo's triumphant grin as she walked the last few feet to the lake. That boy could run. She should have known she couldn't beat him after following him through the forest the other day. Running wasn't her thing, but she'd thought she was in good enough shape to do it anyway. She'd been wrong. Mateo had let her think she was winning, and then he'd blasted past her without looking back, leaving her in his dust. She wanted to blame the loss on the two times she tripped over rocks she couldn't see in the weeds, but she'd seen him stumble a few times as well.

"So you run?" she asked, forcing herself to take even breaths.

"I run."

"Hmm. I didn't take you for a runner."

He smirked. "Why? Because I'm undisciplined?"

She glared playfully at him. "Maybe."

"When you're the troubled kid, people go out of their way to make you do things to replace your anger. My mom got me into running and weight training. It actually helps."

"It was impressive."

He grinned. "Yeah, well, I ran a lot harder than I wanted to so I could totally waste you."

Kaylee smiled. "I hope you get a leg cramp."

"You say that right before we go swimming? If I get a leg cramp, you'll have to save me."

"I wouldn't count on that if I were you." She looked past him at the lake and her mouth fell open. "Wooooow. I've never seen water like that before."

Mateo turned around and his jaw dropped as well. "That has to be magic."

"How did you not see that when you got here?"

"I was busy gloating."

"It's amazing." It didn't look like any water she had ever seen. Kaylee could see the lake floor covered in sand and small shells. The water appeared thicker than any she had seen before. Almost like a thick gel.

"Weird," Mateo said, bending down and scooping water into his cupped hands. He shook it, and it jiggled.

"That's slightly creepy. What are you doing?" she asked as he held it up to his lips. "Don't drink it!"

"I'm thirsty," he said, slurping up the thick water.

She pushed his hands, sloshing the remaining water out of his hands. "What if it's poisonous?"

He wiped at a wet spot on his shirt. "Then I'll die happy. That is the best water I've ever tasted. Try it."

Kaylee squinted down at the water. She hated drinking from any water she wasn't sure was clean. Sure, she had earlier, but that was an emergency. This water didn't look natural. Mateo was already kneeling down, drinking more.

"I'm not drinking fish poop water if I don't have to, especially when it jiggles."

"I don't see any fish."

"There has to be something living in there." She tried to see farther out, but it got darker as the lake went on.

"There is something—odd about it," Mateo said. "I feel different."

"Great. If you're going to spend the rest of the day ralphing in the bushes, that's going to mess us up."

He grinned. "Ralphing? I'm assuming from the context you mean puking?"

She rolled her eyes. "Yes. It's my mom's favorite word for throwing up."

He laughed. "I prefer vomit. Why are there always so many weird words for things that are gross?"

She shrugged. "I've never thought about it."

"I don't feel like *ralphing*. I feel like—I might be able to breathe underwater."

She tilted her head. "I would say you are crazy, but you know more about magic than I do. So how do we test it?"

"I stick my head in the water and take a deep breath. Then either nothing happens or I come up coughing, fall on my boom, and you can laugh at me."

"On your boom?"

He grinned. "Your mom likes ralphing, my mom likes boom. Well, she doesn't like it, but she's really against a lot of other words. It's another thing with way too many words for it. She can handle bum, rear, back end, and rump if she's in a good mood. Then there are a few we can say in Spanish. Anything else will get you a time-out and a stern talking-to. Well, you can say bottom and fanny, but only if you use a British accent."

Kaylee laughed. "I've never heard anyone call it a boom."

"I think my youngest brother couldn't say bum. He said boom once, and we all thought it was funny. I guess it became our thing."

"Bum isn't a Spanish word."

"No, but it happened clear back when we lived in Basura, and Akkronese is closer to English."

Kaylee wished she had siblings. It would be like having built-in friends. "Okay, so back to the whole breathing underwater thing. What makes you think you can do that?"

"I don't know how to explain it. I just feel like I can. Drink some of the water and you'll understand."

Kaylee peered into the lake and frowned. "It might not work for me. I'm not magic."

"I don't think it has anything to do with that. I think the water must be magic."

Kaylee moved her lips from side to side as she weighed her options. If she drank the water and got sick, that would be inconvenient. If it worked, finding the keyhole would be a million times easier than finding it while swimming up and down. The possibility of getting sick really made her nervous. This place still had outhouses... and there weren't any of those over here.

When they'd first come to Riviand and someone had led her out behind the castle to an outhouse she'd been horrified. Since being out here for the last while, she was ready to beg for an outhouse. An outhouse was a lot less unsettling than the bushes.

"Are you going to try?" Mateo asked, interrupting her thoughts.

"After you test it. If you really can breathe underwater, I'll do it."

Mateo bent down and stuck his face in the shallow water. His shoulders moved up and down, and he wasn't pulling his head out. Kaylee's heart was pounding, and just as she was about to pull him up, he lifted his face from the water.

"That was so cool. You have to try it."

Kaylee sighed and kneeled next to the lake. She cupped her hands and dipped them into the clear water. As soon as the water hit her stomach, a cool sensation ran through her entire body. It seemed to flow through her veins and it made all of her fatigue vanish. She looked up at Mateo, her eyes wide.

He smiled. "Told you. I wonder if we could market this stuff. I would pay money to feel like this. It feels so… renewing? Is that the right word?"

"Sounds right to me. So now what? We just walk into the lake?"

"I guess."

"What if it runs out and we can't breathe all of a sudden?"

Mateo shot her a crooked smile. "Then I guess we open our mouths and the water flows in."

She shook her head. "Right. It shouldn't be a problem if we're surrounded by the water."

"You aren't nervous, are you?"

She laughed and ignored the slight shake of her hands. "Me? Nervous?" She rubbed her arms. "I'm completely nervous."

"Me too." He held out his hand, and she hesitated.

"Will we float up? Maybe we should wait until we find Dovin."

"You're stalling."

She took a deep breath. "All right. Let's go. Probably not with boots." She kicked off her boots and pulled off her socks.

"I was going to walk right in with mine on," Mateo said, pulling his boots off.

Kaylee tossed her cloak on top of her boots and made sure the sword was still secure. It would be a pity to come all this way and lose it. She put the last bit of her bread on her cloak and covered it. Mateo threw his shirt and cloak down and Kaylee rolled her eyes and thought about the time Mia told her Mateo had nice arms. Not that he was *that* impressive. He was still a sixteen-year-old boy, after all.

"What?" he asked.

"You're such a show-off."

"What are you talking about?"

Her cheeks burned. "Nothing."

He shrugged, but she could see a sparkle in his eye. "Let's go." He held out his hand again, and she took it. She didn't want to be by herself under the lake.

The first step into the water made her shiver. It wasn't cold, it was just a strange sensation, like stepping into a lake of thick syrup—only not sticky. It was thick enough to make their steps slow, but it felt soothing to her feet and legs.

One step took the water from Kaylee's knees to her waist. She sucked in a breath and tried to ignore the pounding of her heart. They were going to be covered completely, so sooner might be better than later anyway.

Mateo squeezed her hand. "It looks like it drops off again. I'm guessing the next step will take us under. Are you ready?"

Kaylee took a deep breath and nodded. "Let's do it."

18

CHAPTER 18

Claret had never had time where she wasn't doing anything before and she could tell staying in the dungeon was going to be a test of her patience. There was nothing she could do but sit on her bed. She knew she was lucky she'd been given such a nice bed. Footsteps echoed across the dungeon, and she froze. It was probably Odie.

"Dovin?" she said when the man came into view. His hands were tied in front of him and three goblins walked near him. One cut off the bands with a small blade and Dovin rubbed his wrist.

"In here," one goblin commanded. Dovin walked into the cell across from her and shut the door behind himself. The goblins left and Dovin waited a moment and then opened the cell door.

"They have a strange way of keeping prisoners," he said, entering Claret's cell.

Claret frowned. "I'm sorry they caught you."

"Don't be. It actually took a lot of effort to get captured. Goblins aren't the best at patrolling their lands."

"You got captured on purpose?"

He sat at the foot of her bed. "Of course I got captured on purpose. I find it easier to escape from a prison than to break into one."

"You've done it before?"

"A few times."

Claret bit her lip. She should share her plan with Dovin, but it would be embarrassing to say out loud. "I didn't think anyone would come, so I've been trying to make a plan."

"Oh?"

She looked down at her hands. "It probably won't work. The king is making Odious stay down here to guard me."

"That would explain all the stuff in the hall," he said, motioning to Odie's things with his head.

"I don't think Odie is like the goblins even though he might want to be. I think I might be able to get him to help me escape."

Dovin chuckled quietly. "I see."

"I'm almost sure I can... I don't know."

"Use your feminine charms?"

Claret covered her cheeks with her hands. "Ugh. Don't say it like that."

He laughed. "It's actually not a bad idea. If goblins raised Odious, chances are he hasn't been around a lot of women. It might be easier than you think to solicit his help."

"It will be even more awkward now that you are here."

"Sorry to mess with your plan. It's always good to have someone on your side, though. If you can't manipulate Odious, I can try something a little more dramatic."

More footsteps came down the hall and Odie came into view. He looked at the two of them, then sat on his chair at the table.

"The goblins make you stay in the dungeon?" Dovin asked him.

Odie shrugged. "Not usually. I was the one they trusted to do this." He tapped his fingers against the table. "Did you know the man who was standing by the king?"

Dovin raised his brow. "I've never seen him before. You seem worried."

"King Ummi avoids humans. Well, besides me."

"I don't know many people here. Perhaps Claret does."

Claret hadn't seen the man and didn't even know what they were talking about.

"Do you know a man named Garin?" Odie asked.

"I don't believe so." Claret had met a lot of people in her life. As queen, it was expected. Remembering all of them wasn't an easy thing. Her father had tried to teach her to memorize the name of everyone she met. He said that people were loyal to a monarch they knew. It was something she struggled with.

"I think he is someone who should be avoided."

Claret's eyebrows came together. "Oh?"

"I think he might mean harm to your kingdom."

Claret just stared at him. He almost seemed like an entirely different person than she was used to dealing with. He wasn't trying to impress anyone with silly tricks or making ridiculous demands. She knew she was getting weirdly fixated on his messy hair, but it was almost bizarre the difference it made.

"Is this Garin working with your father?" she asked.

"He was standing next to him like an advisor. My father isn't after your kingdom, but I think Garin is trying to get it into his head."

"Why are you telling me this?"

"I just want you to be aware."

She kept her hands clasped on her lap. "There isn't anything I can do about it from here."

He nodded. "I suppose there isn't."

Odie yawned and rolled over in his bed. It was probably morning, but down here in the dungeon, it was impossible to know. The cold air crept over his exposed arm and he pulled it under the blanket. There was one fireplace down here, and it was the only thing giving off light. He had extinguished all the candles when Claret said she was tired and they had all agreed it was probably time for bed. He didn't want to light more and risk waking anyone up before they were ready.

He chuckled to himself. Odie was the worst person in the world to deal with prisoners. He shouldn't be worried about whether they got enough sleep. That made him soft. He turned to his side. Dovin appeared to be sleeping. When the guards had brought dinner, Odie had demanded they bring Dovin a bed. He turned the other way and tried to make out Claret's features. She also appeared to be asleep. Of course they could all be awake and unwilling to get out of their warm beds just like him.

This was a horrid position to be in. He was regretting his part in his father's plan for Claret. It was wrong, and he knew it. He'd tried to tell himself it was all right, that the people of Riviand owed the goblins, but he knew it wasn't true. Now his mind was a mess. If he weren't a coward, he would figure out a way to get Claret out of here. If he did, he would be banished in the least, and he didn't know enough about the rest of the world to know what he would do if that happened.

If someone didn't get up soon, the fire was going to go out. He grudgingly got out of his warm blankets and walked over to the fire. It was on the back wall of the hall. Whoever built this dungeon may have thought they were doing their prisoners a favor by putting in a fireplace, but one was not big enough for such a vast area. He picked up two logs from a pile near the wall and put them in. The flames burned brighter, and he sat in front of them.

He could see Claret climb out of bed from the corner of his eye. She left her cell, her bare feet slapping against the floor. She sat next to him, pulling her cloak tighter. "Do you think it's morning?" she asked.

"Probably. It's hard to tell. I could go ask a guard, but I guess it doesn't really matter what time it is down here."

A piece of hair fell over his eye, and he pushed it back. He should probably go change his clothes and fix his hair. He didn't want to look like a prisoner. Not that he needed to impress anyone. He used both of his hands to try to keep it back.

"You should leave it," Claret said, watching.

"Leave what?"

"Your hair. It looks better when it isn't slicked back."

"Oh." Odie didn't know what to say. No one had ever told him what to do with his hair, so he had tried to copy a soldier he saw once when he was young.

"Just let it be loose," she said, reaching out and moving some pieces to the sides. Odie tried not to squirm. No one had ever touched his hair before, and it was a strange sensation. "There. I think you should wear it like that."

He swallowed and nodded.

She placed a hand on her head. "I guess I shouldn't say anything. My hair must look like a rat's nest."

Odie looked at her, then away. Her hair was messy, but that didn't make her any less pretty. Of course he wouldn't say that. "I can see about getting you a brush if you wish."

She beamed. "That would be lovely."

"I wish I could get you a clean dress, but that would be hard to come by. The tallest goblin would only come to your waist."

She frowned. "Clean clothing would be nice. I feel so disgusting."

"If you want, you can borrow one of my tunics. I could probably find you a pair of britches that might work. They would be short but clean."

She nodded, then laughed. "I just had the funniest image of what I would look like."

He smiled. She had a nice laugh. He better be careful and not let that distract him.

She stood and stretched her back. "Where is Gregor when you're down here?"

Odie was sure the color drained from his face. He smacked himself in the forehead. "Ugh! I can't believe I forgot about him! I'll be back."

He jumped to his feet and tore off down the hall. Gregor was probably so upset. Odie had never left him overnight before. He ran up the stone staircase, trying not to count the stairs as he went. When he reached the top, he was panting. He tapped the secret knock on the door and it swung open. The guards moved out of the way and he ran past them.

He almost tripped when he rounded a corner, but he managed to stay on his feet. When he got to his room, he pulled the door open and scanned the area. "Gregor?" The puffin was nowhere in sight. He always came when he was called. The room was fairly empty since he had demanded all his belongings be taken to the dungeon. Gregor must have gotten out when they were moving his things.

He slammed the door and ran back the way he came. When he got to Tipp's room, he pounded on the black wooden door. "Tipp? Are you in there?"

The door opened a crack and Tipp peeked out. "Hey, Odie. What's wrong?"

"Have you seen Gregor?"

Tipp frowned. "Gregor? You lost him? Hmm... no, I don't think I've seen him."

Odie heard a squawk from inside. He rammed his shoulder into the door. It wasn't hard to push his brother out of the way.

"Hey, you can't come in here!" Tipp protested.

Gregor stood on Tipp's bed, a handful of seeds sitting in front of him.

"What have you been feeding him? I swear, if he vomits, I'm going to rub your face in it."

"I'd like to see you try. I could change you into a toad if I wanted to."

"You're going to make him so unhealthy. Come, Gregor."

Gregor flew off the bed and crashed into Odie's chest. He caught the bird and glared at Tipp.

Tipp held his arms up in defense. "Don't get angry with me. He was wandering around the halls. You're lucky I found him and took care of him."

Odie turned to leave.

"Wait... Odie?"

He glanced over his shoulder. "What?"

"If I tell you something, will you promise not to tell anyone else?"

Odie sighed. Tipp was annoying, but he was his brother. "Of course I won't tell."

"Well... the thing is... I am a little worried about Father's new advisor."

"The human he was with yesterday?"

"Yeah. He's called Garin. I think he's going to be the cause of something bad."

"For Father?"

"Perhaps. He's going to be a bad influence on him, if nothing else."

"He made me nervous when I met him," Odie admitted.

"I've always known Father was greedy, but I don't think he's evil. I think Garin might be."

Saying their father was greedy was an understatement, but Odie had never met a goblin who wasn't.

"I'm afraid he might be trying to influence Father to do things he wouldn't normally do."

"Oh? Like kidnap a queen?"

"I'm sure that was his idea."

"You helped. You are the one who actually grabbed Claret."

Tipp glanced at the floor and traced the cracks of the stone with his toe. "I know. I figured it was all right if we were just trying to get gold. Garin wants more than gold. He wants power. I listen to him talk with Father and I wouldn't be surprised if he wants Queen Claret's kingdom."

"Do you know where he comes from? Does he have any people behind him?"

"I'm not sure, but I bet he doesn't. If he did, why come here? I bet he wants to use the goblins to help him with whatever it is he is trying to do."

"Why are you telling me? You always go along with whatever Father wants."

Tipp shrugged. "Yes, well, I don't think this man is doing things in Father's best interest. He's trying to use him."

"Probably."

"What are we going to do about it?"

Odie patted Gregor on the head. "I don't know if there is anything we can do. Father doesn't listen to me very often, and he listens to you less."

"I think we need to bust the queen out of the dungeon."

Odie had been thinking the same thing but probably for different reasons than Tipp. "What good would that do?"

"Then Garin wouldn't be able to use Father to try to take over her kingdom."

"If that's really his goal, I doubt he'll stop just because the queen runs off."

"Maybe not, but I don't want to be any part of trying to take over the rest of Riviand. Goblins should stick to these mountains where we belong. The last thing we need is a war."

Odie nodded. "Still, you might be wrong. He might only want to work for Father and he isn't a threat at all."

"Did you see his eyes? I'm not sure I can trust someone with eyes like his. Sometimes they have flames."

"You can't judge a person by the way they look."

"I know, but he has a mean smile."

"I'm not sure what to do. We don't really know what his game is."

Tipp scratched the skin on his head. "We should spy on him and find out what he's up to."

"I can't. I have to watch the prisoners."

"I guess I could do it myself."

Odie frowned. "That's a terrible idea. You are horrible at spying." Odie and Tipp had tried to spy on other goblins several times when they were younger. Tipp could never stay quiet and they were always found out.

"Well, I'll make sure I listen when I'm around him. I'll let you know if I hear anything."

Odie nodded. "I have to go." He shut the door and hurried back to the dungeon.

Claret and Dovin were sitting at his table, eating breakfast. He sat by them and grabbed his own plate. Gregor jumped to the floor and went off to explore. This was one place in the castle he had never been, and he loved new places.

Claret looked up from her bowl of cooked oats. "I'm glad you found Gregor."

"My brother had him. He likes to overfeed him. That's why he's closer to the size of a turkey than a puffin," he exaggerated.

Dovin watched the bird hop away. "It's been a long time since I've seen a puffin. I've never seen one that was a pet."

Odie ate a grape. "I found him when he was young and alone. I took him home and fed him and he took to me. I've been training him."

"To do what?"

Odie felt the back of his neck get warm. "To attack my enemies."

Dovin's eyes twinkled as he stirred his oats. "I see. And how is that going?"

"Not as well as it could."

"If you want an animal that you can train to attack, you should have a dragon."

Odie's eyes widened. "I would love a dragon. They aren't easy to get."

Claret turned to Dovin. "Dragons are endangered. It's illegal for anyone to own one."

Dovin tilted his head. "Why? Dragons do well with people. If they are endangered, it would be helpful if people could take them and care for them."

Odie's brows came together. Dovin must not be around a lot of dragons. He'd never heard of anyone who would think taking in a dragon was like taking in a puppy.

Claret speared a piece of melon with her fork. "Dragons are ferocious. It would be dangerous to try to keep one."

Dovin took a sip from his dented goblet. "I have several."

If Odie's eyes had been wide before, it was nothing compared to now. "You have dragons?"

"Yes. They really aren't hard to tame."

Claret's mouth turned down. "Perhaps dragons are different where you are from."

Dovin shrugged. "Perhaps, though I doubt it."

Odie's brows came together. Where was Dovin from? There was nowhere in Riviand that would be very different from another area. He grabbed a cluster of grapes and stood. "I'm going to check on Gregor."

Claret glanced across the table. Dovin was casually eating his breakfast. "You're going to make Odie wonder about you," she whispered. "You don't want him knowing you are from above."

Dovin tossed a grape into his mouth. "Why not?"

"He is the enemy. You probably shouldn't give him ideas about taming dragons, either. I shudder to imagine what would happen if the goblins had control of the dragons."

Dovin nodded. "That would be bad, but that boy's heart isn't the heart of a goblin."

Claret leaned forward. "What do you mean?"

"It's difficult to stray from the way you are raised, but Odie is conflicted. I can see that in his aura. He's being torn between what his goblin family wants and what he believes is right."

"His aura?"

"Yes. Did I not tell you I can see auras?"

Claret shook her head. She had heard of people with that power but had assumed it was dead magic.

"The boy is confused, but I can see that he will do amazing things. Of course, auras aren't as clear as glass, but I believe they will be good things. I don't see any darkness in him."

"He is holding us captive," Claret protested.

"Yes, but he has little choice. He's scared and trying to figure out his feelings."

"Do you see everyone's aura?"

"No. It's random, and I don't always understand them when I do."

"Can you see anything about me?" Claret asked, unsure if she really wanted to know.

"I did when I first met you. I could see that you were struggling with fear and responsibility. At least that is the way I interpreted it. I could also see you have good intentions."

Claret nodded and let out a breath. She was glad she didn't know anyone else with this power. She didn't need everyone to know how unfit she was to rule a kingdom.

19

— · —

CHAPTER 19

This was amazing. Mateo had never experienced anything like it before. They were walking under the lake, just like they would up above. At least, almost like above. They were moving a lot slower. It felt like they were walking through gelatin. He wondered if they could talk, but neither of them had tried.

Green, purple, orange, and blue plants covered the lake bottom. The colors were bright and looked unnatural. Almost like something that would be in an aquarium. They had to walk around some because they were so big. Fish swam past them and didn't seem bothered by their presence. One even bumped into his leg. It was strange to watch them swim. They appeared to be going in slow motion. He could probably reach out and grab one, although he was moving at a snail's pace as well.

Kaylee came to a stop and pointed to the side. Mateo's head turned as fast as he could manage, to see what had caught her attention. His eyes widened as a school of some type of sea creature swam near them. They had heads like dragons and bodies like seahorses. They were gold, green, brown, and tan, and they were bobbing up and down.

"What are they?" Kaylee asked.

"I've never seen them before." Talking felt natural but sounded strange. That was a relief. "I hope these aren't babies. I would hate to run into a grown-up scary version."

Kaylee dropped his hand and took a step closer. "I'm not sure how scary that would be unless they blow fire or something." She stuck her hand out, and the creatures backed away. When she took another step, they started moving up and down with greater speed and their color changed. Now they were all a fiery red or blue.

"Let's go the other way," Mateo suggested.

Kaylee took a step back at the same moment the seahorse dragons opened their mouths, and something long and thin shot from their mouths. Mateo tried to dive to the lake floor, but he was moving too slow. He felt something poke into his upper arm and another in his knee. By the time he hit the ground, another had hit him in the shoulder. He looked up and watched the creatures scurry away.

"That was stupid," Kaylee said, sitting next to him, on top of something that looked like purple moss. "Did they hit you?"

"A few times," he said, pulling a barb from his knee.

"Sorry," she muttered, yanking one out of her arm. "I hope they aren't poisonous."

He pulled out the remaining two. "At least they come out easily. I say we avoid any animal."

"They were so neat, though," she said, glancing at him, then away.

He got to his feet and helped pull her up. "Are we moving faster? I don't feel like we're in slow motion anymore."

"I can't tell. We might be, or maybe we've just adjusted to the way things are down here."

"I guess that's possible." He took a few steps, then jumped over a plant. "Wow!" he said when he landed. "Did you see that? I flew right over that thing."

She tilted her head and smirked. "We are underwater, so it's not that impressive."

"Yeah, but it's different down here. If I did that in regular water, I wouldn't have landed like that, I would have floated or something. Come on!" He grabbed Kaylee's hand and ran a few steps, jumping and pulling Kaylee with him over another plant. She shrieked and then laughed when they landed.

He pointed up at some floating water plants. They were all different heights and colors. "Look at those things up there. Five points if you hit a green one and ten for a brown one."

Kaylee ran forward and jumped, slapping a brown plant. "That's ten."

"Nice." Mateo ran and jumped over a plant and then leaped as hard as he could, hitting a brown one. "This is just like being in a video game."

She giggled. "It really is."

Mateo lost track of time as they ran around the lake bottom, jumping and hitting things and calling out their points. Between the running and jumping, he stopped to itch the places those nasty little sea dragons had gotten him. The spots itched like crazy, and he was getting small red welts.

"Mateo! Try this!" Kaylee called. He watched her jump up and flip.

"Awesome," he said, running and copying her moves. "I bet I can flip twice!" He ran and jumped, spinning two and a half times before he fell on his back.

Kaylee laughed and scratched her arm. "Impressive landing."

He grinned. "At least it was soft."

"WHAT ARE YOU DOING?" a voice boomed. Mateo scrambled to his feet and turned to see a mermaid. He peeked over at Kaylee. Her eyes were wide. The mermaid swam closer, her long blond hair flowing behind her. She had a long green tail, and she wore something that resembled a women's swim shirt. It was bright green with a picture of a wave on it and it went down to her wrists. Mateo frowned. That was an odd thing for anyone to have in this world, and even more odd that she had it in Riviand. It looked like something from Earth.

Kaylee came closer to Mateo, and the mermaid stopped in front of them. She put her hands on her hips and frowned. "I asked you a question."

Mateo looked at Kaylee and she shrugged.

The mermaid glared as her eyes surveyed the lake bottom. "Look at what you've done!"

Mateo glanced around and his face heated. They had made a mess. Pieces of torn plants floated in the water, and plants on the ground were trampled.

"We're sorry," Kaylee said. "We weren't thinking."

She arched her brow. "I can see that. It's your first time here, I assume?"

Mateo nodded. "Yes."

She sighed. "I can understand. I was probably just like you the first time I came down. Now, why are you here? This isn't a place most people come of their own accord."

"Really?" Mateo asked. "It's awesome down here. I'm surprised it isn't full of people."

She looked around. "Yes, I think so, but most people avoid it."

"Why?"

"Because of the wellers, for one thing. I see you met them," she said, pointing at the welt on his shoulder. It was getting bigger.

He scratched his shoulder. "Yes, we met those. Are they poisonous?"

"A little. Not enough to make you sick or anything, but the itch is annoying."

Kaylee nodded. "It's like a mosquito bite on steroids."

The mermaid flinched a little and then her face went blank. "I wear this for a reason," she said, pointing to her swim shirt. "You never know what will happen in the water. Material doesn't stop the barbs, but it keeps them from going in as deep. You should have worn a shirt."

Kaylee grinned, and Mateo shrugged. It still would have gotten him. The one on his knee itched less than the others, though, and it had gone through his pants.

"Where did you get your, uh, shirt?" he asked. "It doesn't look... local."

She threw her head back and laughed. "Doesn't look local? I like that. I'm not originally from Riviand."

Mateo nodded. He had assumed as much. "You fell into Mermaid's Demise?"

She frowned. "I did. I have a know-it-all brother who always told me I would probably fall into trouble someday and he was right. Curiosity got the best of me. I got too close to the whirlpool and when I decided to go back, it was too late."

"We jumped in," Mateo told her.

She cocked her head. "Into this lake, or into Mermaid's Demise?"

"Both."

She rubbed her lips together. "So you are from above?"

"I'm from Boztoll."

"Why would you jump in on purpose? Don't you have families? I know I miss mine every day."

"We do," Kaylee said, pulling the sword from her back. "But some things have to be done."

Her eyes widened. "The Blade of the Phoenix." Her surprise quickly turned to something else, and she frowned. "That is not something you should wave around for anyone to see. I assume you are here to secure the lock?"

Kaylee nodded. "Yes. Do you know where it is?"

"I can take you to it, but first listen well. That blade is no ordinary blade, as I am sure you know. There are many who would love to have it. People who might ignore you at any other time would kill you for it. Don't show it to everyone you meet."

"We don't," Mateo protested.

"You showed me."

"You seem normal."

Her lip twitched, and her eyes sparkled. "Thank you, but many seem trustworthy who aren't. Mermaids can be a... bad choice of people to trust. We all come from different places, different lives, and a lot of mermaids are jealous and greedy. We rarely stay near one another because we all know this. I like to think I'm different, but who doesn't think they are the exception to every rule?"

Mateo itched his knee. "We know about mermaids. About the lockets," he said, pointing at the gold necklace around her neck.

She stroked it with her fingers. "There is such a pull to be in the water. It's almost impossible to resist. I spend very little time in the water now. I regret where it has taken me. Now I only come when I need to think."

"Where did you get the shirt?" Mateo asked. "It doesn't look like anything I've seen up above either."

"I've never seen mosquitos up above either," she said, glancing at Kaylee. "And you are holding the sword. That means you have no magic."

Kaylee gripped the sword. "I'm from... somewhere else."

"Earth?"

"Yes."

She nodded. "My husband was obsessed with Earth. He spent a lot of time there, and I went with him when we were first married. Once my daughter was born, I stopped. I should have stopped going to the ocean as well. Then I would still be with them."

"Is she young?" Kaylee asked.

She laughed. "Oh no. She was grown before I left."

Kaylee looked skeptical. "You don't look old enough to have a grown daughter."

"People live longer here than on Earth," Mateo told her. "They age slower."

"Well, enough about me," the mermaid said. "How did you get the sword?"

"We found it."

"Up above?"

"No. On Earth."

Her eyes lit up. "If someone stole the sword and it ended up on Earth, then that means there is a way to get out of Riviand."

"We hope so," Mateo said. "We haven't figured it out yet, but we will."

"Come with me and I'll show you where the lock is. The sooner the continent is secure, the better. How many more locks do you have after this?"

Mateo frowned. "Only one, and it's near the goblins."

"That's inconvenient. I believe the goblins are behind the sword's disappearance."

Kaylee nodded. "So do we. We were with the queen, and a boy tried to take the sword from me. A goblin grabbed the queen and pulled her through a portal."

The mermaid put a hand to her head. "The goblins took Queen Claret?"

"Yes."

"The boy who tried to take the sword. Did he wear a cape of black feathers?"

Mateo nodded. "Yeah."

"That would be Odious. Did he touch the sword?"

"Yes."

"I suspected he didn't have magic. Come, we must hurry and turn the lock. After that, you will go to the goblin mountains and find the lock and save Claret."

She turned and began swimming. Mateo glanced at Kaylee and she shrugged. They swam to try to keep up. It was a lot easier to swim down here than in normal water. Mateo's mind filled with the stories he had heard as a boy about mermaids. They were usually creatures to avoid. They liked to trick people and drown them, according to the tales. What if this one was trying to trick them?

Kaylee wondered how innocent the mermaid was. Being near her made Kaylee want to tell her all her secrets, and that couldn't be a good thing. It must be some type of mermaid magic. She thought the mermaid was harmless and wanted to help them, but how could she know for sure?

"Here we are," the mermaid said, brushing some seaweed from the lake bottom.

Kaylee looked down at the familiar slit. "Do you think it will work down here?"

Mateo gazed down at the slit. "Why wouldn't it?"

"The sword always bursts into flames. Does it need to do that? Fire can't start under water."

"Someone had to lock it the first time, so it should work."

The mermaid looked at the sword. "It bursts into flames?"

"Yes."

She nodded. "That makes sense. A phoenix is reborn once it burns. It shouldn't be surprising that the sword is the same. When a phoenix is renewed, it is stronger than before. The sword might be as well."

Kaylee pushed the sword into the slit and turned until she felt a click, then she stepped back to avoid whatever might happen. This time, the flash was orange instead of blue. Flames sprang up, undeterred by the water. If Kaylee wasn't imagining things, it was burning higher than before. When the flames died, Kaylee retrieved the sword.

Mateo gave her a thumbs-up. "Once again, Kaylee steals the show."

She grinned. "Yes, and it's so hard to turn something."

"That was magnificent," the mermaid said. "I wish we had time to sit and talk some more, but we need to save the queen. If the queen is in danger, then so is all of Riviand. People need to know she is there or they might fear for the safety of the world."

"And you are going to come with us?" Kaylee asked. She wasn't sure how she felt about that. The woman seemed nice, and she had helped them, but every time an adult was added to their group, it might mean there were that many more people to boss them around. She could take it from Dovin, but he was an exception.

"I'll try to meet you there," she said.

Mateo crossed his arms. "How will we find you? If we can't and we have two different plans, that might cause a problem."

"Don't worry about that now. I can't leave yet. Becoming human doesn't happen as soon as I remove my locket. It's a painful process, and it takes some time. It isn't always the same, so it's hard to plan. I will come as soon as I can. Don't wait for me, but be careful. Are you ready?"

"For what?" Kaylee asked. "To leave?"

The mermaid smiled and thrust her hands out in front of her. The water moved, picking them up, and tossed them violently through the water. Kaylee couldn't think of a time she had ever moved that fast, except maybe on a rollercoaster or on Dovin's dragon. The sword was still in her hand and she hoped she wouldn't land on it. She closed her eyes to avoid seeing the lake bottom pass by at such an alarming speed. Almost as soon as it began, they were dumped onto the shore.

Kaylee shivered as the water retreated back into the lake. She pushed herself up, put the sword on her lap, and grabbed her hair, wringing it out.

Mateo sat up and wiped his face. "That would have been really fun if it hadn't been so terrifying. She could have killed us, dumping us out like that."

She grinned. "Just be happy you landed on your boom instead of your head."

He chuckled. "I am. I'm also glad you didn't stab me while we were flailing around."

"I was worried about that."

Several yards into the lake, the water broke, and the mermaid popped up. "I forgot to tell you," she said loudly. "Time passes differently in the lake. An hour here is a day on land." She waved and disappeared beneath the surface.

Kaylee frowned. "How long do you suppose we were down there?"

Mateo scratched his chin. "I don't know. Three hours, maybe?"

"So we lost three days. We really needed those three days." She hopped to her feet, placed the sword on her back, and walked over to her things. She pulled her cape over her shoulders. Her clothes seemed wetter than was possible and she wondered how long it would take to dry. Every movement felt gross. She'd dropped her bread on the ground. It wasn't much, so she wouldn't try to salvage it. It was probably stale anyway if they had been down there for three days.

Mateo pulled his dry shirt over his head while Kaylee tried to wipe the sand off her feet. She put her socks and boots on. It was disgusting trying to get them over her wet, dirty feet.

"It's too bad all your clothing is wet," Mateo said with a sly grin.

Kaylee glared at him.

"Do you want to know some awesome magic I can do?" he asked.

"I doubt it."

"Watch." He stepped toward her and held out his hands. His brows came together in concentration.

"What am I watching?"

"Can't you feel that?"

Kaylee was about to shake her head when she felt warmth blowing onto her.

"If you turn slowly, this will dry you off."

"Why didn't you tell me you could do this when I asked what magic you knew?"

"Turn slowly so you don't get burned. I learned to do this before my family went to Earth. Dovin actually taught it to me and my brother."

Kaylee turned, glad for the heat. "That's a useful skill."

"I forgot about it because I haven't needed it. I used to do a little magic when my mom wasn't looking, but the place where we lived was warm and even if we got wet, we dried quickly."

"Let me take my cloak and sword off. Otherwise, my back won't dry." She quickly tossed her things to the dirt. "If I could only have one magical power, I would choose teleporting, but this might be the second. I hate being cold. Not that it's cold, but it would be nice to be able to do."

"As soon as we finish all this, I'm going to beg Dovin to teach me everything he knows. If he teaches me to teleport, I'll take you anywhere you want to go."

"Anywhere in Riviand," Kaylee corrected.

"No. We are going to get out of here. I know it."

20

CHAPTER 20

"Does red go with blue?" Odie wondered out loud, holding up a pair of his old blue britches. He had found a trunk of his old things and thought he might find something for Claret. There was a reason he only wore black these days. Black had to match with black, and he didn't have to worry about it. Goblins didn't care about matching, but Odie was the one who dealt with the humans and he didn't want his poor choice of clothing to distract them.

The door opened, and Tipp entered. He was wearing armor. Odie had never seen that before.

"What are you doing here?" Tipp asked. "I had the worst time trying to find you."

Odie glanced around their mother's old room. Queen Hilva had kept everything Odie and Tipp had ever worn or made, and it was all stored here. It wasn't because she was sentimental. It was because she liked things. The room was massive, but it was so full of things that no one had wanted to clean it out when she died last year. There were nice things like golden cloth and gems, but there were a lot of gross things as well. Hilva had kept the skeletons of every pet she had ever owned, and they were all here.

"I'm finding some clothing for Queen Claret."

Tipp snorted. "Why would she want to wear your old things?"

"Because they're clean and most humans prefer to be clean."

"Yeah, I never understood that."

"Why are you wearing armor?"

Tipp grinned and puffed out his chest. "I've been made a captain in the goblin army."

The hairs on Odie's arms stood on end. "There isn't a goblin army."

"Well, there is going to be. Father is organizing it."

"Why? We have plenty of guards. We don't need an army."

"Garin says we do. Once we get all the goblins organized, we are going to take over all of Riviand."

Odie dropped the clothing he was holding. "Why do you look happy about this? It goes against what we were just talking about. I thought you didn't like Garin."

"Things can change. Garin was the one who suggested Father make me a captain. Don't look so concerned. You get to be one too. Your armor isn't ready, but it's being worked on. Garin said it will take at least a year or two of preparations before we're ready to attack."

"You were just telling me we needed to free the queen and now you want to take her kingdom?"

He shifted from one foot to the other. "I don't really, but I love the thought of being a captain. No more talk of freeing the queen, all right?"

Odie nodded. He wasn't surprised. Goblins were all unique in some ways but united in their love for shiny things and recognition. "I've got to take this down," he said, scooping up a pile of clothes, and headed for the door.

"There is something else."

Odie paused and turned his head. "Oh?"

"Garin thinks we should put the other prisoner to death as a warning to anyone who might come digging around for anything."

Odie nodded again and rushed toward the dungeon. His mind was on fire and he couldn't keep one coherent thought. He wouldn't be part of something like this, but what could he do? If he left, there would be no one to protect Tipp, but if he stayed...

He tried to focus on Dovin. He didn't deserve to die. Odie was almost sure. There was something about the man that Odie couldn't place. Something about him made Odie want to talk to him. The man almost seemed familiar to him. He would think it was magic, but a person's magic couldn't be performed in the dungeon.

There was also Claret to consider. It would be a shame to make her stay in the dungeon while her kingdom was under attack. The guards saw him coming and opened the dungeon door. Odie took the steps two and a time, careful of his armful of clothing. Falling wouldn't end well. When he got to the bottom, he ran down the long, musty hallway and stopped when he got to his table.

Claret sat propped up on her bed with a pillow, reading a book he had gotten her, and Dovin was pacing in his cell. He stopped when Odie tossed the pile of clothing onto the table.

"Here are some things you could try," he told Claret. "You can take them into one of the cells down the hall and try them on."

She nodded. "Thank you." She glanced down at her book.

Odie's heart was beating wildly. He was in no mood to be patient. "Aren't you going to go try them?"

"I will in a minute."

"Why not now?"

She peered up and raised her eyebrow. "Does it matter if I do it now or in a minute?"

He jiggled his leg and pursed his lips.

Dovin studied him with an unreadable expression. "Why don't you do it now, Claret?"

She sighed. "I suppose, if it's so important to all of you." She placed the book on her bed and exited her cell, grabbing the pile of clothing. She walked down the dim hallway, glancing back over her shoulder but not stopping.

Odie entered Dovin's cell and stood close to the man. He was hoping to intimidate him, but Dovin was at least three inches taller than he was and his broad shoulders did not name him a weakling.

Dovin grinned and didn't move back. "May I help you?"

"Did you put a spell on me?"

Dovin's brow rose. "Why would I put a spell on you? I can't do magic here even if I wanted to. Believe me, I've tried."

"You could have put a spell on me before we came into the dungeon."

"A spell to do what?"

"To tell you things."

"I have been studying magic my entire life, and I have never heard of anything that could make people do that."

"Then why do I want to confide in you?"

"Ah," Dovin said, stepping back. "I would assume that is because you feel you can trust me."

Odie frowned. He hadn't trusted many in his life. He cared about his family, but he had never trusted them completely. To trust a goblin was foolish and a lesson anyone who dealt with them knew well.

"I shouldn't trust you. I don't know you."

"If there is something you need to say, now would be a good time. Claret will be back soon."

Odie ran his hand through his hair. That was something he'd only started doing the last few days. It had always been too full of goop to do it before, but now he was leaving it down since Claret had suggested it. "The goblins are gathering an army."

Dovin didn't appear surprised.

Odie tried not to fidget. "They want to take over Riviand. Garin is behind it."

"I assumed as much. The goblins I know don't start wars. They only join them."

"My brother has been made a captain, and I guess that is their plan for me as well."

"And you are uncertain?"

Odie rubbed his arm. "Tipp is annoying, but he's my brother. I don't think I can leave him. We talked about how bad it would be if something like that happened, but now he's changed his plan. The perks of being a captain have overtaken his senses."

"Can you change his mind?"

"I usually can, but I have a bad feeling about this. I bet he charges ahead with the army and feels guilty later."

"I've never known a goblin who felt guilty about anything."

"Tipp is different. Perhaps he spends too much time with me. If I don't join the army, he won't have my help."

Dovin sighed and sat at the foot of his bed. "If Tipp decided he wanted to hang from a cliff, what would you do?"

Odie's eyes narrowed. "I would tell him that was dangerous and stupid."

"What if he did it anyway?"

"I would try to pull him up."

"How easy would that be?"

"Not very. Goblins may be small, but they can be heavy."

"It would be easier for him to pull you down than for you to pull him up."

Odie's mouth turned down. "Yes, I suppose."

"To pull him up, you would need his cooperation."

"Yes."

"If you hang off the cliff with him, you won't help him. You will both fall. If you want to help him, you need to stay on top and wait for him to want your help. When he does, you can reach out and pull him up."

Odie focused on the floor as he thought about Dovin's words. They made more sense than anything he had heard in a while. He was going to have to leave Tipp and hope his brother changed his mind.

Claret's boots clicked on the stone floor as she approached them. She donned one of Odie's old blue tunics with a pair of britches he wore when he was twelve. His lips twitched at the sight of the queen without a royal gown. It was different, and different wasn't always bad.

Odie turned back to Dovin. "There is something else. Garin thinks you should be put to death."

Claret gasped and covered her mouth with her hands.

Dovin's eyes twinkled, and he chuckled. "I'm sure he does. He needs to make an example of someone, to make others fear him."

"How can you laugh?" Claret asked. "We need to get out of here."

"I suppose it's time," Dovin said. "Are you coming with us, Odious?"

Odie threw his hands in the air. "You can't just leave. You are in a dungeon guarded by goblins."

Dovin exited the cell and stood next to the table. "We aren't even locked in cells. There are two guards at the top who open the door every time someone knocks like this." He made several quick raps on the table that he must have heard Odie do when he left. "Once the two guards open the door, we have magic again. Two goblins are no match for me. This isn't even a challenge. It almost feels like cheating."

Odie crossed his arms. "It might not be as easy as you think. The guards are ready for anything." He knew it was a lie. The dungeon wasn't as secure as he had thought, although it would be if he locked them in their cells.

"We need to be careful," Claret said, standing tall. "If the goblins are planning on killing you, they won't hesitate to do so if they see you trying to escape."

Dovin gave a half smile. "It takes a lot to kill me or hold me prisoner."

"And how many times have you had to escape from a prison?" she asked.

Dovin looked at the ceiling and tapped his lip. "Let me see... it's hard to say off the top of my head. Six? Possibly seven."

Claret's brows came together. "That many?"

"Yes, and none of them were as easy as this one will be. In fact, I'll let the two of you figure it out if you wish. It might be good to get some experience."

Claret glanced from Odie to Dovin. "I'm not planning on being locked up ever again."

"No one actually plans to be captured, do they?"

"If I help you, we really don't have to plan," Odie finally said. "I can get the guards to open the door."

Dovin nodded. "And then what?"

Odie pulled a small glass vial from his cape and held it up to show them. "I break this on the ground, start it on fire, and the guards will fall asleep."

"You've made a sleeping potion? How clever," Dovin said. He looked sincere. Whenever he showed the goblins his inventions, they usually made fun of him.

Claret tilted her head. "What about us? You break the bottle and we fall asleep as well."

"Right," Odie said, turning the bottle around in his hand. "That was my problem the first time I used it."

Dovin sat at the table and leaned back, watching them.

"Are there others who will hear the glass break?" Claret asked. "Could you break it, set it on fire, and then close the door until the potion settles?"

He shook his head. "The door locks in two ways. One is automatic as soon as it shuts. We would be locked in again."

"Can we hold our breath and run?"

He crossed his arms and tapped his fingers while he thought. "It's possible, but it's also possible they could use magic on us before they fall asleep."

"What if we break it, then teleport?"

Odie laughed. "Teleporting hasn't been done in ages."

"Dovin can do it."

His eyes widened. "Really?"

Dovin nodded. "I can, but it takes some of the fun from an escape."

"Fun?" Claret asked. "You think this is fun?"

Dovin only smiled.

"If you can teleport, that would fix everything," Odie said. "We get out of the dungeon, break the vial, and teleport away."

"We could do that," Dovin said, "but what would you learn from it? If you were ever without me, what would you do?"

Claret pushed a stray lock of hair behind her ear. "So you are training us?"

"I don't think it would hurt."

Odie nodded. "I like to use my brain over something like magic."

Claret sighed. "I have magic. I'm just not terribly skilled at any of it."

"The goblins have magic, but they prefer to fight with weapons," Odie said. "It's more satisfying to them."

"What about lifting the continent? We don't want that to happen because we took too much time trying to escape."

Dovin opened his mouth and then closed it. "I suppose you are right. We don't know how the others are doing without us."

Odie looked down at his boots. "It won't be easy getting to the last lock. My father knows someone is locking them, so the final one will be well guarded. He's probably placed traps."

"Can't you get to it?" Claret asked.

"I don't know. It was easy the first time, but nothing was stopping me. My father didn't share the details with me. I just know he's made it more difficult to get to."

"All right," Dovin said. "I've been sitting idly here for too long. We need to go find Mateo and Kaylee and get this settled. Are you with us?"

Odie ran a hand over his face. "Can we wait until I grab some things? They might be helpful."

"How long will it take?"

"Fifteen minutes. Why don't you stay at the top of the stairs while I'm gone? As soon as I get back, we can take out the guards and be on our way. Someone bring Gregor."

Dovin nodded. Odie took off down the hall and up the steps. He was certainly getting his exercise today. He rapped on the door and bolted down the hall when it opened. The guards mumbled behind them. He didn't know what they had to complain about. If they didn't open the door every now and then, they didn't have anything else to do.

He slowed when he got to a corner and paused when he heard voices. One belonged to his father and the other must be Garin.

"I don't trust him to be useful," Garin said.

King Ummi sighed. "He isn't, but he's still my son."

"But not really."

Odie sucked in a breath. They were talking about him.

"No, but we raised him."

"What good will he do? From what I've heard, he can't do magic and often causes explosions."

"He is skilled with a sword, and explosions can be helpful."

"Not if they aren't done intentionally."

The king let out another sigh. "I know. Odious is rather ridiculous when it all comes down to it."

Tipp's voice joined in. "Odie can't do anything he's supposed to. Why don't you just keep him where he is? Guarding the queen. That way he isn't in the way."

"I don't want him to feel unneeded."

"He won't. What could sound better than guarding the queen? He'll think it's an honor and be out of the way. Odie is easy to fool. I do it all the time."

Odie rounded the corner, his soul on fire. Tipp looked down at the floor and his father frowned. Garin crossed his arms and smirked.

"I have nothing to say to any of you," Odie said, his teeth grinding. "I will watch the queen. That's more important than any of your stupid plans."

He stomped down the hallway, ignoring his father's shouts to come back. He swung open the door to a large closet where he kept supplies. After grabbing a pack that was hanging on a nail, he began filling it with everything it could hold that wouldn't break. It wasn't easy to get supplies like these and he wouldn't leave them behind.

His father's and brother's words stung, but he wouldn't dwell on them. It only made his decision to leave easier. It was time to go where people appreciated him and didn't see him as a joke.

21

—·—

CHAPTER 21

M ateo watched Kaylee run her hand over Willow's back. The alicorn had found them again, and Mateo wasn't sure how he felt about that.

He looked around. "We should have asked the mermaid for directions. We don't know the way to the goblins or the castle."

Kaylee patted the animal. "At least we found Willow. That will save us time if we can get her to fly again."

"I'm not sure that's a good thing unless you know how to steer her."

"I bet it's just like riding, except in the sky. I was too shocked when she flew last time to try anything. This time I'll be ready."

He nodded. "Okay, but that still doesn't help us know where to go."

"I didn't pay a lot of attention to the map, but I noticed the places with the keys are close to the corners of the continent. The castle was close to the middle."

"So if we go straight in the right direction, we should run into the goblin mountains."

She shrugged. "In theory, but we don't know which way that is."

"I don't even know what direction we came from."

"Perhaps I can help?" a voice said from behind.

Mateo and Kaylee spun around to see Vigh and Padmire. Vigh wore his armor but held his helmet in one hand, his sword at his waist. His brown hair was pasted to his head with sweat. Padmire had a sword as well. It was the smallest Mateo had ever seen.

A smile overtook Kaylee's face. "I am so glad to see the two of you."

Mateo nodded, but he didn't like how happy Kaylee was to see Vigh. The soldier wasn't that great. "How did you find us? We've been all over the place."

Vigh came closer. "You were gone too long. Queen Claret said you would all return the day you left. When you weren't home by morning the next day, I sensed something was wrong. We knew you would go to all the locks, so we figured out where they all were and went looking."

Padmire crossed his small arms. "Don't take all the credit. I was the one who told you we needed to go."

Vigh laughed. "That's true."

"It would have been nice if you brought more soldiers," Mateo said. "We need to go to the goblins."

"I don't know," Kaylee said thoughtfully. "Sneaking around the goblins might be easier with fewer people."

Vigh's smile fell. "Dare I ask where the queen is?"

Mateo and Kaylee shared a look.

Vigh shifted. "It's that bad?"

"The goblins took her," Mateo told him.

"What of Dovin?" Padmire asked.

Kaylee shrugged. "We got separated. We don't know where he is."

"I'm sure he's fine," Mateo told her. "Dovin is good at almost everything. He probably can't find us because we've been moving around so much."

"We won't all fit on the alicorn," Vigh said. "I think we are better off walking."

"Clear across the continent?" Mateo asked. "That would take forever. How did you get here? There's no way you walked from the castle to this place in such a short amount of time."

Padmire grinned, showing his pointed teeth. "We came on an alicorn."

Mateo squinted and looked around. "Where is it?"

"Vigh forgot to tie her up, and she ran off," Padmire said. "For being a soldier, he's proving to be rather careless in some things."

Vigh glared at Padmire. "You can't blame me. You never stop talking and it distracts me."

"If you just lost her, she can't be far," Kaylee said, looking around. "She must be bent over chewing on the weeds, so we can't see her. Or I suppose she could have flown away. Where were you when you lost her?"

Vigh scanned the area, his mouth turned down. "It all looks the same to me."

"It was over that way," Padmire said, pointing.

"Go look for her," Kaylee commanded. "I'll stay by Willow to make sure we don't lose her."

Mateo jogged over to the biggest bunch of weeds he could see. It would be easy to lose an alicorn if it was bending over. Some of these weeds were like small trees. He peeked around the weeds. No alicorn. He looked to the side. Vigh was hacking at a weed with his sword. Mateo rolled his eyes. That seemed like a pointless waste of time. It was obvious the alicorn wasn't there.

"Stop hitting that thing!" Padmire's high voice yelled. "Even if she was over there, you would only be scaring her."

Vigh nodded and moved on. Mateo shook his head. Who trained the guards in Riviand? Maybe Vigh was just lacking some knowledge when it came to hunting. Mateo had never hunted in his life, and he knew you should at least try to be quiet. Not that they were hunting, but the loud chopping was sure to scare any animal.

"I don't see anything," Mateo said. "I think some of us should fly back to the castle and the others should wait here." By others, he meant Vigh. "We can send someone to get them later."

"I should go," Vigh said. "I'm the only one here who's trained. If the queen has been captured, it is up to me to save her."

"Well, I'm not staying here," Mateo said. "Kaylee has to go because she's the only one who can hold the sword."

Kaylee walked up to them, leading Willow. "We can all squish. Willow is bigger than any horse I've ever seen. If it doesn't work, we can figure something else out."

"Do you know how to fly?" Vigh asked.

"We did it once, but I don't know how to control where she goes. I think I can do it, though."

"I know how."

Kaylee wrinkled her nose. "I feel more comfortable if I'm in front. Not having control scares me."

"If you don't know how to ride her, then you aren't in control anyway," Vigh argued.

She bit her lip and sighed. "This is why I couldn't ever ride a bicycle for two."

Vigh looked confused. "A what?" He began taking off his armor.

"Nothing."

Mateo grinned. "You're going to have to put your trust in someone. Is it really that hard?" He knew it was. He'd been terrified enough when he'd ridden behind Kaylee, but he knew it would be worse if he was in control.

"I hate to leave my armor, but it's too heavy. Kaylee can be in the front and I can be in the middle," Vigh said. "You are short enough I can probably see over your head. That way, I can take over if needed. I can give you tips on how to fly her."

Kaylee nodded. Great. That meant Mateo was going to be stuck in the back with a view of Vigh's big head. Vigh rubbed a spot on the alicorn's neck and she bent down so they could mount.

"Oh, so that's how you get her to go down," Kaylee said. "I must have done it by accident last time."

Kaylee mounted, followed by Vigh. He put his arms around Kaylee, and Mateo frowned.

"What about me?" Padmire asked. He climbed around Willow's leg and up to her neck. "Overloading an alicorn seems dangerous." He sat in front of Kaylee.

"Come on, Mateo," Kaylee said.

He frowned and climbed on. When he put his arms around Vigh, he sighed. He wished he knew how to ride so he could be the one in the middle, pretending to help Kaylee. He knew he was being ridiculous. Vigh was probably too old for Kaylee, and he'd never said anything to make him think he was interested in her. It was just Mateo feeling competitive.

"Don't fall off the back," Kaylee said as Willow stood.

Mateo muttered something and held on. This was going to be a long ride.

Claret fell to the floor of her throne room and gasped. She was home. Dovin and Odie stood by her side.

Dovin reached down and grabbed her hand, pulling her to her feet. "Teleporting can take some getting used to."

She nodded. She had landed on her feet the other times, but she hadn't been so distracted. As soon as Odie had come back to the dungeon, they had been ready. When the door had opened, Dovin and Claret had come out. Odie had thrown his sleeping potion against the ground and Dovin had hit it with a fireball. It had happened so fast the guards hadn't had time to react. They'd held their breaths and Dovin had grabbed Odie and Claret and the next thing she knew, she was falling on the floor.

Claret yawned. "We need to find Mateo and Kaylee and see what they need. I hope they're here." She yawned again. "I wonder if I inhaled some of the sleeping potion. I feel so tired."

Odie glanced at her. "I doubt it. The first time I got it to work, Tipp and I dropped like rocks."

Dovin smiled. "You tested it on yourself?"

Odie's face turned a light shade of pink. "Yeah, I didn't think it through very well."

The door opened, and Captain Nerman entered. He bowed when he saw Claret. Nerman was the person Claret had left in charge when she was gone. She would normally leave Durdessa in command, but her aunt still hadn't returned.

"Captain Nerman. Do you have anything to report?" she asked.

The captain looked from Odie to Dovin and frowned. He was probably wondering why Odie was here. Odie was rubbing his arm nervously, probably wondering the same thing.

"Everything has been fine," he finally said.

"Have Kaylee and Mateo returned?"

"No."

"Will you find Vigh and ask him to meet us here?"

The captain growled. "Vigh is not here. He left with the little blue turtle thing even though I told him to stay here."

Claret's mouth turned down. "Do you know where they went?"

"I assume they went to find you. He asked for permission and I told him no. He said you should have been back by now. I made it clear if he left, he would be punished. The next morning, he was gone."

"I don't like this," Claret said to Dovin. "We are getting too split up."

Dovin sighed. "Kaylee and Mateo are our priority. They are the ones we need to find. After it is finished, we can worry about Vigh and Padmire."

Captain Nerman took a step forward. "If I may, Your Highness?"

Claret nodded. "Go on."

"Vigh has never been the best of the guards. In fact, he only made it through the training because his father was a guard before him. Anyone else would have been turned away. He is compulsive and lazy. I admit I was surprised when you let him be part of your group."

Claret's brows came together. "He found out visitors when they fell through into Riviand. He was helpful. I didn't exactly choose him. He just happened to be with us when we needed help. He took us to the pyramid when we didn't know where it was."

"There are hundreds of soldiers I would choose to protect you over him."

Claret didn't want to insult the captain. She respected his opinion, but maybe he didn't realize Vigh was helpful. Vigh was young. It was possible he was maturing and settling into his place among the guards.

Odie turned to Claret. "Since he's missing, none of it matters right now. What do we do?"

Claret looked at Dovin. "I don't even know where to begin looking for Kaylee and Mateo."

Dovin rubbed his chin. "I don't think there is anything we can do without rest. I suggest we get washed up and get a good night's sleep and start fresh tomorrow."

"That sounds good to me," Odie agreed.

Captain Nerman cleared his throat. "So now you are taking advice from the goblins' man? I don't mean any disrespect, my queen, but I don't think that is the best idea."

"The goblins captured me, and Odie helped me escape."

The captain narrowed his eyes. "At least that is what they want you to think."

"Why would they let me escape? It makes no sense. They were hoping to get a ransom from me."

"Goblins are devious. Who knows what goes on in their minds?"

"I think Odie will be of help to us."

"I will," Odie insisted. "I am the best one to guide you past the goblins and to the key."

Captain Nerman frowned. "I don't trust him. If you leave, take me with you, or at least someone I trust. I feel responsible for allowing you to leave and get captured."

"I need you to stay here until my aunt returns. Don't worry about me."

"That's not easy."

Claret covered her mouth and yawned. "We can discuss it all in the morning."

He bowed. "Yes, Your Majesty."

Odie scratched the back of his neck and glanced around the enormous bedroom Claret had left him in. He hadn't moved since she closed the door behind him. The room was so... so... clean. Everything was the opposite of his bedroom in the goblin castle. The bedspread was light blue and so was the round rug. The floor was made of light gray stone that matched the walls. He had never been in a place where the main color wasn't black, except for Claret's throne room.

He didn't want to move and get the dirt from his boots on the clean floor. Gregor had already jumped from his shoulder and was busy exploring under the bed. The bird was probably going to be disappointed. He would almost bet it was as spotless under the bed as on top.

"I'm not sure how I feel about this room," he told Gregor when the bird reappeared. "I feel like I need a bath just to look at it." Claret told him there would be servants bringing a bath into his room soon, and he wasn't sure what to make of that. He had spent his entire life bathing in a small pond or stream in the mountains. If Claret was having a bath brought to him, that must not be the way they did it here.

There was a tap on the door, and it opened. Four servants carried in a large basin and put it on the floor of his room.

"We'll be back with the water shortly," one man said.

Odie just nodded and frowned at the basin. The men shut the door on their way out and he stepped closer to the basin and peered inside. "This is odd. What do you think, Gregor?"

Gregor squawked and chewed on the rug.

A few minutes later, the door opened and several servants came in, carrying large buckets of steaming water. They poured it into the basin and promised to come back with more.

He glanced at Gregor. "Do you think I'm supposed to get in there?"

Gregor was too busy pulling on the rug to pay attention to Odie's inner turmoil. Getting in that thing just seemed awkward. What if someone came in? What if they came in and that wasn't what it was for? The servants kept coming until the basin was almost full.

"There you are," said a man, handing him a thick white towel. "Will there be anything else?"

"No. Uh, what am I supposed to do with that?" he asked, pointing at the water.

The man raised his brows. "Wash off, sir."

Odie nodded. He wouldn't correct the man and tell him he was a prince, not a sir. A goblin prince probably wasn't the most popular thing to be at the moment.

The man exited the room and Dovin stuck his head in before the door closed. "All settled in?"

Odie shrugged. "I guess I'm going to sit in that thing," he said, pointing.

Dovin nodded. "It's called a tub. Almost everyone uses them."

"It seems odd to me and a lot of effort."

Dovin laughed. "Don't goblins bathe?"

"In the stream. Or the pond."

"Ah. Well, this should be more pleasant. Just latch your door so no one barges in, and I will see you in the morning." The door shut behind him, and Odie moved toward it and latched it. He pulled on the handle to make sure it was secure, then he turned back to the tub and sighed. Humans really did some strange things.

22

— • —

CHAPTER 22

Kaylee's eyes popped open when Willow landed. She must have fallen asleep. It was a good thing Vigh had been there to take over when she couldn't control the alicorn. Trying to control an animal that large was difficult. She was glad Vigh and Padmire had found them. They could have been lost for a long time. Vigh had taken them back to Claret's castle. With luck, Dovin would be here and he could help them decide what to do next. Padmire was asleep on her arm.

Mateo slid off, followed by Vigh. She was quick to get off before either of them offered to help her. Kaylee placed Padmire on his unsteady feet and he yawned. She rubbed her eyes, then stretched. She hoped she hadn't slept long. What if she drooled on Vigh or something gross? It was probably better not to know.

"Wait here a moment, and be ready to leave if we have to," Vigh said. He walked toward the castle.

Two guards met Vigh, and the three of them began talking. Kaylee couldn't hear them, but Vigh was waving his arms around as he explained something. The guards

257

both grabbed one of Vigh's arms and began pulling him toward the castle door.

"That doesn't look good," Mateo said. "Should we follow?"

Kaylee frowned. "I don't know. Those guards didn't look happy."

Padmire leaned against Willow's leg. "It's because the captain of the guard told Vigh to stay here and he didn't listen. He snuck out even though he was told he would be punished."

"That shouldn't affect us then, right?" Kaylee said, hurrying after Vigh. "Hey! What's going on?" she asked the guards. Mateo was right behind her.

One guard turned. "It isn't your concern. If you follow us, we will let Queen Claret know you're here. She wanted us to come right to her if there was any word of your whereabouts."

"She's here?" Kaylee asked. The guard nodded.

"Nice," Mateo said. "That saves us some time."

Kaylee had to take big steps to keep up. "Is Dovin here?"

"The man you came with? He's here."

Kaylee could feel her entire body flood with relief. She'd been more worried about Dovin than she had wanted to admit, and with Claret already here, that meant they could go right to the goblin mountain to look for the lock and not worry about a rescue mission.

Queen Claret came rushing toward them. She was wearing a light blue robe and her bare feet slapped against the stone floor. She hastily tied her wet hair into a messy knot. "I am so happy to see you!"

Kaylee smiled. "We were just stopping to rest, then we were going to go looking for you."

Mateo nodded. "It's good we all ended up here. It would have been annoying if we had missed one another."

Claret's eyes narrowed as she looked at the guards. "What are you doing with Vigh?"

They still had a grip on his arms. They both let go and bowed.

One stepped forward. "The captain wants a word with him."

"Not tonight," Claret said, holding her head high. "From the looks of them, they could all use a good night's sleep and a bath. I will deal with the captain if he has a problem with this. Vigh will accompany us wherever we end up going tomorrow. You are dismissed."

The guards nodded and scurried away.

"Thank you, Your Majesty," Vigh said, bowing.

"We will probably need all the help we can get," Claret said.

Kaylee looked at Claret. "We need to go somewhere near the goblins to find the last lock. From what we've heard, the goblin mountain is large, so it could be anywhere."

She nodded. "Odious is here with us. He can help."

Mateo frowned. "Who's Odious?"

"He's the boy we saw near the giants' village. He was wearing all black."

"The one who took you?"

"No, that was a goblin."

Kaylee nodded. "He's the one who tried to take the sword."

"Yes. He's had a change of heart. He's going to help us."

Kaylee wrinkled her nose. "That's unexpected. At least we know he can't do magic since he could touch the sword."

"Yes, I believe he is the one who stole it. It's a long story. He knows where we need to go. Why don't we rest and talk about it tomorrow?"

Odie forced himself to stand tall and not fidget when he met Claret's friends. They didn't seem happy to meet him, and he couldn't blame them. He rubbed his ribs when he remembered the hard kick Kaylee had given him in the forest. Both of them glared at him as they all got ready to leave the next day. The glares they gave him were nothing compared to the looks the guard called Vigh gave him.

They all stood in the back courtyard of the castle. The wind blew their capes, but the sun was bright.

"You can't take the bird," Mateo said, pointing at Gregor. "It isn't safe and he might get in the way."

Odie pursed his lips and nodded. He wasn't stupid. He knew all the training in the world wouldn't make Gregor ready to sneak up on anyone.

"I can watch him," Padmire said. Odie wasn't sure how he felt about that. Padmire was the strangest-looking creature he had ever met, and his gaze sent a chill down his spine. "Animals love me."

"He is safe with Padmire," Dovin assured him.

Padmire motioned to Gregor, and the puffin wobbled over to him and allowed himself to be patted on the head.

Claret was wearing a tunic and trousers. She must have realized it was more practical than a dress. She also had a sword at her side. Odie wondered if she knew how to use it. As a princess, she had probably been trained. Odie's father had made sure he and Tipp learned sword fighting from a young age.

"Should we take this many people?" Odie asked. "It will be hard enough to get past the goblins without a large group parading around."

Mateo crossed his arms. "And who would you leave behind?"

Odie's eyes scanned the group. Kaylee had to go because she was in charge of the Blade of the Phoenix. Claret probably didn't need to be there, but she looked determined. Odie could lock it, but he knew there was no way this group was letting him touch the sword. Odie had to go because he knew where the lock was. Vigh was the warrior. He wasn't sure what Dovin was, but he thought he might be the one holding everything together. He wanted to say Mateo would be the best one to leave behind, but the glare Mateo was giving him made him rethink that.

He shrugged. "I suppose we can all go, but it's going to be difficult."

Vigh glanced at everyone. He was holding something heavy, wrapped in gray material. He placed it on the ground and unrolled it, exposing a small pile of weapons. "I think it would be wise to have everyone armed, whether or not they have magic. I wouldn't put anything past the goblins. They are devious creatures."

Odie tried to push away the anger rising in him. Vigh wasn't wrong, but it was hard to hear. He had considered himself a goblin most of his life. Mateo was smirking at him. Well, let him smirk. It wasn't like anyone had ever appreciated Odie much in his life.

Claret nodded and studied the weapons. "I think those without magic should probably choose first."

Kaylee tapped the sword at her side. "I already have the Blade of the Phoenix."

Odie swallowed. He was the only other person without magic. He stepped toward the weapons and watched the others watch him. It was obvious they didn't trust him, but he didn't know how to fix that. If he were them, he wouldn't trust him either. He grabbed a thin sword and scabbard that was on the top. He wouldn't take time sorting through the weapons while they all stared at him.

Something in the trees caught his eye. A woman darted away when she saw him look at her. All he noticed was her curly brown hair. Odie thought back to his childhood and remembered the woman who watched him from the trees on several occasions. He wondered if this woman was the same person. She had never seemed like a threat, but it was strange that she was here, so far from his home.

He put the scabbard around his waist and sheathed the sword while the others rifled through the weapons. Odie wasn't a stranger to having a sword at his waist, so it had probably been a good choice. He had never been in an actual fight, and most of his practice had been with Tipp.

"Odie?" Dovin said, pulling him from his thoughts. "Is there anything you want to tell us?"

He blinked and wondered if Dovin could read his mind. He didn't really want to admit that he might not be the best warrior. "About what?"

"About getting to the lock? Anything we might need to know?"

"Oh, uh, they didn't guard it heavily before the lock was turned. It probably is now, and I wasn't part of the planning, so I have no idea what measures have been taken."

"Well, that's helpful," Mateo muttered. Kaylee bumped him with her shoulder, and he shrugged.

"One thing you should know is that goblins like to fight," he said, fidgeting with the hilt of his sword. "They like to fight with or without weapons, but not with magic."

Dovin rubbed his chin. "They don't use magic to fight?"

"They will if they need to, but they would prefer using their fists or a weapon. That is how they'll start. They won't turn to magic unless they think they're going to lose, and they won't think that if they see us. We'll be an easy mark."

Kaylee tilted her head. "You mean they'll think we'll be an easy mark?"

Odie tried to smile, but it probably looked like a grimace. "I suppose that we might be able to put up a fight since you have the blade, but our best chance is to get through without being seen. Goblins don't hold back when they want something."

"Is invisibility an option?" Kaylee asked Dovin.

Dovin shook his head. "I have never figured that out. I don't think it's possible."

Mateo held up his pointer finger. "But the creatures at the pyramid said the person who unlocked it there was invisible."

They all turned to Odie. Sweat beaded up on his forehead. "I assume you all know I am behind the locks being turned." They all nodded, and Mateo crossed his arms. "Well, King Ummi has a way of making a person invisible. It's a rare type of magic that requires very odd and exotic ingredients. They're scarce, even for the goblins, and they don't have any more. I used it all when I was unlocking the continent."

Dovin scanned the group. "If we need to sneak, perhaps Odie is right and we should have a smaller group."

Mateo stepped forward. "Maybe just me and Kaylee. We're the ones who need to do it, after all."

Vigh squinted. "Why?"

"We were like, chosen to do it, or something like that. Dovin saw it in our auras."

Dovin shook his head. "I wouldn't say 'chosen.' I saw that the two of you would come here, though I didn't know why. When you found the sword, it seemed like the most logical explanation, but that doesn't mean you were chosen to do this.

Kaylee watched him. "What would have happened if you hadn't brought us here?"

Dovin shrugged. "There's no telling. I saw you would come, and I interfered. Would you have been destined to come here if I hadn't interfered? It's anyone's guess. I think you would have ended up here somehow, but that is my opinion. Is the Blade of the Phoenix the reason you were supposed to be here? I don't know. And were you supposed to come here, or was that just what was going to happen?"

Mateo shook his head. "Raise your hand if you feel confused." He raised his own. Everyone else just looked at him.

"Claret should stay here," Vigh said. "She shouldn't leave the kingdom and put herself in danger."

Claret rubbed her temples with her hand. "It's my responsibility to protect Riviand."

Vigh raised his brows. "And you can do that better if you stay alive."

She let out a breath. "I suppose that is true. I'll stay."

Vigh smiled at her. "That's a brave decision."

Claret blushed, and Odie frowned. Did she like the guard? Vigh was tall and attractive in an odd way. He could see how he might have turned the queen's head. Still, there was something about him Odie didn't like. Besides, a guard wasn't right for a queen.

"That is wise," Dovin agreed. "If we fail, it would be good to have a backup plan, and that might be your soldiers."

Claret nodded. "With my aunt away, it is probably for the best. If something happens to me, the kingdom will be in chaos."

Dovin glanced at the sky. "I'll teleport us there, but then I think I'll wait for you. That leaves only four people sneaking around. If you aren't back in an agreed amount of time, I will come."

Odie felt a slight disappointment. Dovin was probably the one with the most knowledge and skill. Still, the fewer people, the easier it would be.

"Odie, are you sure you are up for this?" Dovin asked. "You may end up fighting your friends."

Odie looked at his boots and kicked at the ground. "The goblins all think I'm a joke. Even my family. I would hate to fight my father or brother, but they won't be there. They stick to the castle."

"All right, it's settled," Dovin said. "Claret will return to the castle with Padmire, and the rest of us are off."

Claret sank down into her desk chair and rested her chin on her hand. She hated being left behind. She had never felt like a part of a group until now, and she wanted to be with her new friends. At least she hoped they were her friends. She always struggled with figuring out who genuinely wanted to be around her and who felt obligated to be.

Selfishness had been the only reason she had wanted to go in the first place. Her life had been void of adventure, and she longed for a life that was more exciting. Of course this wasn't good excitement, but she would like to help protect Riviand. The more she thought about it, the more she realized what a poor decision leaving would be.

Succession was a funny thing in Riviand. If there was no heir, then the person in command at the time of her death would take the throne. Durdessa was usually the one left in command, but the last few times, it had been Captain Nerman. Claret trusted the man as much as she trusted anyone, but he would not be a good ruler.

She smiled when she thought about the look of concern Vigh had given her earlier. It was probably the concern that any of the guards would feel for their queen, but she liked to think there was some man out there thinking about her. She wondered why he had never caught her attention before. He was handsome, and he had done some great things for Riviand since Mateo and Kaylee had come.

She shook her head. She was the queen and didn't have time to think about things like this. Vigh was only being a good soldier. She drummed her fingers against her desk and sighed.

A rap on the door startled her. She got to her feet and hurried across the blue rug. It was a rare thing to have someone come to her door. It only happened when something was wrong. She pulled open the door and looked up to see Captain Nerman.

She gave him her most diplomatic stare. "Yes?"

He held his helmet in his hands, slowly turning it. "I fear your friends have just walked into danger."

Claret arched her brow. "I think they know that."

"I don't mean from the goblins."

"Oh?"

"I think you need to come see this."

23

—·—

CHAPTER 23

Mateo crouched behind a boulder and peeked over the top. Dovin had taken them to the backside of the goblin mountain and they had begun the climb up. The mountain was so high, and the clouds were so thick, they couldn't see the top. It was the first time he'd seen a black mountain. Odie told them the main village was on the other side. There were smaller goblin settlements around the mountain, but there weren't any over here.

They'd hiked quietly up for over an hour when they heard a sound. Now they were all hiding and waiting to see if anyone appeared. Mateo looked to his side. Kaylee was squatting by him, her hand on the Blade of the Phoenix. She looked calm, but she was breathing deeply, causing him to believe she was as nervous as him. Vigh and Odie were behind a boulder to the west of them, and he couldn't see them well enough to make out what they were thinking.

"Is anyone coming?" Kaylee whispered.

He shook his head. "Not yet." The sound had probably been an animal, but it was smart to be cautious. It also gave them a chance to rest. Mateo wouldn't admit it, but his legs were getting tired. The mountain was steep. He was in better shape than Kaylee and probably Odie, but they weren't complaining.

"I think we should keep going," Vigh said, coming up to them. "I don't see anything."

Mateo nodded and stood straight. Kaylee popped up just as fast. He couldn't believe she didn't seem tired. Exercise was a big part of his life, and his legs were still throbbing. He glanced down the mountain and then up. They weren't even halfway.

They started moving again. Mateo was beginning to think a big part of adventures was walking. No one ever talked about the boring parts. "This is going to take forever. I still can't see the top."

Odie looked up. "We aren't going to the top."

"We aren't?"

"No. The lock is in a cave. It isn't too much farther."

Mateo sighed with relief. "Nice."

Odie bit his lip. "My guess is that the goblins will let us get in the cave, and that is when they'll try to stop us, or that is where the traps will be. These mountains are hard to patrol, but the cave only has one entrance."

Kaylee kept her gaze forward. "Do you know the cave well?"

Odie rubbed the back of his neck. "I know it, but I avoid it."

"Why is that?" Vigh asked.

"The snakes."

Mateo came to an abrupt halt. "Snakes? I do not do snakes."

A glint of amusement sparked in Odie's eyes. "I don't mind snakes, and they aren't venomous or anything, but I don't want one dropping on me."

Kaylee's eyes were bright. "What kind are they?"

"We call them bat snakes."

Mateo frowned. "They look like bats?"

Odie's lips curled up in what Mateo would call a nasty smile. "No. It's because they hang from the mouth of the cave and catch bats as they fly by."

A chill ran down Mateo's entire body, and he shuddered. He rubbed the goose bumps on his arms and forced himself to go forward when everything in him wanted to run the other way.

Kaylee grinned at him, then looked at Odie. "What's the cave made of?"

"Limestone."

She turned to Mateo. "There are snakes on Earth that live in limestone caves. The limestone is porous, so the snakes can crawl around inside. We call them cave-dwelling rat snakes. They catch bats, so they might be the same thing."

Mateo's stomach sank. He wasn't sure he could force himself into a cave with snakes like that. "You aren't making me feel better."

"They're a subspecies of a beauty rat snake. Does that help?"

He rubbed his arms again. "Calling something a beauty does not make it so."

Kaylee laughed softly. "I can see the hair on your arms standing up. Don't worry. I won't let them eat you."

Vigh shook his head. "Snakes aren't a threat. Let's keep up the pace."

"It's just around here," Odie said, leading them around a pile of rocks.

Most mountains Mateo had seen were covered in trees. This one had tons of rocks and only the occasional group of trees. When they rounded the rocks, a cave came into view. The opening was only about eight by eight feet and Mateo couldn't see anything past the mouth.

"You've gone pale," Odie said with a small smile.

Mateo narrowed his eyes, but he didn't have anything to say. This reminded him of a time his brother Miguel had dragged him along to a haunted house. It had taken everything in him to get his legs to take him inside. This might even be worse. He knew the things in the haunted house were fake. The snakes were not.

"Are the snakes only at the entrance?" Mateo asked, scanning the opening.

Odie shrugged. "I wasn't paying a lot of attention when I went in."

"How do they get up so high?"

Kaylee's eyes were twinkling. "They're semi-arboreal."

"Making up words isn't helping me."

She chuckled. "It means they spend a lot of their life up high. They even eat and sleep off the ground. They're great at climbing."

He shivered. "I didn't know snakes could climb."

She patted him on the back. "Even if they bite you, it won't be hard. They aren't aggressive unless you bother them."

"How do you know? They could be a different species. You don't know anything about snakes in Riviand."

"That's true, but I bet they're the same."

"Are we going to stand here debating or go in?" Vigh asked.

Mateo took a deep breath and pulled his sword from its sheath. No bat-eating snake was going to get him.

Kaylee was doing her best to keep her amusement to herself. She could tell that Mateo was completely freaked out. They walked into the cave with no snake sightings. Mateo and Vigh pulled up orbs of light, and the Blade of the Phoenix glowed in Kaylee's hand. The walls were gray with white stalagmites and stalactites. She wished she had a camera. It was beautiful.

"Keep your eyes moving," Odie said, scanning the walls. "If anything looks out of place, stop."

Kaylee hoped it wasn't far. Her legs weren't used to walking uphill, and they wanted to wobble. Mateo, Vigh, and Odie had all gone up the mountain like it was nothing and she refused to be the only one to complain.

A snake moved by Kaylee's foot, and she held the sword near it. It was green and brown, with black scales near its tail. Definitely a rat snake. Mateo was looking the other way, so she kept it to herself. She didn't need him running to the exit.

Vigh scanned the ceiling and floor. "How far do we go?"

"Just around that bend," Odie said, pointing ahead. They turned right and entered a ten-foot cavern. In the center was the lock.

Vigh squinted as he peered around the cave. "Why haven't we run into any traps?"

Mateo moved near the lock. "Maybe there aren't any."

"Don't count on it," Odie said. "We aren't going to walk out of here without something happening. I've spent my entire life with goblins. Don't let your guard down."

Kaylee pushed the Blade of the Phoenix into the lock and turned it. The flash of blue and orange was brighter than it had ever been. A fierce wind knocked her to the ground, and she covered her eyes when the sword burst into flames. The fire climbed up to the cave ceiling and Kaylee coughed as the smoke filled her lungs. She could hear the others coughing near her, but smoke had quickly covered the cavern and her eyes were watering, making it difficult to see anyone.

Someone grabbed her arm, causing her to jump. She glanced up and could just barely make out Mateo. He pulled her to her feet, and they ran from the cavern. Smoke was billowing through the rest of the cave. Vigh and Odie were in front of them, bolting to the exit.

Kaylee tried to stifle another cough, but that only made her eyes water more. "What about the sword?" she croaked.

"Leave it," Mateo said, pulling her from the cave. Once outside, they all collapsed to the side of the opening and gulped in the clean air. Smoke rolled from the cave's mouth and up into the sky. "I guess it's a good thing there aren't any trees to catch fire."

Odie watched the smoke lift into the air. "Nothing else should catch fire. There is nothing flammable in the cave."

Kaylee tried to swallow, ignoring the scratchy pain in her throat. "That smoke will let all the goblins know we're here."

"I'm sure they already know," Odie said. "They probably did something in the cave to make it burn like that."

Vigh took a raspy breath. "We need to get the sword."

Kaylee frowned. "I don't see how. Did you see how big those flames were?"

"We can't leave it here or we are allowing the goblins to have it."

Odie pushed his bangs back. "There isn't a goblin alive who can't do magic. None of them can touch the sword."

Vigh shook his head. "I still don't like it. The Blade of the Phoenix belongs in its place in Tyran."

Mateo raised his brow. "Great, and how do you suggest we get it? It's on fire."

"Kaylee is going to have to go back."

Kaylee's eyes widened. "You want me to run into fire and grab something that is on fire? I don't see that turning out well."

Vigh glanced at the wild smoke and ran a hand over his face. "We can't allow it to burn forever. Think of what the smoke will do to the entire world. Odious can try."

Odie frowned. "I'm confused about why you think that would work better."

"You are expendable."

Odie glared at Vigh. "Expendable or not, it won't work."

Kaylee didn't want to work with Odie, but it was mean of Vigh to say that. "We're going to think of something, but running into a burning cave is not the solution. I'm sure Dovin will see the smoke and come up here soon. He might have an idea. No more talk about a suicide mission."

Vigh sighed and looked at the ground. "You're right, I'm sorry. I don't want to let Queen Claret down."

"None of us do," Kaylee said. "And we won't. We just have to be smart about it."

Vigh nodded and then threw out his hands, knocking Mateo to the ground with magic Kaylee couldn't see. She screamed and ran at Vigh. He had one hand pointing at Mateo, and he turned the other toward Kaylee.

"What are you doing?" Kaylee screeched, coming to an abrupt halt.

"Not another step or I will blast both of you."

Mateo lay on the ground, not moving, but Kaylee could see him glare. Odie stood, his eyes moving from Mateo to Vigh.

Vigh looked at Kaylee. "You and Odie will both go in and get the sword. I have to keep Mateo down, you understand. I can't have him using magic. When you come out with the sword, I'll let him go."

Odie let out a hollow chuckle. "Just because you're threatening us doesn't mean we are going to be able to get the sword. It's just as impossible to get now as it was before."

Kaylee breathed deeply and frowned. "Think about this, Vigh. You don't want to do this."

Vigh smiled. "You seem to think I'm conflicted about all of this. I'm not. Go get the blade."

"And then what? You can't touch the sword."

"No, I can't. You will carry it, as before."

"Do you really think Claret will be happy with your choice?"

His eyes twinkled. They actually twinkled. Kaylee wanted to kick him in the face, but that would be a Mateo solution. "I don't care what the queen thinks. We aren't taking the sword to her."

Kaylee's eyes widened. "Dang it! You're a Prince Hans!"

Vigh's eyes narrowed. "Who?"

"You are the hot guy who seems good but has some dark, dirty secrets!"

Mateo lifted his head an inch from the ground and grimaced. "I knew there was something off with him. He wasn't as good as Prince Hans. That was the shock of my life. This guy gave off signs."

Odie glanced at Kaylee. "Who is Prince Hans? The only royalty in Riviand is the queen in Tyran and the goblin king."

"It's a fictional character. It doesn't matter," she said, waving her hand in dismissal.

"Come on, man," Mateo said. "You don't want to do this. Let me up."

Vigh shook his head. "I'll let you up as soon as they bring the sword."

Kaylee took a deep breath and looked at the smoke pouring from the cave. She couldn't see any way this was going to end well.

"I guess we're going to have to try," Odie said, walking toward Mateo, his hands in his pockets. "Can I just take Mateo's sword?"

Vigh's mouth turned down. "Why? You already have a sword."

"Yes, but Kaylee doesn't."

"You don't need a sword."

"What if Kaylee and I enter the cave together? We hold our breaths and go in fast. When we get to the sword, we both lift it out of the lock by propping the swords under the blade's hilt. As soon as the blade leaves the lock, the fire will probably stop."

Kaylee frowned. It might work, but with all the smoke and flames, it was going to be hard to see what they were doing.

Vigh nodded, his hands still at the ready. "That might work. Take his sword."

Odie stood next to Mateo and pulled his hand from his pocket. He threw something with great force, smacking Vigh in the face. "Run!" he yelled at Kaylee. Kaylee ran toward them, and Odie pulled Mateo to his feet. Whatever Odie had hit Vigh with had caused him to lose his hold on Mateo. Something blue was running down the guard's face.

"What did you do?" Vigh demanded as they began running downhill.

"You have two minutes to wash it off before you die!" Odie yelled over his shoulder.

Kaylee glanced back to see Vigh frantically wiping at his face. Kaylee's heart was probably bruising her chest. It was pounding so hard. They had to take careful steps to avoid falling down the steep mountain. The turn in the path put Vigh out of view.

"Sliding might be safer," Mateo said, dropping like he was going down a slide. Kaylee and Odie joined him. Now all they had to do was avoid boulders.

"I thought Dovin would come!" Kaylee exclaimed. "I hope he's all right!"

Mateo got to his feet as they came closer to the bottom of the mountain. It wasn't as steep here. Kaylee and Odie were also getting up. He dusted off his pants and tried not to feel irritated. Even if Vigh hadn't made him useless up there, he didn't know how to do anything that would have helped much.

They came to a cluster of trees at the base of the mountain. Dovin should be waiting behind them. They rounded the trees and came to an abrupt stop. At least ten unconscious goblins lay scattered across the dirt.

Dovin sat on a boulder, reading a small book. He glanced up at them. "Oh, good, you're back."

Odie's eyes were wide as he walked around the goblins, staring into each one's face.

"What happened here?" Mateo asked.

Dovin shut the book and dropped it in his small brown pack. "The goblins were going after you, I assume. I couldn't have them following you."

Odie swallowed. "Are they…"

"They are fine, though I wouldn't be surprised if they woke up with headaches," Dovin said, waving his hand. "Where is Vigh?"

"Up there," Mateo said, pointing. "He's a traitor."

Dovin nodded. "Can't say I'm surprised."

"Why am I the only one who is?" Kaylee asked.

Mateo shrugged. "I guess you were too distracted by the fact that he's hot."

Her eyes narrowed. "What are you talking about?"

"When we were up there, you said he was the hot guy." Mateo knew it shouldn't bug him, but it did.

She rolled her eyes. "He didn't distract me."

"Shouldn't he be dead by now?" Mateo asked Odie. "You said if he didn't wash that stuff off in two minutes, he would be."

Odie grinned. "Nah, it wasn't anything, really. I just hit him in the face with a stink bomb. I figured he wouldn't have time to think it through, so I let him panic so we could run."

"Nice," Mateo said. He still didn't trust this guy, but he didn't know where they would be without him.

"I thought you would come up when you saw the smoke," Kaylee said to Dovin.

"I was going to, but then I had to deal with the goblins. By the time that was over, I saw the three of you coming down the mountain. I'm sorry it had to come to this. Do you recognize any of them, Odie?"

Odie nodded. "Sure. Goblins aren't like humans. They don't all look the same. They're all part of the king's guards."

Mateo side-eyed him. "The goblins all look almost exactly the same."

Odie shrugged. "If you say so."

Dovin glanced at Kaylee. "Where is the Blade of the Phoenix?"

"When I turned the lock, the fire blazed out of control. It didn't stop like the other times, so I couldn't take it out."

"So that explains the smoke. It's still burning?"

"As far as we know," she said. "What do we do?"

Dovin rubbed his chin. "I'm not sure, but we can't leave it here."

Mateo frowned. "If we stay too long, more goblins might come. Or Vigh."

"I'm not scared of goblins or Vigh."

"That's because you have crazy good magic. That isn't reassuring to the rest of us. Even if I use my sword, I'm going to be like a little kid just smacking at things. I don't actually know how to use it."

"After this is all resolved, I need to give you some lessons."

Mateo's heart sped up. "In sword fighting or magic?"

"Both."

24

— · —

CHAPTER 24

Claret was in the guard's quarters just outside the castle. She sat on a lumpy straw mattress and held a crumpled paper in her hands.

Captain Nerman stood in the doorway, still clutching his helmet. "I knew there was something going on with Vigh. He's a lower-ranking guard, but he kept finding himself in positions he shouldn't be in. He never should have found your friends when they fell into Riviand. That boy is never where he is supposed to be."

Claret glanced back down at the paper. It was a letter to Vigh from his mother. She read out loud for the second time. "Dearest Vigh. I have been as patient as a mother can be. Get the Blade of the Phoenix at all costs and bring it to me. I don't care if you have to kill the queen, just get it. The power that the weapon wields is beyond anything else in Riviand."

"I can take soldiers and go after him," Captain Nerman offered.

Claret put a hand to her head. "I should have gone with them. Now my new friends are in danger." She stood and tossed the note to the ground.

"Putting yourself in danger wouldn't help, Your Majesty. We also found these," he said, handing her a shiny blue gem. "He had several sapphires hidden among his things."

She turned it in her hand. "Hmm. I wonder where they came from." She placed it on the bed. "If we send soldiers to the goblin mountain, the goblins will think we are coming to attack. We don't want a war." She left the dim room and stepped outside, the captain following her. She was going to have to go alone.

When they entered the castle, her eyes widened. Durdessa was leaning against the wall. Her hair was mussed, and she appeared exhausted. When her eyes fell on Claret, they lit up.

"Auntie! I thought you would never come back. So much has happened."

Durdessa opened her arms, and Claret flew into them. "I was worried about you. When I was out visiting, I overheard a rumor that you were missing. I came as quickly as I could."

Claret nodded. "I was in the goblins' dungeon for a while."

Durdessa pushed her back, held her at arm's length, and looked into her eyes. "The goblins cannot influence us. We must cut off all contact with them."

"I need to go there. My friends are there and I think they might be in danger. One of the guards is a traitor, and he's with them."

"What friends?"

"I don't even know where to begin. Some people fell into Riviand. They had the Blade of the Phoenix."

Durdessa didn't look surprised. "Go on."

"They've been turning all the locks. There was only one left, but they left with a guard named Vigh. Captain Nerman just found out Vigh is trying to steal the blade and take it to his mother. I fear for the safety of those he travels with."

Captain Nerman handed the crumpled note to Durdessa. Her eyes skimmed over it, and she frowned.

"You cannot go rushing after someone who might hurt you," she said, looking up. "The kingdom needs you. I never should have left. I'm sorry."

Claret hugged her aunt again. "No, you needed to be out there with the people."

Durdessa frowned. "I needed to be here. I won't leave you again."

"I really do need to go."

Durdessa and Captain Nerman shared a look. Claret's mouth turned down. She hated when they did that. It felt like she was the naïve child they didn't quite know what to do with.

Captain Nerman's eyes pleaded with hers. "Let me take a few guards. You stay here."

Durdessa swayed, and Claret put her hand on her arm. "Are you all right?"

"Fine. Just tired."

"Perhaps you should lie down."

"If I do, you will be gone the next instant."

Claret pursed her lips. Durdessa wasn't wrong. "I can't let Vigh hurt Kaylee, Mateo, and Odie. The least I can do is warn them if it isn't already too late."

Durdessa squinted at her. "Odie? As in Odious?"

Claret nodded. "He helped me escape the goblins."

She sighed. "That does not make me trust him." Durdessa sank to the floor, her pale yellow dress puffing up around her.

Claret squatted down. "Auntie? What's happening? Are you sick?"

"Perhaps a little."

"You must rest."

"Only if you promise to stay near me."

Claret bit the inside of her cheek. "I'll stay but only until you are rested."

The castle door creaked open, and a guard peeked in. He bowed. "Queen Claret. The people who possess the Blade of the Phoenix just appeared in front of the castle. Should I bring them in?"

"Is Vigh with them?"

"No, Your Highness."

"Show them in."

The door shut after him, and Claret turned to Durdessa. Her aunt had risen to her feet. "Are you well?"

"I will be. I am not up for company, so I will meet your friends later."

Captain Nerman bowed. "I'll escort your aunt to her room."

Claret nodded and waited for her friends. She hoped calling them friends wasn't a lie. They hadn't been here long, but they were the closest thing she had ever had to friends.

Odie sat on the roof of the castle and measured a cup of moakberries and dumped them into a mixing bowl. The mixture was a sickly shade of yellow-green and it smelled almost bad enough to be a stink bomb. Why did everything he made stink? He stirred the berries in, turning the mixture light brown.

"Is it supposed to smell like rotten cabbage?" Claret asked, glancing over his shoulder.

He crushed up a dry leaf from a barla tree and tossed it in. "I don't know." Padmire had rattled off a list of ingredients that he claimed would make a mixture that could put out even magical fire. "The smell might be the reason Padmire told us to do it outside."

Claret leaned on a four-foot wall that went around the roof of the castle and gazed out at her kingdom. Her long blond hair blew in the wind and Odie realized he was watching her and not working. He shook his head and began stirring again. It was stupid to think about Claret. She was the queen of Riviand, for goodness' sake. He could argue that he was technically a prince, but the prince of goblins didn't mean much around here.

"I love it up here," she said, not turning. "I can see so much."

He put a few scoops of salt into the bowl. "It's a pleasant view."

"I bet you can see everything from the goblin castle. It's so high on the mountain."

"It's pretty impressive," he said, dumping a green gel into the mixture. He wrinkled his nose. The smell was not improving.

"I'm sorry you can't rest like the others."

Odie shrugged. "I'm glad to be useful." Odie actually felt proud that he had been chosen to mix the concoction. When Padmire had given them the ingredients, Dovin had suggested Odie mix it. It was nice that someone actually recognized his talent. He'd been inventing things for years, and the goblins had always mocked him. Even his father had felt embarrassed by him.

"What are you going to do once this is all over?" she asked.

Odie's mouth turned down. He'd been trying not to think about that. The only life he knew was with the goblins, and now that he had betrayed them, he wouldn't be able to go back. "I'm not sure," he said. His arm was getting tired from all the stirring.

"Kaylee and Mateo are going to have to figure out how they fit into this world," Claret said, glancing back at him. "Maybe the three of you can figure out something to do together."

Odie laughed, but there was no humor in it. "I don't think they like me."

"They weren't glaring at you when you returned. Perhaps their opinions are changing."

"Perhaps." He squeezed some juice from a mavie fruit and accidentally got it in his eye. He wiped at it, trying not to wince from the sting.

"You helped them all escape from Vigh. That has to count for something."

"I think they trusted me more after that, but things could change any second."

"I don't see why."

Odie just smiled.

Mateo finished his bath and pulled on a pair of pajamas. He would probably fall asleep as soon as his head hit the pillow. He needed all the sleep he could get if they were going back for the sword tomorrow. Right before he could climb into bed, someone knocked. He sighed and went to the door, then threw it open. Kaylee stood there, her black hair dripping onto her fluffy white robe.

"What's up?" he asked. "You should be resting. Who knows what we're going to have to do tomorrow?"

"I know, I'm just worrying myself and I'm afraid I won't be able to sleep."

He stepped back and let her enter. "Worrying about what?"

"What happens after this? What if we can't leave? I don't have anything against this place, but I don't see where I would fit in."

"I'm not too worried," he said, moving to his bed. He could almost hear the bed begging him to fall into it and not move until tomorrow. "Odie obviously got out of Riviand, so there must be a way out."

"He helped us today, but I still worry about trusting him."

Mateo yawned. "He could have thrown that stink bomb and run, but he paused to help me up. He didn't have to do that."

"I guess."

He pulled back the blue blanket and jumped back. "Snake!" A green and yellow snake slithered across the sheets.

"Awwww," Kaylee cooed. "My room didn't come with a snake."

Mateo moved back and watched Kaylee pick up the horrifying creature. "Throw it outside! Hurry!"

Kaylee laughed as the snake coiled around her hand. "You're only a little guy, aren't you? You're so precious."

Mateo crossed his arms tightly and rubbed them as a chill spread over his body. "Precious? There is seriously something wrong with you. Now I'm never going to sleep."

"I'll go release him."

"How do you know it's a him?"

She rolled her eyes. "I don't. I'm guessing."

"I don't see how you can hold it. What if it bites you?"

She smiled and shook her head. "Look how small his head is. Even if he bites me, it won't hurt."

"Why was it in my bed?"

She tilted her head. "Odie."

"Odie?"

"That's my guess. When we were out by the castle, I saw him put something in his pack. I didn't see what, but when he saw me watching, he looked super guilty. I bet it was this little dude."

"I'm gonna punch him so hard."

Kaylee gave him a pointed look. "You are not. You don't solve your problems like that anymore. It's a harmless prank."

Mateo let out a breath. "I'm gonna harmless prank his face next time I see him."

Kaylee frowned. "We don't need any more problems."

"What if he'd put spiders in your bed?" He almost grinned when he saw Kaylee shudder.

"That's different."

"Why?"

"Snakes are sweet and spiders are creepy."

Mateo shook his head. "You're crazy."

"I want to be a herpetologist someday."

"You want to study herbs?"

"Herp, not herb. It's someone who studies reptiles and amphibians."

"Hmm. Sounds terrifying. How do you get a job with something like that?"

She frowned. "It isn't easy. From what I've researched, there aren't a lot of jobs in it. My mom wants me to do something else. I think I'll breed snakes or something like that. My mom wants me to be a lawyer."

"I could picture that."

She shook her head. "I would be a terrible lawyer."

Mateo shivered when the snake moved up her arm. "Can you please take that out of here? Then come back and check for more." He felt like a baby saying it, but he wouldn't get any rest otherwise.

She giggled. "Sure, but you owe me."

Kaylee released the snake into the bushes near the castle and watched it slither away. She smiled when she pictured Mateo's face when he saw the baby snake. A noise to her left caused her to look up. She squinted into the trees and Vigh came into view. She sucked in a breath and took a step back. He smiled. Kaylee reached for the sword, forgetting it was gone. She turned and rushed to the castle and threw open the door. When she looked behind her, he was gone.

25

—·—

CHAPTER 25

The sun shone in Odie's eyes the next morning as he waited outside the castle for the others. A large bucket of goop sat near his feet. It had taken a lot of stirring to get it to the right consistency. He turned when he heard someone walking and gulped. Mateo looked rested and more intimidating than normal. His tunic hugged him, emphasizing his muscles, and the sleeves had been torn off. His black cape blew behind him. Odie wondered if he chose a tunic that was too small just to intimidate him. Mateo was walking toward him, his eyes never leaving Odie's face.

Odie smiled, trying to look natural. "Good morning."

Mateo stopped in front of him and arched his eyebrow. "Morning." He crossed his arms, his eyes still fixed on Odie's.

"I trust you slept well?" He refused to look guilty.

"Yes, lucky for you."

Odie squirmed but didn't respond.

Mateo's eyes narrowed. "I want you to know that you owe Kaylee a thank you."

Odie's brows came together. "Why?"

"She made me promise I wouldn't hurt you."

He knew.

"Why would you want to hurt me?"

"Don't play dumb. You put that snake in my bed."

"Why would I do that?"

"How should I know? Don't ever do it again. I can take a joke but not a snake. I'll give you a pass this time for Kaylee but never again. Do you understand?"

"But I—"

"No!" he boomed, holding up a hand to silence him. "Don't pretend to be innocent. I'll let it go, but you better promise."

Odie dropped his head. "All right, I promise. And I'm sorry."

Mateo nodded. "You're lucky you saved us yesterday. If you hadn't, even Kaylee wouldn't have been able to help you."

"So are you and Kaylee—"

Mateo raised his brow and Odie let the sentence die.

"Kaylee's my friend. That's all."

Odie nodded. He believed it. He saw the way Mateo watched Kaylee, but Kaylee seemed indifferent.

Kaylee joined them. Her eyelids looked heavy, and she tripped when she came near them.

"Are you okay?" Mateo asked her.

She yawned. "Fine."

Mateo cocked his head. "You look tired."

Kaylee glared at him, her eyes scanning his clothing. "And you look like a dork, but I wasn't going to point it out."

Odie turned his head to hide a smile. He wasn't sure what a dork was, but he was sure it wasn't a compliment. He needed to be careful around Mateo until he forgot about the snake.

Mateo held out his arms. "What?"

She raised her brow. "It looks like you were shopping in the toddler section, and where are your sleeves?"

Odie tried to hold in a laugh, but a snort came out. Mateo shot him a warning look.

Kaylee sighed. "I couldn't sleep last night after I saw Vigh. What is it with bad guys? He seemed perfectly normal, but now that we know he isn't, he has to get all creepy."

"Where's Claret?" Odie asked.

"I convinced her to stay here. It wasn't hard. Her aunt came back yesterday and isn't well. I guess she's worried about her."

Dovin came jogging toward them. "Sorry to be late. Have you tried the muffins? Delicious."

Odie nodded. The castle did have good muffins. Everything at the castle was good. The best thing about it, it was all clean. Goblins didn't care if a little dirt fell into their food while they were cooking.

"Well, let's get going," Dovin said. "Mateo, what are you wearing? You look ridiculous."

Kaylee snickered, and Odie hid a smile.

Mateo crossed his arms and didn't respond.

"Everyone, grab on to me," Dovin commanded.

Odie grabbed the bucket and touched Dovin's arm. Odie had always been jealous he didn't have magic, but now that teleporting was a thing, it was even worse. Teleporting was the best thing ever. Dovin took them straight to the cave, which was a relief. That saved a lot of climbing. Smoke was still billowing from the entrance.

Dovin watched the smoke pour out of the cave and into the sky. "I must admit, I thought there would be more goblin activity."

Odie nodded. "So did I, but I am almost positive the sword burning like that was their doing. I thought there would be traps, but there weren't."

"Now what?" Kaylee asked. "I don't think all of us should go in."

Dovin nodded. "Kaylee and Odie will go in. Odie can throw his mixture on the fire and Kaylee can grab the sword."

Mateo frowned. "What if it's hot?"

Kaylee shrugged. "It never was before."

"What if it isn't the sword that's on fire? It might be something around it."

Dovin rubbed his chin. "I'm more concerned about the smoke. I could blow the smoke back, but since it's in a cave, it won't have anywhere to go and will probably just circle the cave and come back around."

Odie watched the black smoke. It was going to be difficult to see. "We can try holding our breath."

Dovin snapped, and two wet handkerchiefs appeared in his hands. "I prepared these before we left. Tie them around your faces."

Odie grabbed one and awkwardly tied it. Kaylee did the same.

"Let's hurry," Kaylee said.

"If you aren't out in two minutes, I'm coming in," Dovin said.

Kaylee held out her hand, and Odie stared at it. He'd never held anyone's hand before. She rolled her eyes. "I won't bite you."

"Right," he said, grabbing it. "Let's go."

They charged into the smokey cave. Odie hoped Kaylee could see better than him. When the smoke hit him, he had to close his eyes. Kaylee was practically dragging him. He hoped he wouldn't prove useless.

Kaylee yanked him in a different direction, and he opened his eyes. Flames filled the cavern and he could only just make out the Blade of the Phoenix. He released Kaylee's hand and grabbed his bucket with both hands. He threw the mixture at the flames. A hissing sound filled their ears and the flames immediately sputtered and died. The smoke was still thick. Kaylee grabbed the sword, and they began running to the exit.

Odie's lungs burned, and his eyes felt dry but were watering at the same time. His head felt funny, and he wasn't sure what happened, but he wasn't running any-more. Something pressed against his face, but he wasn't sure what it was.

Kaylee dropped the sword to the ground when Odie went down. They needed to get out fast. She grabbed Odie under the arms and pulled as hard as she could, dragging him along the bumpy cave floor. Her lungs were on fire. The smoke wasn't clearing out as fast as she hoped. She burst from the cave, dropped Odie, and fell to her knees.

Dovin grabbed him and moved him to the side of the cave entrance. Coughs began racking Kaylee's body, and she felt Mateo lift her up and move her away from the smoke. The clear air was having a hard time getting into her lungs. He sat her on a boulder and she leaned over as she continued to cough.

"Are you going to be okay?" he asked, shoving a canister of water into her hand.

She pulled the handkerchief from her mouth and took a sip, cringing when it went down funny, causing her to cough even more. Her head felt fuzzy. Mateo was talking to her, but she was only paying attention to the gunk in her lungs.

"The sword is in the cave somewhere," she croaked. "I dropped it when Odie went down."

Dovin glanced away from Odie. "We can get it when the smoke clears out a little more."

"Is Odie okay?"

"He's breathing, and his eyes are open. Odie, can you sit up?"

Odie groaned, then coughed. "Probably," he croaked.

"The castle staff are going to hate us," Mateo said. "We're all going to need baths again. I'm sure they are tired of hauling water to our rooms. We should teach these people about plumbing."

Kaylee took another sip of water. "Do you know how to install pipes? I sure don't."

"We would have to build them, too. I'm pretty sure I don't know how to even start. Maybe we could hire someone."

Kaylee shook her head. "I can imagine that conversation. Hello, would you like to go to a magical world, jump in a whirlpool, and install some plumbing?"

Mateo grinned. "We wouldn't have to go to Earth. Basura has plumbing."

Dovin motioned for Odie to drink more water. "I don't see any of them jumping in a whirlpool, either. Even if they wanted to, Riviand is down here for a reason. They don't want visitors."

Mateo ran a hand through his hair. "Those were the people who took it down here to begin with. We don't know what the people who live here now think."

Dovin nodded. "True."

"What if the people all decided they wanted Riviand to go back up? Would that be possible?" Mateo asked.

"It's hard to say. Magic was a lot more powerful when Riviand first came down here. Trying to raise it now would probably be a disaster."

"Can we talk about this later?" Kaylee asked. "I feel awful."

26

— · —

CHAPTER 26

Claret stood on the castle roof and watched for the others. There wasn't anything else to do, and she was anxious. She touched the sword at her side and rubbed the hilt. Recent events made her feel nervous, and the sword helped with some of it. She was also following Kaylee's example and wearing britches. They were so much easier to move in. She wouldn't wear them every day, of course. Just when she wasn't meeting with anyone.

Something caught her eye, and she turned to see Dovin, Kaylee, Mateo, and Odie walking toward the castle. She smiled. They were faster than she expected and they must have succeeded because Kaylee had the sword. Claret hated being the one left behind, but she understood the importance of keeping safe. If something happened to her, it affected all of Riviand.

She spun around to go meet them and found herself facing Vigh. She resisted putting a hand to her chest. Letting him know he had scared her wouldn't do. She held her head high and glared at him. How had he gotten past the guards? "Why are you here?"

He grinned and stepped closer. "I assume you've gone back for the sword."

"I haven't."

"But the others have?"

Claret narrowed her eyes. "You need to leave."

"I will but not without the sword."

"You can't even touch it."

He took a step closer. "That doesn't mean I can't haul it in something."

She held out her arms. "I obviously don't have it."

"But you know where it is."

Her eyes narrowed. "I don't understand you, Vigh. What would you want with the blade? You want Riviand to rise?"

He took another step. "Of course not. Why would anyone want that? The blade is more than just a key. It's also a powerful weapon."

He was getting too close. Claret pulled her sword from its sheath and held it in front of her with both hands. "Why would you need a powerful weapon?"

"I don't. My mother wants it, and what Mother wants, she gets."

"You're willing to throw away all your hard work with the guard to get the sword for your mother?"

He stepped forward again. "The reason I became a guard was to get the sword."

"Stop coming closer."

"My mother doesn't actually want you to survive. It's dark, I know."

Claret swallowed. "What does she have against me?"

"Absolutely nothing. She's a bit of a collector. The sword will look lovely above her mantle. She also enjoys war. Killing you will give her the sword and cause a war."

She hoped he couldn't see the sword shaking in her hands. "Is that what you want?"

He shrugged. "I don't care about war or collecting things. I care about money. Gold. Anything I can use to live comfortably."

"Why wait until now?" she asked, hoping to buy herself time. "Why not take the sword earlier?"

"I wasn't able to get near it. Captain Nerman never let me guard it. Once the goblins stole it, I figured we better get everything locked before I took it."

"I don't see how taking the sword will give you money."

"My mother will pay me. I've come out ahead even without the sword. Why do you think Kaylee and Mateo lost me in the pyramid? I was busy filling my pack with sapphires."

Claret bit the side of her cheek and concentrated on keeping the sword steady. "Why would your mother want a war?"

"You know how witches are. They're only happy when others aren't. If there is a war between Riviand and the goblins, it will make her day. If I kill you and we blame the goblins, there will be a war."

"Your mother is a witch?"

"Yes. A dreadful witch. I can't stand the woman and I'm pretty sure she can't stand me."

Claret's forehead wrinkled. "But you do her bidding."

"I'll do anyone's bidding—so long as they pay. Now, where is the sword?"

Claret gave him her best glare. "If you are going to kill me anyway, why should I tell you?"

He grinned and pulled his sword from its sheath. "Because then it ends here. I don't have to go after your new friends or your aunt."

"I don't think you want to do this. Please think it through."

He laughed. "I thought you would go with, 'Please, Vigh. Let me offer you more money than your crusty old mother will,'" he said in a high falsetto voice. "Don't try to prick my conscience. It won't get you anywhere. You can bribe me, or I can kill you."

"I'm sure that sounded great in your head, but that's the stupidest thing I've ever heard," Odie said.

Claret's head whipped to the side as Odie and Dovin entered the rooftop door and let it crash shut.

"Ah, the goblins' little messenger. I owe you for this," he said, pointing at a slight cut under his eye. "I've visited too long and made things complicated."

He turned and took several fast steps toward Odie and Dovin, his sword in the air. Dovin pulled his sword out and pushed Odie behind him. Vigh's sword crashed into Dovin's and the two began exchanging blows.

Odie rushed over to Claret. "Quick, go inside." He grabbed her arm and tried to pull her.

"No! I'm not leaving Dovin." Claret didn't know how to explain it, but in the small time Dovin had been here, he was healing the ache of losing her father.

"He's doing fine. Look. Vigh is no match for him."

Claret's eyes watched as the two men's swords clanged. Dovin seemed to have the upper hand. She tried to think of any magic she might do that would help. Most of what she knew was for convenience, not violence.

Dovin swung at Vigh, knocking the villain's sword to the ground. Vigh's eyes widened, and he stepped back, but not before Dovin punched him in the face with his free hand. Vigh fell dramatically to the ground and rolled. His palm flew up and blasted a ball of fire at Dovin. Dovin jumped to the side but tripped and fell, his sword dropping from his hand.

Vigh grabbed the fallen sword and raised it above his head, ready to strike Dovin. Claret ran forward and thrust her sword forward, stabbing it into Vigh's back. He yelled out, and his sword clattered on the stone roof. Claret covered her mouth in horror as she watched the blood run down his back.

Everything was moving in slow motion and Claret felt tears spill over her cheeks. There was no way Vigh was going to survive this, and she was the cause. Vigh's eyes narrowed as he slowly turned, his gaze locking on her. Someone, probably Odie, put a hand to her shoulder.

Dovin jumped onto his feet and flung his hands out toward Vigh, a powerful wind blowing from them. Claret let out a scream as Vigh plummeted over the wall and off the castle roof. Her vision felt foggy, and she felt like she was dreaming.

"Come," Odie said, taking her arm. She nodded and let him lead her to the door. Nothing would ever be the same again.

Mateo stared at the Blade of the Phoenix. It rested on a small oak table in Dovin's room. Kaylee, Odie, and Dovin were also looking at it. The room smelled like smoke because none of them had taken baths yet. Claret had been taken to her aunt's room.

It was hard to believe Vigh was dead. Not that he didn't deserve it. Now maybe everything in Riviand could go back to normal. They'd turned the locks, and the goblins hadn't shown their faces.

"What now?" Kaylee asked. "If we put the sword back, the goblins will know where it is."

"We could take the sword back with us," Mateo said. "That way, no one would know what happened to it."

"The goblins found us when we were at the school," Kaylee said.

"That's true, but they must have known it was around there. We could hide it on Earth."

Dovin looked at Odie. "That is only possible if we figure out how to leave Riviand."

Odie laced his fingers together, and he glanced down at them. "I can't help you leave."

Kaylee leaned forward. "Why not?"

He glanced up at her, then back down. "I don't know how."

"But you did."

He sighed. "After I stole the blade and unlocked the locks, my father told me we had to take the sword somewhere no one would ever find it. He used magic on me so I couldn't see or hear until I ended up on one of the upper continents. I don't have any idea how I got there."

"No idea at all?" Mateo asked. He didn't feel overly worried, but Kaylee was thumping her knee up and down and wringing her hands.

"None."

"How did you get to Earth?" Dovin asked.

Odie scratched the back of his neck. "There was a goblin that met me up top. He opened a portal, and I threw the sword through. Some of my father's guards went through after it to keep watch over it. I didn't know where the portal went, so I thought that would make it really well hidden. I wouldn't be able to tell anyone where it was, even if I wanted to. The only one who would know was Vork."

Dovin sighed. "Vork? I should have known he was lying when he told us he didn't know how to get down here."

Odie arched his brow. "You know Vork?"

"We go way back. We went to him for help when we were trying to get down here. He said the only way was through Mermaid's Demise."

"I'm sure he knows other ways," Odie said. "He's my father's brother, and he comes down all the time."

Mateo leaned forward. "At least we know there's a way out. We just have to find it."

Odie nodded. "I think the way is connected to the goblin mountain or the castle, but whatever magic my father used on me made me confused, and I can't be sure. I don't know if I got there quickly or if it took a long time."

"Is everything we need to do finished?" Mateo asked Dovin. "We locked the continent, but what about Vigh's mother? Is she a threat?"

Kaylee tapped her fingers on the table. "And what about the goblins? I don't think they're going to slink away and stop trying things."

"The goblins would normally quit now," Odie said, turning a black ring on his pinky finger. "Goblins are greedy to a fault, but they lack motivation. Garin, on the other hand, has something in motion. He's pushing the goblins and they are listening to him. I don't know what his goal is, but he is going to be a problem."

Kaylee slouched in her chair. "I don't think we should leave until things are more settled. Since we don't know how to get out of here, we might as well stay and see how we can help Claret."

Mateo's lips turned up. He was glad to hear Kaylee say that. He wasn't ready to go back.

Odie glanced up at Dovin, then back at his ring. "Can I ask something?"

Dovin steepled his fingers under his chin and rested his elbows on the table. "You want to know why I knocked Vigh off the castle?"

Odie nodded. "It seemed unnecessary. He was going to die, anyway."

"Yes, he was," Dovin said, his eyes locked on Odie's. "But I felt that the way he died might be important."

"Oh?"

"Claret stabbed him and the wound would have killed him. Instead, he died from the fall."

Odie's brows came together.

"Claret didn't kill Vigh. I did."

Odie's eyes widened. "You did it so Claret wouldn't have to live with killing him."

"Yes."

Mateo wasn't surprised. It sounded like something Dovin would do.

Odie let out a long breath. "That makes sense, but now you have to live with it."

Dovin waved his hand in dismissal. "It was necessary. I'm used to doing what needs doing."

Mateo rested his folded arms on the table. "I'm going to say this quest was a success. We locked the continent down, got rid of a threat, and our mentor didn't die. I think we're ahead of the game."

Dovin's mouth turned up slightly. "Yes, but what are we going to do about the sword?"

"Hide it and make a fake one. Put the fake sword in the lock and guard it. We won't even tell the guards it's fake."

Dovin rubbed his chin. "That might work."

Odie raised his hand. "I'll make the sword! I've always wanted to do that."

Kaylee tilted her head. "Do you have any experience?"

"No, but we can't have the blacksmith do it. Then he would know."

Mateo nodded. "I'll help Odie."

Odie got to his feet. "We can get the ore and smelt it and everything. I bet there's a book about sword-making in the library."

"It's not going to work," Kaylee protested. "It has to look convincing."

"I bet we can figure it out," Mateo said, getting excited. He loved working with his hands, and this could be fun. "I made a knife once. It wasn't great, but I was young." He didn't add that a professional had been there to help him every step of the way.

"This is going to be amazing," Odie said, his eyes dancing. Kaylee rolled her eyes, and Dovin shook his head.

Mateo smiled. "Best idea ever."

27

— · —

CHAPTER 27

"**T**his was the stupidest idea anyone has ever had," Mateo said, wiping sweat from his brow.

Odie sat back on a boulder and took a drink from his canteen. "I agree." They had been digging in the ground near a mining area for three hours, hoping to find some ore. Odie's arms were about to give up.

"Are you sure this is how you find ore?" Mateo asked.

"I don't know," Odie admitted. "The book just said to mine the ore." They had found two books on sword making in Claret's massive library.

"How do we even know if we find any? What does it look like?"

Odie shrugged. "Some type of metal?"

Mateo threw his shovel to the ground. "This is a waste of time."

That was what Kaylee and Dovin thought. Claret had agreed when they told her the plan. Odie didn't want to go back and tell them all they were right, especially after such a short amount of time.

Odie leaned on his shovel. "We could ask some miners what to do. Perhaps someone will sell us some? I don't want to go back and tell everyone we failed."

"Neither do I. I can already picture Kaylee's smug grin."

"What if we go to the blacksmith and see if he has the materials? He might let us use his things if we pay him."

"Let's try. Do you know where the blacksmith is?"

Odie shook his head. "There must be one in the city. I bet we can ask anyone for directions. Everyone needs a good blacksmith every now and again."

Mateo kicked at the dirt they had shoveled. "Fine. Let's go."

Mateo and Odie stared at the blacksmith's door after it slammed in their faces.

"That was rude," Mateo said. "He could have just said, sorry, you have the wrong place."

Odie nodded. "If a blacksmith doesn't make swords, who does?"

"The other blacksmith," a woman said, passing by them. "Just up there."

Mateo looked at where the woman was pointing. "Thanks."

The woman nodded and hurried away.

Mateo wished they hadn't been so adamant about making the sword themselves. He walked to the second blacksmith's shop and Odie followed. They rapped on the door and it popped open. A large man with a black apron and an unkempt beard appeared.

"Yes?"

"Are you the blacksmith who makes swords?" Mateo asked.

The man smiled. He was missing a few teeth. "Yes, I am Trio. From the looks of you, I assume you have already met my brother. He's the other blacksmith. He thinks making weapons is a disgrace."

"We met him," Mateo muttered.

"So you need a sword made?"

"We actually want to make a sword," Odie said. "Can we pay you and use your things?"

Trio rubbed his beard. "Do you know how to make swords?"

Mateo shook his head.

"So you are going to come in here and guess?"

Odie scratched his head. "That didn't work so well when we tried to mine the ore."

Trio threw his head back and laughed. "Is there a reason you need to make one yourselves?"

Odie and Mateo shared a grimace.

"I guess we don't have to do it. If we could help a little, that would be enough," Mateo reasoned.

"Why do you need to be involved? I can make a sword pretty fast, but not if I've got inexperienced help."

Mateo shrugged. "If we could do any of it, even a bit, it would be fine."

Trio tilted his head. "I could let you help a little, but I want to know why?"

Odie stepped forward. "We told some girls we were going to make one, and we don't want to tell them we failed."

Mateo pushed his shoulder into Odie and glared at him. Didn't he know when to be quiet?

Trio laughed again. "Now that I can get behind. What type of blade are you thinking of? Something easy, I assume."

"Oh, I don't know," Mateo said. "Maybe something that resembles the Blade of the Phoenix."

Trio's brows rose. "Well, that is about as complicated as they get. You want something similar or something that could be mistaken for the sword?"

"As close as we could get would be nice," Mateo said.

Trio rubbed his beard again. "Come in."

They followed him into the sweltering shop. A fire was burning in one corner and soot covered everything. Mateo wrinkled his nose as the smell of coal and body odor assaulted him.

Trio walked to a wall that held several swords. He pulled one down and held it out to Mateo. "How about this?"

Mateo's hands flew behind his back. The sword looked exactly like the Blade of the Phoenix.

Trio laughed. "This is only a replica. You can touch it."

Feeling foolish, he took the sword. It was heavier than the sword he'd been carrying.

"That is perfect," Odie said, leaning forward to see.

"Why do you have this?" Mateo asked.

Trio tilted his head. "You aren't the first kids to come by wanting one of these. I sell at least two a year, so I keep some around. If you want to be able to say you worked on it, I can let you heat it up and beat on it a little. We wouldn't want to embarrass you in front of your lady friends."

Heat crept up Mateo's neck. It was probably better that Trio thought that was all there was to it. They didn't want him to know they were going to put it in the place of the actual sword.

"I figure a couple of whacks should count," Odie said.

Mateo nodded. They were getting off easy.

Kaylee and Claret sat in the castle kitchen, at a small table that only the maids usually used. Claret had been quiet, but that might be normal. Kaylee didn't really know her very well. A cook had given them both a warm cup of something that smelled like nutmeg and a pastry that Kaylee wasn't familiar with. It had cinnamon and icing, and it was too soft to be eaten without a fork.

"I'm sorry you can't go home," Claret said, stirring her drink.

Kaylee shrugged. "I'm sure we'll figure it out, eventually."

"Will your parents worry?"

"No. Dovin told them we might be gone for a long time, and we locked the continent down pretty fast. Maybe we can help you if the goblins cause any more problems."

Claret's mouth turned down. "My father was the king for so long, and he never had problems like this. Everything was peaceful. I'm doing something wrong. Now there are problems with the goblins and possibly a witch. That's not even mentioning the man who is working with the goblins. I didn't meet him, but from what I've heard, we should be careful."

Kaylee took a sip of her drink and winced. It wasn't very good. "Things can take a bad turn fast. Don't blame yourself."

The queen stared into her cup. "I can't believe I stabbed Vigh. I'm going to remember that forever."

"It had to be done."

"I know. My father always taught me that ruling a kingdom required sacrifices. I still feel funny about it."

Kaylee didn't know what to say. She would probably feel bad as well, but it was hard to know. She'd never done anything like it. "What did your aunt say?"

"She said not to dwell on it."

"Is she still sick?"

"Yes. Durdessa is always busy. She rarely rests. Every now and again, she tours the kingdom for me. Whenever she comes back, she's always in poor shape. I tried to get her to stop, but she won't."

"Is she old?"

Claret cocked her head. "I'm not sure how old she is. She's looked the same since she came."

"Someone said people here live longer than where I'm from. I bet that makes it harder to know someone's age."

"I hope she isn't old. My father was always touchy about age, so I never dare ask anyone. Durdessa is one of the best people I know. I'll have to introduce you once she feels better."

Kaylee nodded and wondered if she would offend anyone if she didn't finish her drink. "Do you trust Odie?"

Claret frowned and stirred her drink some more. "I don't know. I spent so long feeling nervous about him, so it's hard to say I trust him completely. He spent a lot of time helping the goblins rob Riviand. I don't blame him entirely. The goblins are his family and I think it took a lot of strength to go against them."

"He's an interesting person," Kaylee said, not knowing how to describe him. She thought he was earnest about wanting to do what was right, but that still didn't mean he was trustworthy. They hadn't been around him enough to know what he was really like. "Do you think Odie and Mateo are going to be able to make a sword?"

Claret smiled. "I doubt it."

"So do I. It might be funny to watch."

"I wonder if we even need a sword."

"What do you mean?"

She stirred her drink again. "What if we build something around the place the sword is supposed to be and then let people think it's inside? Like as another precaution to keep it safe."

Kaylee stirred her own drink. Maybe that made it taste better. "That might work." She sipped the drink. It wasn't better. The pastry wasn't very good either. She wondered if there was a way to dispose of it all when Claret wasn't looking.

"May I ask you a personal question?" Claret asked after she sipped her drink.

Kaylee tried not to look too curious. "Sure, I guess. Do I get to ask you one back?" She didn't have anything to ask Claret, but she didn't want the queen delving in too deep.

"Are you and Mateo connected?"

Kaylee sat back and pretended to sip the drink. "Connected? What do you mean?"

Claret's cheeks turned pink. "Are you courting?"

Kaylee snorted and let a small laugh slip out. She placed her cup down. "Courting? I've never heard anyone use that word in real life. No, we are most definitely not courting."

"But you fancy each other?"

Kaylee's mouth turned up. She loved the accent in Riviand. "I haven't known him very long. We kind of just got thrown into this together. I don't *fancy* him. He's all right and I think we're becoming friends."

Claret raised one eyebrow. "He likes you. I can tell."

Kaylee blew out a long breath. "I don't know. He might. That's somewhere I don't want to go right now. What about you? Is there someone who grabs your attention?" She wasn't really sure what to say when she talked to Claret. They could understand each other fine, but there were times she suspected they were both only guessing what the other person meant.

Claret's eyes went back to her cup. "No. I was never allowed to interact with boys my age. I'm unsure how to act around them."

"Do you have to marry a prince or something? In every princess story I ever read, that was a requirement."

"I've read stories about that as well, but down here, it would mean never getting married. The ruler of Riviand rules the entire continent, except for the goblins. That means there aren't any princes to marry."

"Isn't Odie the goblin prince?" Kaylee asked with a mischievous grin. "That would make him royalty."

Claret laughed, but her face was more red than before. "That would probably cause more problems than marrying the stable boy."

"So who does royalty marry?"

"There isn't a rule. It's usually someone from the courts, but it isn't necessary. My mother was a duchess."

The cook came back into the kitchen. She was an older woman who looked like she enjoyed eating her cooking. She had a bright smile and a head full of curly white hair.

"Enjoying your treats?" she asked.

"Yes, thank you, Cook," Claret said, smiling.

Cook bowed and left the room.

Claret stood. "Her name really is Cook. I guess her parents weren't very creative. They were both cooks when my grandfather ruled." She walked over to the door and opened it. Kaylee was surprised to see that it went outside. Claret tossed the contents of her cup out the door. "If you want to toss yours, now is your chance."

Kaylee hurried to her feet and the liquid from her cup joined the wet spot from Claret's in the dirt. Claret shut the door, then grabbed both of their pastries. She tossed them in the garbage bin and then covered them with some potato pills.

"Cook has been here forever, but she isn't what you would call a talented cook."

Kaylee grinned. "I was wondering if I could find a way to get out of finishing."

"Cook is in charge of all the cooks and rarely does it herself. That saves us all from her inventions. The nutmeg drink always comes out when she thinks I'm sick or upset. I bet she made some for my aunt and had some left over. Durdessa can drink anything and not even flinch. I asked her if she liked it once and she said she didn't, but she didn't want to hurt Cook's feelings."

"Do you have cookies here?" Kaylee asked. She could go for a big chocolatey cookie right about now.

"I've never heard of one. What is it?"

As Kaylee was nearing the end of describing a cookie, the door swung open, and Mateo and Odie entered the room. Mateo was holding a sword that looked almost identical to the Blade of the Phoenix.

"We've got it," he said, holding it up.

"Impressive," Kaylee said, trying to keep the skepticism from her voice. "I thought it would take longer."

Odie rubbed the back of his neck. "Well, when you know what you're doing."

Claret's eyes sparkled. "That was faster than it takes the blacksmith, and you had to find the ore and smelt it. We should put you both in command of sword making."

Mateo sighed. "We have the sword. Does it really matter who made it?"

Kaylee and Claret both laughed.

"I think it will do nicely," Claret said.

Mateo turned the sword, inspecting it. "What have you two been doing?"

"I was just telling Claret what a cookie is," Kaylee said.

"I could go for a cookie right now. They don't have them here?"

"No."

Mateo's eyes sparkled with excitement. "I am the king of making cookies. Is there any chocolate here?"

Claret glanced at Odie. "I've never heard of it. Have you?"

Odie's mouth moved from side to side as he thought. "I don't believe so."

Kaylee was positive a world without chocolate was a sad place to be stuck for eternity. "What about cocoa beans?"

Mateo grinned. "If you want me and Odie to try to make cocoa beans into chocolate, you're going to have to give us a while. We haven't recovered from trying to find ore."

Kaylee and Claret giggled.

"Hey, *Minecraft* makes it look so easy."

Claret grabbed a small stepping stool and placed it near a row of cupboards. She stepped up and grabbed a canister from the top. When she got down, she opened the canister and held it out to Kaylee. "We have this. We call it cocoam. Is it the same?"

Kaylee pulled out a jagged piece of what appeared to be dark chocolate. She popped it in her mouth and wrinkled her nose. "It's bitter."

"There are all sorts of things you have to do to make it taste good," Claret said. "I'm not really sure what."

"Baking and lots of sugar," Odie said. "I use it when I make cakes."

Claret raised her brow. "You make cakes?"

"Occasionally. Baking is a lot like my alchemy experiments. Goblins don't like to cook, so I started experimenting when I was young."

"I hate cooking," Kaylee said. "If we end up stuck here forever, we could open a pet shop and bakery. We could call it Snakes and Bakes."

Mateo shook his head. "That sounds so unsanitary. You can't have animals around food."

"It could be one shop with two rooms." Kaylee had been joking when she first said it, but she liked the sound of it.

Mateo tapped the sword on the floor. "That still sounds gross. Who is going to buy food when they come into a shop and it smells like animals? We could just make cookies in the shape of snakes."

"We better put the fake sword in its place soon," Claret said, changing the subject. "Once it's there, it should comfort everyone who knew it was missing."

"Good idea," Kaylee said. "The actual sword is cool and all, but I'm getting tired of lugging it around."

"Did we ever decide where to put the real sword?" Odie asked.

"No," Claret said, returning the canister to its place. "It has to be somewhere secure."

"I could keep it," Kaylee said. "It isn't ideal, but then we would know it was safe."

Mateo frowned. "Not necessarily safe, just accounted for. If someone sees you, they'll know you have it. It's a pretty fancy sword, and it's famous here."

Claret sank into her chair. "I have an idea, but I don't like it. We could take it to the fairies."

"What are you saying about fairies?" Dovin asked, entering the kitchen.

"That we should take the Blade of the Phoenix to the fairies for safekeeping."

Dovin frowned. "I have never met a fairy that I could trust, and I've met a lot of fairies."

Claret nodded. "Fairies are constantly causing mischief, but they don't want Riviand destroyed any more than we do. No one bothers the fairies because the less attention you get from them, the better. I think they will keep it safe if we ask."

"I don't like it," Dovin said, "but I can't think of anything better. You are the queen, and we will trust your judgment."

Kaylee found the thought of fairies intriguing. "I haven't seen a fairy since we've come."

"Fairies stay away from people," Odie said. "They're all around, but they keep out of sight unless they're up to something. I tried to catch one when I was younger." His face turned pink. "I wouldn't recommend that."

Kaylee and Mateo grinned. They would have to hear that story someday.

"So we find a fairy?" Dovin asked. No one answered. "Wonderful. We'll do it tomorrow."

28

CHAPTER 28

C laret spread the news across Riviand, letting people know that the Blade of the Phoenix had been found and was secure. Kaylee had put on a great show of placing the sword back in its place in the middle of the city. All of Riviand was celebrating. People danced in the streets and sold food and drinks off of mobile wooden carts. It reminded Mateo of a Renaissance Faire his mom had taken him to once.

While people were celebrating, Mateo, Kaylee, Odie, and Claret were out looking for fairies. Dovin had tried to get Claret to stay behind, but she wouldn't. She thought the fairies might listen to her over the others. Mateo couldn't help thinking this world needed the internet. So many things would be easier. Then they could just search for 'Where can I find fairies?' It would also be helpful in learning to make swords...

He scanned the treetops as they walked through the dense foliage. "Where should we be looking?"

"Anywhere," Odie said. "Some live in trees, some in lakes or streams. I've even heard some live underground."

Claret nodded and said, "My tutors informed me that there is a large fairy village underground. However, only fairies may go down there, so we should probably search for other options."

"The times I've seen them were usually by the water," Odie said. "They like to jump around on the rocks in the streams."

Kaylee's eyes lit up. "How many have you seen?"

"Dozens."

"Really?" Claret asked. "I've never seen one."

"Do you spend much time outside?"

She shook her head. "Almost none. There is a stream nearby. Should I take us there?"

Mateo tripped on a rock and tried to pretend he hadn't, but Kaylee's eyes were shining. She must have seen. "Might as well. We don't have any other ideas."

Odie was fidgeting with the hilt of his sword. "I probably should have stayed behind with Dovin and Padmire. This isn't something we all need to do."

"Yeah, but that would be boring," Mateo said. "I think I hear water."

Claret nodded. "It should be through these trees."

Mateo was nervous about finding a fairy. The girls both seemed excited, but Odie looked a little green, and he was the only one who had ever seen one. A small stream came into view and they rushed over to the edge. It was only a couple feet across and probably only six inches deep.

"Now what?" he asked. His eyes raked over the water and the surrounding area, but he couldn't see anything noteworthy.

"We could call out?" Kaylee suggested. "That sounds embarrassing."

"I'll do it," Claret said, straightening her pale blue dress. She had insisted on dressing well because she said it made people respect her position more. She was even wearing a small diamond-studded tiara.

She stepped forward and cleared her throat. "I am Queen Claret of Riviand," she exclaimed. "I need to speak with the fairies if you please." She waited a few moments. "It is about a matter regarding the safety of every creature that lives in Riviand. Please. We need your assistance."

She looked over at Kaylee with worried eyes. "Perhaps we should move downstream and try again."

"No need for that," said a voice near Mateo's head. He jumped back and almost swiped at a small fairy. Her tinkling laugh pierced his ears. "Isn't this exactly what you were expecting?"

"Sorry," he said. "You startled me."

She flew over next to Claret and Mateo watched with his mouth hanging open as she grew to the same size as the queen. She pushed silkie black hair over her shoulder and smiled. Mateo had never seen anyone as beautiful as the fairy in his life. She wore a long yellow dress and had little white flowers in her hair. Her long silver wings shimmered in the sunlight.

"My name is Arelia. Why do you seek the fairies?" she asked. "The Blade of the Phoenix was found, and the locks were secured."

"How do you know that?" Mateo asked.

"It's hard to keep anything from us, and we assisted you."

Mateo frowned. "Assist us? What are you talking about?"

Arelia smiled at him. "We don't like to interfere unless it's completely necessary, but we felt it was a few times."

Kaylee tilted her head. "You were the ones who helped Mateo and me get out of the hole. You lowered a rope."

"Not me specifically, but it was a fairy. A fairy guided the alicorn to you when you were lost and pushed her toward you again a second time."

"We appreciate it," Kaylee said, and Mateo nodded. "Who made the hole?"

The fairy shrugged. "Probably a hunter. Now why are you searching for us?"

Claret stepped forward. "We fear the Blade of the Phoenix is still in danger."

"Yes, we know you put a false sword in its place."

Kaylee pulled the sword from its sheath. "We were wondering if you could help us protect the real one so that no one will steal it again."

Arelia puckered her lips and moved them from side to side. "I cannot take it, if that is what you want. We are bound by the same laws as anyone else. We cannot touch it because of our magic."

Claret nodded. "Do you have any suggestions?"

"The sword should be safe. Most in Riviand cannot touch it, and you travel with the one who stole it to begin with," she said, glancing at Odie.

Odie looked at the ground and sighed. "I'm trying to make up for that."

"Yes, we know that. That is why we believe it is safe. Who else could take it?"

"We don't know," Mateo said, "but we know the goblins will keep trying."

Arelia looked up at the sky and rubbed a finger over her lips. "That is a worry. The goblins now consult with a man who could bring ruin to Riviand. Can you show me the sword?" she asked Kaylee.

Kaylee held the sword out so Arelia could inspect it. She turned it slowly in her hands as the fairy peered at it.

"I have an idea. What if you cover the hilt with something? A hard clay, or even melt metal and pour it over. You could change the way it looks and keep it with you, and no one will know. It also might make it possible for someone with magic to hold it, so that is a concern."

Kaylee bit her lip. "Is that safe? That might mean anyone could steal it."

"That's true, but no one would know what it was, so they wouldn't want to steal it. Make it ugly and ordinary, and I think that should do."

"Perhaps it would be better to destroy it," Claret said. "Then the locks would stay locked forever."

"Do you not know the legend of the blade? It cannot be destroyed."

Mateo's brows came together. "Says who? The person who made it? Maybe they only wanted people to think that."

"You have witnessed the consequences of touching the sword with magic. Just think of what might happen if someone tried to destroy it. Do you want to chance it?"

Mateo thought for a moment and shook his head. He still remembered the sword throwing and burning him. "If we change the way the sword looks, that means Kaylee will have to do it, since she's the only one who can touch it."

"I'm not sure that's something I would be good at," Kaylee said, sticking the sword back in its sheath.

Odie crossed his arms. "She isn't the only one who can touch it. I can as well and I can probably figure something out that would work."

Arelia nodded. "The goblins' human might be correct. He has a talent for many things. He trapped a fairy one time. That isn't a simple thing to do."

"And I'll never do it again," he said, his face turning red.

She smiled. "I would think not. Your punishment was severe."

Mateo grinned. "What was it?"

"I don't want to talk about it," Odie muttered.

"I am sorry I cannot help you more," Arelia said. "When trouble comes your way, it would be best to avoid looking to fairies for help. Most fairies are not as... likely to help as I am." Faster than they could blink, the fairy shrank to her normal size, and she disappeared into the trees.

"It sounds like fairies hear everything," Kaylee said. "It makes me nervous."

Odie stared at the trees where the fairy had gone and shook his head. "They don't hear everything, but I never say anything that I wouldn't want a fairy to know if I'm out in the woods. Let's hurry back to the castle and work on disguising the blade. I have some ideas."

As soon as the castle popped into view, Kaylee came to a stop. There was a man sitting on the steps. "Who do you think that is?" she asked, pointing ahead.

Claret squinted. "I'm not sure. He must not be a threat because the guards arc ignoring him. Perhaps he is only resting from all the dancing." The villagers were still dancing around and having a great time.

The man stood when he spotted them. He was Black, with broad shoulders, and he was tall. That was about all Kaylee could make out. They walked through the crowd toward the man, but he didn't make any move to meet them.

"Hey, I think that's the teacher from school," Mateo said. "The one who helped us."

Kaylee's eyes went wide. "Coach Williams? I think you might be right." She frowned and picked up her pace. Coach Williams had not seemed overly excited about leaving Earth, so something must have happened.

"Kaylee! Mateo! Good to see you," he said as they drew nearer. "Where's Dovin? I asked the guards, and they don't seem to be in a talkative mood." The two guards standing to the side of the castle door didn't respond.

"I think he's inside," Kaylee said. "What are you doing here?"

"Can we find Dovin first? I don't want to explain it twice."

Claret glanced suspiciously at Coach Williams.

Kaylee stepped forward. "Claret, this is Coach Williams. He's from the upper continents. Coach Williams, this is Queen Claret of Riviand." Kaylee wasn't sure how to announce royalty, but Coach Williams bowed and Claret nodded, so it must not have been too bad. "And this is Odie," she said, hoping he didn't realize she had almost forgotten him.

"Come, let's go somewhere we can talk," Claret said, leading them up the stairs. The guards opened the door, and they filed in.

"You can all call me William," Coach Williams said. "Everyone does."

Mateo grinned. "Your name is William Williams?"

He laughed. "No. I've always hated my first name, so I started going by Will when I first went to Earth."

"I don't think I can call you William," Kaylee said. "Maybe Williams."

The doors slammed behind them, and Kaylee jumped. "What's your real first name?"

He shook his head. "Nope. I'm keeping that one a secret."

Claret motioned to a door on the left. "We can talk in my council room. We never use it."

"I'll go find Dovin," Mateo said, taking off down the hall. Kaylee wondered if Claret would rebuke him for running in the castle, but she didn't seem to notice. The rest of them entered a room with light stone walls and a large red rug. On the rug was a table with ten padded red chairs.

"Sit," Claret told them all. She went to the head of the table and pulled out her chair. The rest of them sat. Before a minute had passed, Dovin and Mateo joined them.

Dovin frowned. "Williams, what are you doing here?" He sat at the table opposite him.

Williams rested his arms on the table and clasped his hands. "I've had a bit of an adventure since you all left. I went back to the school the day after we parted and I heard someone scream. When I ran over to see what was happening, there was a goblin running down the hall. Nobody was too upset because they all thought it was some sorta prank or something."

Kaylee's eyebrows came together. "Why would a goblin stay at the school?"

Williams leaned forward. "I don't know. He isn't the smartest creature I've ever met. I cornered him and told him I was going to turn him into a bat if he didn't come with me. He didn't suspect I didn't have magic, so he followed me to my office. It took me a while, but I got him to confess."

"To what?" Mateo asked.

"He said the goblin king has been taking advice from a man named Garin. A lot of the goblins who know about it aren't happy, but they're afraid of angering the king. The man convinced the king to get someone to take the Blade of the Phoenix and left some goblins on Earth to make sure no one found it."

Kaylee nodded. "We've already found all the locks. Riviand is safe for now."

"That was fast. The way the goblin described Garin made me think the man is bad news. Not the kind that gives up after a failure. I went to the upper continents to see what I could learn about him. I didn't want to leave you all down here unprepared."

Mateo narrowed his eyes. "How did you get there?"

"There are a lot more people on Earth from this world than you know. I called in a favor from a friend. I went to the city of Akkron and found my cousin Brake. He's your cousin Graham's dad," he said, looking at Kaylee. "He helped me ask around. Garin is originally from Akkron and it wasn't hard to find information about him. He's wanted just about everywhere."

"For what?" Claret asked.

"Mostly theft. He was a superb pickpocket as a teenager and he moved on to bigger things as he got older. He left Akkron as a young man and went across the ocean to the Northern Kingdom. Brake and I went there to ask more questions. Garin worked for the captain of the guard while he was there. It seems he kept on thieving and eventually was lost over the edge of a ship. People presume he is dead."

"He's here," Kaylee said.

Williams nodded. "I assumed as much, from what the goblin said. I spoke with the captain of the ship. Garin didn't go down with the ship. He jumped over the edge and swam into the fog at Mermaid's Demise. He left on purpose."

Mateo leaned his elbows on the table. "He was trying to get to Riviand."

"I think so. The ship's captain said he had some other passengers do the same just recently. I figure it was you guys."

Dovin grinned. "Was it Oscar?"

"Yes, I think that was his name. I asked him if he would take me to Mermaid's Demise and he flat out refused. He said he was tired of coming back without all of his passengers."

"So how did you get here?" Dovin asked.

"Brake teleported us to the goblin mountain. He went and talked to a goblin named Vork and after a lot of arguing, he agreed to help me get to Riviand if I let them blindfold me. I let them, and I don't know what else they did, but time seemed to have no meaning for a while. I felt like I was floating. When the blindfold came off, I was still at a goblin mountain, but it was a different one. It was in Riviand. Vork was there with me. He opened a portal and sent me here."

Relief flooded through Kaylee. She'd believed Odie when he told his story, but it was nice to have someone she knew and trusted confirm it. There was a way into Riviand that didn't involve the whirlpool, and that meant there was a way out. They might not know exactly where, but they would figure it out.

Dovin rubbed his chin. "I suppose you're stuck down here with us until we figure out how to get the goblins to let us leave."

Williams sighed. "I think so."

Claret stood. "I will make sure you have a room and anything you need."

"Thank you."

Kaylee turned to Odie. "Are you ready to try to disguise the sword?"

He jumped to his feet. "Yes, let's go."

He rushed out of the room, and Kaylee followed. She wondered if he was anxious when people talked about the goblins. He had been one of the key players in their scheme, after all. Kaylee still wasn't sure if she completely trusted him.

CHAPTER 29

The mess in the kitchen was getting bigger, but Odie ignored it. Claret had led them here so they could work at the table and because the kitchen was the only place in the castle without rugs that he could ruin. A woman called Cook had not been happy about it, but when Claret had explained Odie's need for a clean space to do something important, the woman had eventually given in. By the end, Cook looked ready to spit nails and Claret looked like she might cry.

He hoped he was long gone before Cook saw the mess he had made in her spotless kitchen. Claret had taken a list from him and gathered all the things she could find. He hadn't been completely sure what he was going to do, so the table was full of all sorts of things. Most of it he hadn't touched, but he would rather be overprepared and not have to go searching for things.

Odie had tried a few times already and failed. He made a silver clay that hardened really fast. They had stuck it all over the hilt of the sword and made it smooth, so it looked like there was no decoration on the hilt. As soon as it dried, Kaylee had picked it up, and the clay cracked and made a mess all over the floor. He tried to make something that hardened slower, but it never hardened and it had taken twenty minutes to clean it off. Another try had made a bubbling concoction that seeped all over the table and floor and when he tried to wipe it up, the rag stuck to it and they couldn't get the rag off the floor.

Kaylee had fallen asleep with her head on the table. Odie didn't blame her. There wasn't a lot he needed help with. Having anyone else try to do what he was thinking in his head never turned out well. It was like letting a toddler help make a cake. It might be a good experience for them, but it made the process longer and more painful.

Being around people was interesting. Odie had interacted with people a lot in his life but never as anything more than the goblins' spokesman. He was finding it difficult to know what to say to them. Looking into his bowl, he frowned. He couldn't think of anything to do. Every mixture he made was a random guess of things he thought would go hard.

Odie flinched when he looked over and saw Kaylee staring at him, her head still resting on her arms on the table. Talking to people was hard, but talking to girls was even harder. He hadn't dealt with many in his life, even among the goblins. Almost all the goblins in the castle were men.

Kaylee lifted her head and stretched her arms. "What if we dip the hilt in hot, melted metal? Then it would cover all the markings."

Odie leaned against the table. "I thought about that, but it takes a lot of heat to melt metal. We wouldn't be able to make a fire hot enough."

"Could we do it at the blacksmith's?"

Odie scratched his head. "Perhaps... he would be suspicious, though."

"I think he already knows."

"Knows what?"

"That we put his fake sword in the lock."

"Why would you say that?"

"When I was sticking the sword in and the villagers were all watching, I saw a man watching me and smiling. He winked at me. When I pointed him out to Mateo, he said he was the blacksmith."

"I don't think he would know just from looking at it."

"You don't think he would recognize his own work?"

Odie shrugged. "It was a good replica. It looked almost exactly the same as the actual sword."

"If nothing else, I bet he suspects. He met you and Mateo, and he saw us all standing there to return the sword."

Kaylee was probably right. Trio had probably seen them standing there and realized they had the fake. But would he tell?

"If you don't like that idea, then what if we wrap the hilt with thin twine? That would cover it and make it so someone else might be able to hold it."

Odie's mouth turned down. It might work, but he wasn't sure he wanted to do something that was Kaylee's idea. He wanted to be the one who came up with something because he knew he was the one nobody trusted yet. If he could be helpful, he could earn their respect.

"You don't think it will work?" Kaylee asked.

He tilted his head and studied the mixture in his bowl. "It might, but it would have to be wound really tight. I could make a type of glue, and then we could wrap the twine around that, just to make it more secure."

She nodded. "That sounds like a good idea."

Odie grabbed the mixing bowl and dumped its contents in the garbage. He had already invented an extremely sticky glue years ago. He could make it again now and it would look like he had come up with it really fast. In reality, it had taken him weeks to perfect.

Kaylee hopped up from her chair. "I'll go see if I can find some twine."

She rushed from the kitchen, leaving Odie to himself. His gaze ran over the table. He had everything he needed. He grabbed a clean bowl and began mixing things as fast as he could. The mixture might have taken him a long time to invent, but now that he knew how to do it, making it was a snap.

He tossed things into the bowl and made sure he didn't over-stir the mixture. The door creaked open, and Claret and Kaylee entered. They were laughing about something. Odie pretended not to care about what.

Claret had a spool of twine in her hand. "Kaylee said you need this," she said, placing it on the table. "Do you need help?"

Odie shook his head. "This is really sticky. If it gets on skin, it's almost impossible to get off. We're going to have to throw the bowl out when we're done. Sorry about that."

"It's not a problem," Claret said, peeking into the bowl.

"I need to move fast, or it won't work. Can someone hand me a butter knife or something I can spread it with?"

Claret hurried to a drawer and pulled it open. The clanging of utensils filled his ears as he grabbed the Blade of the Phoenix. Claret shoved a butter knife into his hand and he scooped some of the goop onto its dull blade and wiped it across the hilt.

Kaylee wrinkled her nose. "I hate to think of what this is going to do to the sword. It seems like ruining an artifact."

Odie kept spreading. "I don't think it will ruin it, but it will be hard to get it off if we ever need to. Can someone cut me a long piece of twine?" he asked. "Or maybe hold the spool while I wrap it?"

"I will," Claret said, taking it from the table.

He dropped the knife into the bowl and took a piece of the twine. He began wrapping it as tight as he could around the hilt.

"I'm gonna go get Mateo," Kaylee said. "He can try to touch it when it's done."

"I can do it," Claret volunteered.

Kaylee shook her head. "Mateo already said he would do it. I'll be back." She hurried away, leaving Odie alone with Claret. It was getting harder and harder to talk to her. Now that he wasn't trying to manipulate her, he had nothing to say.

Claret wasn't exactly what he had always thought. When Cook talked to her, you would think she was a naughty little girl. As the Queen of Riviand, Claret should be able to use her own kitchen without having the staff argue with her. She had seemed unsure and apologetic and at the end looked like she might fall apart. He'd never seen her like that—well, unless you counted the spiders.

He wondered if Claret wasn't as confident as she had always seemed to him. The look on her face while talking to Cook remained etched in Odie's mind. What if she had had the same look every time she had spoken to him when he came for the goblins? The thought made him sick to his stomach. Everyone assumed a queen was in control of her emotions, but no one stopped to think that she was a person like everyone else.

"You shouldn't let the staff talk to you the way Cook did," he said as he kept winding the twine.

She grimaced but then made her face passive. "Cook is a little—passionate about the kitchen."

He kept his eyes on the hilt. "But it's your castle. You're the one who says what goes, not the staff. You pay them, and they work for you."

"I know," she said, still holding the spool. "But I want everyone to be happy. If everyone is comfortable, they work better and they're more pleasant."

"I'm not saying you should mistreat them or anything, but they need to respect you and Cook doesn't."

She sighed. "Cook is a special case. She was born in the castle. Her parents worked here. We all put up with more from her than we should."

He let it go. He was probably being a bit of a hypocrite. The goblins who worked at his father's castle were always being rude behind his back and loud enough that he could hear them, and he'd done nothing to correct their behavior. Still, he didn't like to see anyone treat Claret that way.

He grabbed a small knife from the table and cut the twine, then pushed the last bit down. "There. How does it look?"

She put the spool on the table. "Great. No one will suspect it to be anything other than a plain sword."

She was exaggerating a little. The bottom of the hilt still looked fancy, but no one was going to think it was the Blade of the Phoenix.

"The glue is already dry," he said, turning the sword.

"That's amazing. It was clever of you to come up with something like that."

Odie ignored the heat creeping up his neck. "I hope it works."

The door opened, and Mateo and Kaylee entered.

Mateo yawned. His hair was flat on one side and there were pillow lines on his cheek. Claret's eyes were on him, and Odie forced himself not to sigh. Mateo was one of those people who looked good no matter what condition they were in. Odie didn't have that going for him.

"Is it ready?" Kaylee asked. Odie nodded and handed her the sword. "Nice. It looks good."

Odie tried not to look too proud. "I think it's going to work. No one will suspect."

"Now we just get Mateo to touch it," she said with a sly grin.

Mateo flashed her a smile. "You just want to see me get blasted across the room."

Kaylee giggled. "With luck, you won't. Maybe we should wait for Dovin. Then if you end up bleeding all over, he can help."

"Funny," Mateo said, holding out his hand. "Give me the sword."

"I don't think you should take it," Kaylee said. "Just poke it or something. Then, if it doesn't work, it might not blast you as hard."

"We have to know it works. What if I can poke it but not hold it? When it hit me in the nose, it only shocked me."

"It's your funeral," she said, holding out the sword.

Mateo grabbed it, and a flash of orange blinded them, and he went flying into the air. He fell onto the table, causing the bowl with glue to soar high and fall wrong side up, splattering the glue on all of them.

Mateo lay on the table, staring up at the ceiling. "Ouch."

Kaylee and Claret ran to him and helped him sit up. Odie hoped everyone realized the twine was Kaylee's idea. The table was a mess. All the ingredients Odie had been using spilled and were dripping to the floor.

He put a hand to his hair and felt glue. It was hardening fast. Kaylee had glue in her braids and on her tunic, while Claret's dress was completely covered in it. Their faces and arms were covered in tiny specks. Multiple things covered Mateo, since he was the one who hit the table.

The door swung open and Cook stuck her head in. "What is going on in here?" she demanded. The four of them looked back and forth between each other, and at the mess on the floor.

Kaylee covered her mouth, and a small giggle escaped her. When she tried to keep it in, she snorted, and that made Claret, Mateo, and Odie burst into laughter.

"My kitchen is a mess!" Cook said, placing her hands on her hips. "How can you laugh at something like this?"

"It's my kitchen," Claret said, glancing at the woman. "And we will clean it."

Odie nodded, and Cook stormed away. Cleaning it wouldn't be as easy as they might think.

Kaylee sat in Claret's council room and tried not to smile as she watched Mateo rub his cheek. He had a stubborn spot of Odie's glue that he couldn't get off, and it was red where he kept rubbing it. It had taken them hours to clean the kitchen, and then they had all gone and taken baths. Mateo didn't help clean because he had gone to see the healer. The burn on his hand was worse than last time. Adler had covered it in salve and wrapped it.

Kaylee ran a hand over her scalp. She'd had to take out her braids, and now her head was sore from the change. She'd had those braids in for over two weeks, and it always felt uncomfortable when she first got them and when she took them out. It had been necessary because of the glue. The first few times she'd gotten dirty here, she had washed her hair with the braids in, but they had been too gross this time. She pulled her shoulder-length curls back and put them in a ponytail.

"Who cut your hair?" Claret asked her.

Kaylee smoothed a piece of hair back. "No one. I took my braids out. They were fake."

Claret and Odie stared at her, their brows furrowed.

Kaylee laughed. "On Earth, you can have extensions put in your hair. They braid it together with my real hair and it makes it look longer."

"How interesting," Claret said. "I would love to see someone do that."

Odie had red spots on his face where he'd scrubbed and so did Claret. Claret had been lucky and not gotten any in her hair. Dovin sat at the table with his elbows resting on the edge. He'd already lectured them all on the dangers of doing something like they had without his approval.

"Where's Padmire?" Kaylee asked. She hadn't seen much of the bungle.

"He's enjoying the castle," Dovin said. "He said he has the softest bed he's ever felt, and he's spent a good deal of time there."

Kaylee nodded. The beds here were nice. "Now what? Do you think the people suspect the sword is fake?"

"I don't think so," Dovin said. "I'm not worried about that. Keep the twine on the actual sword, just don't let anyone touch it. How is your hand?" he asked Mateo.

He held it up and looked at the bandage. "It hurts, but it's okay."

"I can ask Durdessa for some of her salve," Claret offered. "It works well on cuts and burns. It's better than anything the healer has."

All the color drained from Dovin's face and he leaned forward. Kaylee frowned. He looked like he might puke.

"Durdessa?" he asked.

"Yes, my aunt."

He swallowed and rubbed his hand over his face. "Your aunt's name is Durdessa?"

"Yes. She's feeling better. She said she'll meet you all tomorrow at breakfast."

Dovin closed his eyes and put his hands over his face. "Are names repeated in Riviand?"

Claret frowned. "What do you mean?"

"On the upper continents, no one has the same name. Baby names are registered, so there are no repeats."

"We don't have that here."

"Are there others named Durdessa?"

"Yes, it's actually becoming popular."

Dovin wiped his brow. "I see."

Kaylee had never seen Dovin like this. "Are you okay?"

He sat back and smiled. "Yes, of course. Now I think you all need to rest. You have done great things for Riviand, but I fear there are more trials to come."

Mateo frowned. "With the goblins?"

"Yes, and possibly Vigh's mother."

"Who is a witch," Odie muttered. "Witches make me nervous."

"I don't get what makes someone a witch here," Kaylee admitted. "If everyone has magic, doesn't that make all of you witches?"

Claret's mouth pulled down. "Of course not. Witches use magic for evil and are often more skilled in magic than the normal person. They dedicate their lives to becoming more powerful."

"So we are going to fight goblins and witches," she said. "My life is sure going in a direction I didn't expect."

Mateo grinned. "But you have to admit it's exciting."

"I'm not sure if it's a good type of exciting."

"Sure it is. You get to spend time with me and skip algebra."

She smiled and shook her head. Mateo was growing on her. "I'm surprised Dovin hasn't been giving us school lessons so we don't fall behind."

The color had come back to Dovin's face and his eyes sparkled. "Funny you should mention that. While we are preparing for whatever happens next, I think you should do schoolwork. I even talked to Coach Williams about it. He's willing to help. I'll teach science and math, and he will do gym and history. Odie and Claret, you may join us if you wish."

Mateo winked at Kaylee. "Sounds like a party."

Kaylee smiled. It might not be a party, but it was going to be exciting.

— · —

ALSO BY KRISTY DIXON

<u>Cozy Mystery</u>
Murder With a Side of Bacon
Murder With a Hint of Cinnamon
Murder With a Fudge Brownie to Go

<u>Young Adult</u>
Akkron (The Silver Eclipse Book 1)
Boztoll (The Silver Eclipse Book 2)
The Other Continent (The Silver Eclipse Book 3)
The Amethyst Crown
More Than Once Upon a Time
Trapped In Once Upon a Timen
The Beginning of Once Upon a Time

<u>Coming Soon!</u>
Mermaid's Demise (Riviand Lost Book 2)
Dragon's Cove (Riviand Lost Book 3)
Murder With a Splash of Vanilla
Murder With a Drizzle of Syrup

ABOUT THE AUTHOR

Kristy Dixon started writing stories when she was seven and never stopped. She enjoys writing cozy mysteries and YA. At home, she spends her time playing board games with her husband and kids and writing. Occasionally she takes part in a Super Mario marathon. She has six chickens and a cat that help keep life amusing. If she isn't playing with her kids or writing, she is usually eating cookies, or wishing she was eating cookies.